**“I never thoug**
**of person who w**
**but I do.”**

Maggie stopped looking away from him. “I was foolish to run away from everything, Will. To run away from you.”

He reached out, stroking his fingers along the underside of her jaw. “Then don’t run away anymore. Stay. Stay here tonight. You realize, don’t you, that all the old attraction is still there between us? Let’s do something about it.”

“I’m not sure that’s a good idea. As you pointed out very clearly, we’re completely unsuited for one another.”

He swayed forward until a kiss, like a cool little snowflake, floated against her cheek. “Opposites attract, remember? And we’re about as opposite as two people can get.”

Dear Reader,

Readers often ask where an idea comes from. To tell the truth, sometimes I just don't know. Inspiration can be anywhere, and sometimes it springs from the most mundane roots. Writers love to play "What if..." In fact, that's often the best part of writing a book!

I knew I wanted to set *The Missing Mom* in Florida, my home state. I wanted a free-spirited heroine, Maggie, who would be at odds with her straight-arrow, no-nonsense hero, Will. To boost the conflict, I felt Maggie needed goals and interests in something Will would find a little unorthodox. Researching oddball careers led me to professional aquarium cleaners, a nasty job that seems to pay well if you're willing to do it. From there, I discovered companies that specialize in designing custom aquariums. Aha! I thought. Here's something creative Maggie could really sink her teeth into. And the added bonus for me–I've always found tropical fish fascinating (and goodness knows, living in a state surrounded by water, you run into a lot of them). For me, it's also very important that my stories have good visual elements. I want readers to "see" key scenes in their heads, just as I do.

I hope I've succeeded with *The Missing Mom.* As you read, I hope you can close your eyes and be there with Maggie and Will–seeing the world through their eyes and loving every minute of it. And of course, rooting for them to find a way back to one another.

Please feel free to share more stimulating images with me at my Web site, www.aboutannevans.com. I love hearing from you.

*Ann Evans*

# THE MISSING MOM

*Ann Evans*

TORONTO • NEW YORK • LONDON
AMSTERDAM • PARIS • SYDNEY • HAMBURG
STOCKHOLM • ATHENS • TOKYO • MILAN • MADRID
PRAGUE • WARSAW • BUDAPEST • AUCKLAND

ISBN-13: 978-0-373-71468-1
ISBN-10: 0-373-71468-8

THE MISSING MOM



This edition published by arrangement with Harlequin Books S.A.



www.eHarlequin.com

**Printed in U.S.A.**

## ABOUT THE AUTHOR

Ann Evans has been writing since she was a teenager, but it wasn't until she joined Romance Writers of America that she actually sent anything to a publisher. Eventually, with the help of a very good critique group, she honed her skills and won a Golden Heart Award from Romance Writers of America for Best Short Contemporary Romance of 1989. Since then she's happy to have found a home at Harlequin Superromance.

A native Floridian, Ann enjoys traveling, hot fudge sundaes and collecting antique postcards. She loves hearing from readers and invites them to visit her Web site at www.aboutannevans.com.

**Books by Ann Evans**

**HARLEQUIN SUPERROMANCE**

701–HOT & BOTHERED
752–THE MAN FOR HER
805–HOME TO STAY
870–DREAM BABY
957–THAT MAN MATTHEWS
1136–AFTER THAT NIGHT
1215–THE DAUGHTER DILEMMA
1262–HOME TO FAMILY
1331–MISFIT FATHER
1370–THE RETURN OF DAVID McKAY

## *CHAPTER ONE*

ON A TERRIFIC Florida morning like this, there was only one place Maggie Tillman wanted to be.

The beach. And she knew just who she wanted to be there with.

She hopped out of bed, dressed quickly in her usual T-shirt and shorts, then galloped downstairs. The house lay silent. Since her older sister, Alaina, had married a big-deal doctor last year, Maggie had lived with her parents in this rambling two-story Victorian that sat on a deadly dull cul-de-sac on the stuffy side of North Miami Beach.

She skidded to a halt just inside the kitchen. "Good morning," she called out to her parents. "Have I missed anything?"

Her mother was at the stove, making pancakes. When she glanced up, one brow went as high as it could go. Her father stood at the counter, engaging in his usual impatient staring contest with the coffeemaker. He made a point of looking at the clock. Both James and Connie Tillman were early risers. Maggie knew that the fact she'd dared to sleep until nearly nine o'clock wouldn't sit well with either of them.

"The morning's half gone," her father said before turning his attention back to the coffee.

"Well, it's still beautiful," Maggie said in her brightest tone. She threw her arms wide, nearly knocking over one of her mother's carefully constructed flower arrangements from atop the baker's rack. "I feel like I could be in one of those old movies, where the woman wakes up and breaks into song."

"Spare us, dear," Connie Tillman said, adjusting the blooms so that they were perfect once more. "We've all heard you sing."

Her father said nothing.

Maggie resisted a sigh. Why did it have to be like this? Why couldn't her parents accept that she would always be different from Alaina? She didn't have her sister's clever tongue and vivacious good looks. She knew she was clumsy, spoke too fast, laughed too loud. She might never set the world on fire.

But Maggie didn't think she was *completely* the impulsive, irresponsible slacker they often accused her of being.

Last night at the dinner table, Mom's best meat loaf had gone stone-cold while their weekly disagreement played out. Some boring junk about her unwillingness to change her college major and get her mind wrapped around the idea of heading back to school. But she was nineteen, for Pete's sake, and she was achingly aware that spring break was nearly over.

There was plenty of time to think about the degree in marine biology she wanted. *Later.*

Determined not to allow that unpleasantness to spoil this morning's lovely possibilities, Maggie swept past her parents, giving them both a kiss on the cheek as she made her way to the fridge. She rummaged through its contents, eager to get out of the house and head for the beach. She grinned when she found a carton of orange juice hiding behind the milk.

"Do you want pancakes?" her mother asked, then frowned at Maggie. "Use a glass, for heaven's sake. You weren't brought up in a barn."

Maggie returned the juice to the refrigerator. Yep, the beach was looking better and better, and right there and then she decided neither of them needed to know where she was going. "No pancakes for me, thanks. I've gotta run. Lots of business to take care of."

Her father looked up from his cup, letting his eyes travel slowly over Maggie from her sandaled feet to the ponytail that held back her pale blond hair. "Dressed like that? Why don't you spend a whole dollar on your outfit next time?"

James Tillman might be comptroller for one of the largest corporations in the Greater Miami area, but he had the communication skills of a drill sergeant—at least when it came to Maggie.

"Don't start, Dad," she said, trying to keep the annoyance out of her voice. She didn't want to fight. She wanted to feel warm salt air on her cheeks and the tide tickling her toes. "I've got three Go Fish calls to make, and then—"

"Go Fish," her father said with a look of such disdain that Maggie wished she had simply walked out the front door and never stopped for a sip of juice. "What kind of silly name is that for a business? Like I said last night—"

"James..." her mother cautioned. "Come eat your pancakes."

Maggie watched him concede to his wife, but she felt her own resentment swell. She refused to be bullied about the decisions she'd made, and he really was ruining this beautiful day.

She looked her father right in the eye. "Give it up, Dad. I'm never going to change my major to accounting. I hate math, and I don't want any career that puts me behind a desk forty hours a week. I need a creative outlet for my talent."

"What talent? You never do a task long enough to develop any." He lifted his hand, spreading his fingers. "You gave up tennis after three lessons. The art classes we spent thousands of dollars on supplies for, you ditched after a month." He ticked off each item. "Fencing. Kayak camp. You think those are careers?"

"No, but with a degree in marine biology, I think I can morph Go Fish into one."

Her father made a face. "Oh, ridiculous. You think something called Go Fish is going to support you?"

"Actually, Dad, by the end of this year, Go Fish is going to put enough money in my pocket to get me out of this house. Permanently. So I don't think it's very silly or ridiculous at all."

The beginnings of a blustering response came from the kitchen table, but Maggie had already turned and marched out of the room, smiling to herself. She didn't often get the last word with her father.

She drove her beat-up convertible down A1A. She loved this strip. It had so many moods as it wound past the faded glory of hotels that had been built in the sixties and through canyonlike corridors of condominiums that hugged some of the most expensive beachfront property in Florida. Every so often she caught a glimpse of the Atlantic, shining like a sliver of mirror behind the buildings, and her heart quickened, so eager was she to get there.

Finally, she turned into Will Stewart's driveway. Her bad mood evaporated, replaced by the usual regret that she couldn't seem to get along with her parents, couldn't seem to be the daughter they wanted. But replaced, too, by a solid resolve to have some fun today, no matter what.

The service calls she needed to make for Go Fish could wait. Tomorrow was soon enough to get back into harness and be responsible, wasn't it? After all, she was her own boss and set her own hours.

Sometimes she was still amazed that her love of exotic fish had turned her summer job into a viable enterprise. Go Fish, her home aquarium service company, only existed because of the determination and hard work she'd poured into it over the past year, all while trying to get used to freshman routines at the University of Miami.

The rich might enjoy the look and luxury of having large tropical tanks in their homes, but they certainly didn't want to take care of them. That's where she had found a niche. Customers all along the coast paid her fifty dollars an hour just to scrape algae and change water, and whether her father wanted to admit it or not, business was good. Nearly every day she fielded calls from prospective clients. By year's end, she intended to turn a profit. A hefty one.

*So there, Dad. Why isn't that good enough for you?*

The front door opened as she hit the stoop, and Will Stewart was suddenly there, looking drop-dead gorgeous in a dark suit. She'd met him six months ago at a local trade show where she'd been passing out business cards. He didn't own an aquarium, but he was the only one who'd come back to ask questions about Go Fish. They'd been together ever since.

Maggie went into his arms eagerly. "Kiss me," she said, nuzzling his neck and inhaling expensive after-shave. "I need to know someone cares."

He laughed at that and pulled her close. He kissed her with such great and tender skill that she felt as if she were going to die.

But when she brought her hands up to his chest, he caught her fingers. "Don't play with my tie," he ordered. "I just got it the way I want."

She looked down at it, wrinkling her nose at the bland, dark blue material. Last month, she'd bought him one with iguanas painted on it by an artist friend of hers, but she'd yet to see him wear it. "Too conservative."

"Then it's perfect," he said with a smile.

She loved having Will for a boyfriend. Full of charm and confidence, he was as handsome as any woman could want, but blessed with absolutely no arrogance about his looks. Just out of school, he'd recently been hired by one of Miami's most prestigious architectural firms. He wasn't the kind of man Maggie would have expected to be attracted to, but right now she thought she was one lucky girl to have him in her life. And every day she found herself wanting more.

She longed to sink deeper into his embrace, but Will pulled away, letting his hands rest on Maggie's hips. She caught movement in the background and realized that Lisa, his thirteen-year-old sister, also stood in the foyer.

"Hi, there," Maggie said with a waving ruffle of fingers. "What are you up to today?"

"Chores," Lisa complained. She pointed to her brother. "Make him stop being mean to me."

Will kept his back to his sister and seemed immune to her claim of abuse. "Say hello, Lisa. Then get busy cleaning your room."

After their parents had died in a car accident three years ago, Will had assumed responsibility for Lisa. Maggie knew there had been mutiny brewing in the girl lately but she felt a little sorry for her. Lisa was at a tough age, and didn't like being ordered around by her big brother, but sometimes Will just didn't seem to understand.

Instead of responding, Lisa snorted, crossed her arms and remained where she was.

Deciding it was best not to be dragged into whatever beef Lisa had with her brother, Maggie turned her attention back to Will. "Play hooky today," she begged him. "Come to the beach with me."

"Can't. I've got a big presentation to make for Watkins and Company." He glanced at his watch. "I'm supposed to be in Pompano Beach in twenty minutes."

Maggie frowned. Will would be a fine architect someday, but so far, he was still interning and considered strictly second-tier. "*You're* presenting?"

"Don't sound so shocked. I'm doing part of it, anyway. Jacobson thinks I can connect with Watkins because he and my father were both Yale grads."

That didn't sound promising beachwise, and there was something unbendable in Will's manner. But Maggie was nothing if not inventive. With one fingertip, she played with the edge of his mouth. "So can't you slip away after a while? Meet me at our usual spot? You know which one I mean?"

She lifted her brow, reminding him of the quiet, secluded section of the beach she had in mind. The place they'd discovered just last week, in fact.

Will caught her finger and touched his lips to it. "Yes, I do, but the answer is still no. I can't go today. I have to play nice with Jacobson. And don't you have service calls to make?"

"I do. But fish aren't as particular as stuffy businessmen. They'll wait."

"Blowing off customers. That's not the way to get rich."

Maggie scowled. "Why are you so uncomfortable with self-indulgence? You sound like my father. And anyway, who said anything about wanting to get rich?"

"If Will can't go, can I come with you instead?" Lisa said behind them.

They both turned to look at the girl. "Sure," Maggie said, at exactly the same time that Will said, "No."

"Why not?" Lisa whined to her brother.

"Yeah. Why not?" Maggie chimed in. She liked Lisa, and the girl was very low maintenance.

She realized immediately that she should have kept quiet. Will, wearing a harassed look, tossed her a quelling glance before he turned to his sister. "You know why not. Because I've spent good money to have a math tutor come to the house today to help you get your grade up. She'll be here any minute."

"But it's spring break!" Lisa complained. "Nobody studies at spring break."

"You do. And even if this woman wasn't coming, I've already told you that I want your room cleaned up. It's a pigsty in there."

"I know where everything is."

"That's not the point."

Maggie could see that Will wasn't likely to give on this. He was in full parental mode. She knew that he often worried about whether he was making the right decisions, doing what his mother and father would have wanted. Maggie had once pointed out that his parents would never have given him custody if they'd had any doubts. But she wasn't sure he'd ever be completely convinced of that.

She touched his shoulder, eager to avert a budding argument. "Will, if it helps any—"

He shook his head so quickly that her lips parted in surprise. "Don't *help* anymore. I'm sorry to be the bad guy, but Lisa can't go to the beach today and neither can I and that's that." There was a momentary deafening silence, then Will sighed, clearly feeling contrite already. "Maybe we'll all go this weekend, but not today."

"I don't want to wait until the weekend," Lisa cried. "You're the meanest brother ever!"

On that angry outburst, she stormed off. A few moments later, they heard a bedroom door slam shut.

Will raked a hand through his hair. "Thanks a lot. Lisa and I have been going at one another all morning about her responsibilities, and you just made it worse." He sounded calm, but the muscles in his jaw betrayed him. They pulsed the way they always did when he was tense.

"Sorry," Maggie said. She offered an apologetic smile, but couldn't help feeling a little stung. "It wasn't intentional, you know. I just felt like going to the beach, and I really didn't think about anything else."

Her father might have added that she didn't think,

*period,* but thankfully Will made no such comment. He merely looked down at his watch again.

"I have to go," he said. He scooped his car keys out of a bowl on the foyer table. "Let's order pizza tonight. Then the three of us can make plans for the beach. All right?"

She nodded, and he gave her a quick kiss as he closed the front door behind them. Together they walked toward their cars. Morning sunlight bounced brightly off the vehicles, but the fun had gone out of the day as far as Maggie was concerned.

"Stop sulking," Will said as he unlocked his car door. "The weekend will be here before you know it."

Maggie made a face at him. "I hate delayed gratification."

"It's good for you," Will said. "It builds character."

And with that, he roared out of the driveway.

THREE HOURS LATER, Maggie had already completed two of the three service calls she'd originally scheduled for today. After Will's unwillingness to play, she'd considered going to the beach alone simply on principle, but, really, what fun was that? Better just to accept the fates that had aligned against her and make some money.

She was just heading for the last job on her list when her cell phone rang. It was Will's house number, but it was his sister on the line.

"What are you doing?" Lisa asked.

"Working." Maggie felt sorry for the girl, stuck

inside at home on a pretty spring day like today. "How's the math tutoring going?"

"It's not. Right after you and Will left, my tutor called and said she had to cancel until tomorrow."

"Uh-oh." From experience Maggie knew that Will had two pet peeves in life—people who were chronically late, and people who canceled appointments at the last minute. "Your brother's not going to like that."

"He doesn't know because I didn't call him," Lisa said. "But I think he'll be happy. I cleaned my room and the kitchen and even put away the laundry. I've done everything that was on the stupid list he gave me, and now I deserve a reward. Can I go to the beach with you?"

"I'm not going to the beach. I told you, I'm working."

"But we could go later, couldn't we? After you finish."

Maggie shifted a strand of hair out of her eyes. She'd put the top down on her convertible because she loved the feel of the breeze and that seemed to be the closest she was going to get to really enjoying the day. "Will was pretty clear, Lisa. No beach today."

"But that was before everything worked out the way it did. It's not my fault my math tutor didn't come. And I've done what I'm supposed to do. If I stay here the rest of the day by myself, I'll just get into trouble."

Maggie laughed. "You know that for a fact, do you?"

"I thought you wanted to be my friend," Lisa said, and her unhappiness came through loud and clear. "Can't we do stuff together today? Even if it's work. I'd be a good helper, I swear."

"I don't know…. Your—"

"*Please.* I promise to do whatever you want. Pleeeeeeease."

Maggie thought a moment while Lisa waited. Since she'd been dating Will, she'd come to understand how important his sister was to him, and Maggie had wanted to become a friend to the girl. If she and Will had any hope of forming a long-term relationship, didn't she need to get to know Lisa better? And wasn't it preferable for Lisa to be with Maggie than home alone, doing stuff she shouldn't?

"All right," Maggie said, making a U-turn at a gas station. "I'll pick you up in ten minutes. In the meantime, call your brother and let him know where you'll be."

Lisa agreed with a whoop of pleasure.

Because of traffic, it took Maggie twenty minutes to get back to the Stewart house, and she'd no sooner pulled into the driveway than Lisa came running out the door.The girl jumped into the passenger seat, all smiles, then threw a small duffel bag in the back.

"What's that?" Maggie asked.

"My bathing suit," she replied with a mischievous look. "Just in case we get done with work early."

Maggie grinned. The kid was as opportunistic as she was. "Did you call Will and tell him where'd you'd be?"

"I had to leave a message with his office. He's still in Pompano Beach."

"I suppose we can try him later," Maggie said as she backed out of the driveway.

"Where are we going?" Lisa asked excitedly.

"I'm going to work your butt off. You'll wish you'd stayed home and watched the soaps."

"And then maybe the beach?"

"Maybe."

Maggie caught the interstate, then took the cross-town back roads that led to Key Biscayne, one of the most desirable, exclusive parts of south Florida. Just across the bridge were at least a dozen clients of Go Fish, but they weren't Maggie's favorites.

In the sprawling mansions and high-tech condos along the beach there were four- and five-hundred-gallon custom-designed tanks filled with angel rays and harlequin rasboras, living coral and rainbow-colored dottiebacks.

Maggie almost felt sorry for these beauties. Their owners hadn't purchased them for personal enjoyment. They'd been bought to impress guests and business associates. To make statements about wealth and power. Or maybe just because they were a pretty backdrop for the right furniture. Maggie much preferred dealing with a ten-gallon tank housing a handful of guppies that had all been individually named by the kid who owned them. But she couldn't deny the reality that the wealthy provided a lot of her income.

Her last stop was for a bi-weekly cleaning of a four-hundred-and-forty-gallon crescent tank that separated a huge foyer from its adjacent living room. True to her word, Lisa helped Maggie cart equipment out of the car to the front door of the ridiculously large Mediterranean villa. They were met by the housekeeper.

"Hi, Mrs. Walker," Maggie said as she and Lisa entered the house. "Brought a helper today."

The woman smiled a welcome and disappeared, leaving Maggie to her own devices. Maggie didn't mind. One thing about service calls to these huge showplaces—the owners were seldom around to get in her way and ask a bunch of silly questions. Besides, she didn't really like this particular client—a middle-aged guy named Huckabee, with teeth that were too shiny, a tan that looked as if it went all the way to the bone, and a smirky, smoke-frayed laugh that always set her teeth on edge.

"Wow," Lisa said, as she stared at the enormous aquarium. "They've got a *lot* of fish."

"Too many," Maggie remarked as she began to lay towels out on the floor in case she spilled any water on the expensive parquet.

On previous house calls, she'd told Huckabee that he needed to stop buying more exotic fish. She'd explained to him that the fish he had were social creatures, community dwellers, and that in spite of the tank's size, they were displaying signs of stress from overcrowding. But the man had just laughed.

Huckabee was clearly not the kind of guy to take direction from a nineteen-year-old woman.

She and Lisa worked for almost an hour. Maggie showed the girl how to check pH levels, how to scrape algae without scratching the acrylic, the best way to move rocks but keep from creating a muddy cloud in the water.

Lisa proved to be a surprisingly quick learner and best of all, she actually seemed to enjoy the tasks Maggie assigned her. She peppered Maggie with questions. She didn't turn her nose up at the more unpleasant duties, and she didn't complain. The time went fast, and Maggie felt as though they were really bonding.

"Can you get me about a quart of tap water?" Maggie asked, handing the girl a small bucket. She pointed toward the back of the house. "The kitchen is through that door."

Lisa nodded and disappeared down the long hallway. Maggie, whose right arm was immersed up to her shoulder in the aquarium, kept mounding rocks in one corner, intent on making a natural hiding place for some of the smaller fish. An inquisitive brown-striped kuhli loach came up to investigate one of her fingers, and Maggie noticed that a tiny portion of its caudal fin was missing.

"Poor little guy," Maggie crooned to the fish. "Are those big boys beating up on you?"

The fish didn't let her stroke it—by nature the breed was too shy for that—but she thought it was actually listening to her. It was a funny little creature, one of her favorites in spite of the fact that it looked more like a worm. Long ago, she'd become convinced that some fish really did have distinct personalities, that they could connect with their owners. They weren't just pretty pieces of living art as Huckabee seemed to think. They needed love and attention. Just like people.

She was glad Lisa had come with her on this call. From some of the things the girl had said, Maggie suspected that she might need an older female in her life. She wasn't a child anymore. She was a teenager discovering so many new things about her body, feeling her way through the baffling intricacies of womanhood. Maybe tonight, Maggie thought, she should spend a few minutes trying to explain that to Will.

But right now, where was Lisa with that water? Frowning, Maggie slipped her hand out of the tank and dried her arm with a towel. The girl should have been back by now.

She hoped Lisa wasn't pestering the housekeeper. And had Maggie told Lisa that she mustn't ever venture farther into a client's home? The room holding the aquarium, the kitchen or bathroom were fine, but everything else was off-limits. She couldn't afford any accidents in one of *these* homes.

Maggie hurried to the kitchen. The room was techno-shiny with stainless steel equipment, but empty.

"Lisa," Maggie called in a half whisper.

No one answered, and a premonition of trouble

flared at the edge of Maggie's mind. If the girl had been foolish enough to explore, Maggie would make her sit in the car once she found her. And definitely no beach. Even if Lisa hadn't been told the rules, she ought to know better....

Maggie left the kitchen and went into the formal dining room. Nothing. She walked into the next room, obviously Huckabee's domain since it was dominated by a huge home theater setup and enormous workout equipment that made the space look like a torture chamber from some medieval castle.

The room led off to the back deck and pool, and Maggie caught movement there. It was Lisa, all right. Standing beside a patio table, chatting with a barefoot man in a white terry-cloth robe who had his back to Maggie. She recognized him as Huckabee—no mistaking that slick blond haircut—and the girl had obviously disturbed him during his sunbathing. He had his hands on his hips, and Maggie wondered if he was annoyed. She knew *she* was. God, she was going to kill Lisa for bothering a customer—even a jerk like Huckabee.

She made a move toward the French doors, not understanding why in that moment goose bumps rose along her arms. Halfway there, Maggie stopped. She realized suddenly that Lisa wasn't talking at all, she was listening. And the look on her face was so wary, so anxious, that Maggie immediately knew something was wrong.

And in the next moment Maggie discovered what it was. While she watched, stunned, Huckabee slipped the knot from his robe and pulled apart the edges to expose himself to Lisa.

The air left Maggie's lungs in a rush as a wave of nausea rippled at the back of her throat. Even as she strode toward the door, galvanized by an anger so deep and strong that she could hardly see the handle for the red haze in front of her eyes, she knew that everything was about to change. Everything.

Nothing would ever be the same again.

Not in her world.

Not in Lisa's.

## *CHAPTER TWO*

*Eight years later*

MAGGIE WAS on her computer, creating a six-hundred-gallon wave tank on her AutoCad program, when Zack Davidson strode into her small office. He must have come directly from his workshop behind the building, because a paper face mask still dangled from the string around his neck and bits of sawdust clung to his brown hair like a sprinkling of snow.

He was a tall, good-looking man with impressive biceps from years of carpentry work. He'd been Maggie's partner in Sapphire Seas Designs for four years, and right now, he didn't look happy.

"I just got off the phone with Lou Myers," he said. "Did you tell him he could have cherry instead of oak cabinets?"

"I did," Maggie replied absently. She used her mouse to erase an errant line from her computer design. "He wants the cabinets to match the waiting room furniture he bought yesterday."

"Damn it, Mags," Zack said as he shook a tiny

shaving out from underneath the collar of his shirt. "Why didn't you tell him it was too late to change his mind? You know I've already cut the wood."

Maggie tilted back in her chair. She smiled up at Zack, though she couldn't really see his features because the Key West afternoon sunlight coming through the window cast his face in shadows. "I know. But remember customer service?"

"We won't have any customers to service if you drive us out of business by wasting inventory. What am I supposed to do now with a bunch of oak cut for cabinets we haven't sold?"

"Zack, do you know what Lou Myers does for a living?"

"Dentist?"

She shook her head at him in playful disgust. They'd been friends since high school, even when he was making moon eyes at her sister, Alaina, and getting the brush-off. After he'd moved down here to Key West, she hadn't seen much of him, but eight years ago, when she'd had no place else to go, he'd been there for her. She owed him a debt of gratitude she could never repay, but he drove her crazy sometimes.

"This is why you're still back in the workshop, you know." She saved her design in the computer, then shut it down. "Because you won't take an interest in the customer side of the business."

He came to her desk, letting his weight settle against the edge so that one jean-clad leg could dangle as he crossed his arms and stared at her. "I'm back in the workshop because I like to build things. What's your point, partner?"

"Lou isn't just any dentist. He's head of the Pediatric Orthodontia Society of America. That means he talks to thousands of kiddie dentists all over the country. The guy's excited about the Atlantis theme we're building for his front office. Really excited."

"So?"

Maggie sighed heavily. "So once he has pictures of the finished product, he's going to be showing them off at every convention he goes to." She tapped her monitor for emphasis. "And he goes to a lot, according to the research I did on him. Some of his colleagues may want aquariums for their own offices. And I want Lou referring them to Sapphire Seas. He'll do that if we go this extra mile for him." She offered her friend a consoling look. "Cut the cherry, Zack. We can always save the oak for another project."

Zack remained thoughtful for a long moment. Then he cocked his head at her. "Do you ever stop hustling for business?"

"No, and neither should you. Not if we're going to put Sapphire Seas on the map this year."

"Do you know who you sound like?"

"Who?"

"Your sister."

That surprised her a little. Alaina's name rarely came up between them. Partly because Maggie so seldom saw her family anymore, even though they were only hours away in Miami Beach. But mostly she avoided talking about Alaina for Zack's sake. Her sister had broken his heart years ago, and he could pretend all he wanted, but Maggie knew he was *still* in love with her. He just wasn't willing to do anything about it. Of course, Alaina was married, so maybe that was just as well.

Maggie shuffled the latest stack of bills on her desk. "Good," she said in a deliberate tone. "It's taken me twenty-seven years to turn into Alaina. Too bad Mom and Dad aren't here to see it. Like they'd ever bother to come down for a visit."

"Like you'd ever invite them." Zack snorted. "Hell, no. *You're* not bitter."

He was right, and Maggie knew it. The fiasco of eight years ago was like a scar that wouldn't fade. Just to be civil, she kept in contact with her parents. But it wasn't much of a relationship, and none of them tried very hard to change it.

She stopped fiddling and stared up at him. "I'm *trying* to grow this business. To stick with the game plan. What's wrong with that?"

"Nothing," Zack said with a shrug. "If it's the *right* game plan. If it doesn't keep you from enjoying yourself."

Lately Zack had been giving her grief about her social life—or the fact that she didn't have much of one. But after what had happened in Miami so long ago, after she'd had to depend on someone else's kindness just to keep from ending up on the streets, Maggie had learned that there were a lot of different ways life could beat the crap out of you. What was wrong with being…cautious?

"I am enjoying myself," she shot back. "Now stop pestering me. I've got work to do."

"I liked you better when you were Alaina's wild and crazy kid sister. You were a lot more fun."

"Wild and crazy and fun doesn't put food on your table or money in the bank. It only gets you into trouble."

She suddenly realized she sounded like her father. Wow. Maybe you really could mature.

"You need to lighten up, Mags. You've been pushing hard for months now—"

Before she could cut him off, the phone did the job for her. She looked at Zack to see which one of them was going to answer it.

"Let it go to the machine," Zack said.

She shook her head at him again as she snatched up the receiver. Really, sometimes Zack was the least motivated businessman she'd ever met. "Sapphire Seas Designs. This is Maggie Tillman."

It was Teddy LaCrosse's office up in Miami—a call she'd been holding her breath for. An entrepreneur with the attitude of Jimmy Buffett and more money than Midas, Teddy had loved the aquarium designs she'd pitched for his new South Beach project. He'd even come down to check out their studio and workshop. Maggie was ninety-five percent certain Sapphire Seas would get the job. The bid had been fair, and her designs innovative.

She crossed her fingers and raised them to Zack, mouthing who was on the line. It wasn't LaCrosse, but his assistant, Susan. Close enough, Maggie figured. As long as the answer was yes.

They exchanged pleasantries, then Susan said, "Miss Tillman, Mr. LaCrosse asked me to call. He'd like to schedule a time when the two of you could talk. It's about the designs you submitted for the South Beach property...."

Maggie felt her heart drop. Right then and there, she knew the answer was going to be no. She had a gut instinct about this sort of thing. Maybe because she'd been hearing the word an awful lot lately. She couldn't control her disappointment and shock. "Oh, hell," she said. "He went with someone else, didn't he? I can tell by your voice."

"Miss Tillman, I'm not at liberty to discuss this matter with you. I'm only—"

"Just tell me, Susan. I know the kind of assistant you are. There isn't a thing that goes on in Teddy LaCrosse's office that you don't know about. Who did he go with? Was it Coastal Communities?"

"I'm sorry. I really can't give you that information. Please..."

"Okay, you're right," Maggie said in a quick, conciliatory tone. "I'm sorry I put you on the spot. It's just that getting this job is very important to me."

Maggie spent the next few minutes being professional and polite with the woman—when all she really wanted to do was yell or throw something.

She'd spent weeks coming up with those designs. She'd furnished LaCrosse with enough testimonials from happy clients to choke a horse. She'd practically had to take out a bank loan in order to wine and dine him properly. She'd done everything to get this job except sleep with the man, and she'd be lying if she said the thought hadn't crossed her mind. And now, she knew it. It was all going to be for nothing.

"Then it's set," Susan said. "Mr. LaCrosse will be in touch with you tomorrow at two."

Maggie shook her head at Zack, indicating failure. "There's no way I can speak to him today?" *This minute,* she wanted to add.

"I'm afraid not. Right now, he's holding a press conference regarding his plans for the resort."

By the time Maggie tossed the telephone receiver back in its cradle, she could hardly contain her disappointment. She cupped her face in her hands and swore softly.

"You don't know it's a bust," Zack said.

"In all the years we've been doing this, have I ever been wrong about whether or not we got a job?"

"No."

"I can read between the lines. I got lots of practice when I lived with my folks, trying to guess when and where the next argument was going to come from."

Zack stood, settling his tool belt on his hips. "So we don't get the contract. We've been shut out before."

"This was big, Zack. We could have bought the

new oven. We could have stopped subcontracting to that toad Jefferson."

The commercial-sized oven they needed to heat acrylic so they could seal joint seams properly was a particularly sore spot for Maggie. Although the equipment was horribly expensive, no aquarium design firm worth its salt relied on outside help for that sort of thing.

But ever since their ancient, secondhand oven had bitten the dust a year ago, Sapphire Seas had been contracting out the work. To a squinty-eyed jerk up in Marathon who thought that every bit of oven time he sold Maggie ought to come with a free overnight stay in her bed. So far she'd been holding him off, but purchasing an oven of their own would have stopped that nonsense forever.

Oh, well. Goodbye to that dream. For now.

She flung a disgusted glance around the office. "Why didn't I try to clean this place up before Teddy came down here? Everything looks so shabby. The *remodeling* needs remodeling, for pity's sake."

"Mags, stop."

Maggie rubbed her fingers along her jaw. "Who do you think he went with? Coastal's the only outfit in the state that could handle a job that big." She sat up straighter suddenly. "Wait a minute! Susan said he was holding a press conference today. You know what that means?"

"Media coverage."

Maggie nodded. "Whatever decisions have been

made could be on the Miami paper's Web site by tonight."

Zack headed back to his workshop and Maggie spent the rest of the day watching the clock. By six that evening she could check the Internet. LaCrosse's press conference probably wouldn't divulge who'd gotten the green light for the resort aquariums—too small a job in the grand scheme of things—but Maggie was hoping for something, *anything* that might tell her what to expect from Teddy's conversation with her tomorrow.

By the time she closed the office, the first streaks of a pink and purple sunset were sifting over the palms that lined the short driveway to Sapphire Seas. Back at her desk, she paged through the top news stories of the day on her computer. It took very little time to find what she was looking for, and when she did, Maggie's mouth parted in surprise. Then absolute, flat-out shock. She settled back in her chair, staring at the screen and feeling nothing but…numb.

Zack came into the office. "Find out anything, Sherlock?"

Maggie jerked her chin toward the monitor. "Take a look."

There was a good-sized picture of Teddy LaCrosse smiling out at them from behind a podium. Although he was backed by a wall of three-piece-suit types, he wore a Hawaiian shirt and his hair clearly hadn't been trimmed since the last time Maggie had seen him.

Zack quickly scanned the article below the picture,

then looked at Maggie. "It doesn't say anything about specific contractors. Nothing to indicate we lost out."

"We're not getting the job, Zack."

"How do you know that?"

Maggie ran a finger gingerly across the screen, then let her fingertip rest on one of the men standing behind and to the left of Teddy. Oh God, she still couldn't believe it.

Zack frowned. "Who's the bean counter?"

Maggie hardly heard him. She couldn't take her eyes off the man's face. Could barely allow her finger to make contact with the image, as though it might burn her right through the glass. "He's not a bean counter," she said. "He's Teddy LaCrosse's chief architect. From Jacobson and Duquette Associates. His name is Will Stewart."

"Will Stewart," Zack repeated thoughtfully. "Why do I know that name? Will—" He shot a quick glance her way. "*Your* Will Stewart? The guy who—"

"One and the same."

Zack blew air through his lips. "Oh, damn. You think he advised LaCrosse to go with another company because you two—"

"I think *advised* might be too polite a word. You know architects work closely with all the contractors. If he found out I was behind the Sapphire Seas bid, I'll bet he threw a fit at the thought of coming within a hundred miles of me."

"Are you going to ask LaCrosse when you talk to him tomorrow?"

Maggie moved suddenly, snapping off the computer. She rose, pulled her purse out of the bottom drawer of the desk and grabbed her car keys. "Nope. I'm going to find out right now. Tonight."

IN THE END, Maggie didn't make the four-hour drive up to Miami that evening. Even if she'd known where to find Teddy LaCrosse, tracking him down, forcing him into a midnight conversation, would look unprofessional and probably wouldn't win her any points. She'd spent years trying to get a handle on her impulsive nature. No sense letting her emotions get the best of her now.

But early the next morning, as she drove up the long stretch of US-1 that connected the mainland to the Keys, it wasn't how to win over Teddy that ate at her nerves.

It was the thought of Will Stewart.

All Maggie could think about was how her gut had kicked to see his face again.

Eight years seemed like a long time, and yet she could recall every detail of that bright spring afternoon as though it had happened yesterday. Huckabee's arrest. Lisa, white-faced and trembling as they sat together at the police station. Someone handing Maggie a cup of coffee that spilled and burned her fingers because she, too, was shaking so badly.

Most of all, she remembered Will striding into the detective's office, rigid with anger and fear. He had pulled his sister into a hug so tight that Maggie imagined she could hear bones creak. She felt as if she were in a dream, the kind where a person can only watch, not move or speak. She saw Will enfold Lisa, saw his head bending. It almost made her weep to witness the exquisite tenderness with which his fingers traced her face as he crooned comfort to her.

"What the hell happened?" he had demanded at last, and even his voice was white-hot.

Oh, those words. In the pit of Maggie's stomach, something twisted even tighter. He hadn't addressed the detective. He swung to face her, fixing her with a stare that would have scattered some men like petals on the wind. Right then, in that moment, she knew it was over between them. She felt as though some support in the pit of her stomach had been abruptly ripped away.

It took a little while, of course. There were charges to be filed and court appearances to make. It could have been worse, she supposed. Huckabee turned out to be a repeat offender. His attorney tried to persuade him to throw himself on the mercy of the court. Instead, thinking money could fix almost anything, the fool made the mistake of attempting to bribe the judge. He found himself in jail in record time.

Lisa weathered all of it surprisingly well, thank God. After three sessions with a child psychologist who pronounced her very resilient, she seemed none the worse for what had happened.

But for Will and Maggie...there was no hope.

It was clear that Will held her responsible for everything. He didn't say it. At least, not at first. But their time together took on a new unnatural formality, a masquerade performance for Lisa's benefit. Words between them marched and maneuvered like tense soldiers. When Maggie tried to find a way to make it right again, she was met only with Will's cast-iron composure, so that eventually, she, too, was forced to take refuge in blank-faced complacency.

And then one night a month after the incident, everything just erupted. They opened a door between them that was impossible to shut. The argument was quick, hot and horrible. They stepped on each other's sentences without waiting for responses. Will's dark, fenced-in manner gave way to harsh accusations, until Maggie felt bludgeoned and desperate and the healthy instincts of self-defense rose up in her.

But his anger was fully unleashed at last, and he would hear no explanations, no excuses. They were like stars separated by unimaginable distances and would never see eye to eye. Her impulsive, immature behavior had put Lisa in danger. Maggie was the adult. She should *not* have given in to his sister that day, knowing how he felt.

In the end, every nugget of hope was extracted from their relationship, and there was nothing left to do but finish it. Nothing in her life had been easier than loving Will, and nothing about leaving him could have been harder. They traded one last, searing look. Operating on numb disbelief and adrenaline, Maggie walked out of Will's house and did not glance back.

She went home, weighed down with a misery she

could barely comprehend. Deep inside where it counted, she felt withered and betrayed. Grief made her unapproachable for days. She stayed in her room over the objections of her parents, who begged her to come out. She cried a flood of tears, got angry and resentful all over again, then wept into her pillow for hours. It had been unbearable to be nineteen and heartbroken, and when Maggie finally did emerge, she had thought she would never be the same again.

She was right.

A week after that final argument, she learned she was pregnant with Will's child.

The green interstate sign announcing her approach to Miami brought Maggie back to the present. Just as well. She didn't need to think about the mess her life had been eight years ago. She needed to stay focused on getting the LaCrosse contract. There had to be some new way to persuade Teddy to go with Sapphire Seas.

Since the South Beach project was en route to Teddy's office, Maggie stopped there first. She saw his sleek, red Lamborghini with the vanity plates parked just outside the main construction trailer and pulled to a halt nearby. Drawing a decisive deep breath, she reapplied lipstick, swept the wrinkles as best she could from her mauve skirt and tucked her bid file under one arm.

The site hummed with activity. The LaCrosse Restoration Project—a massive resort, condo, shopping and dining complex—spanned an entire city block and seemed to be moving ahead quickly. Months ago, the land had been cleared and concrete poured. The hotel section, nearly complete, towered impressively, and Maggie glimpsed the guts of the lobby shaping up beneath it. Now, if only Sapphire Seas could be part of the excitement.

Maggie entered the trailer. Because of the strong morning light, it took a moment for her eyes to adjust. Then she spotted Teddy, lounging in a high-backed office chair behind a desk laden with blueprints, tools and a storm of paperwork that probably kept some construction boss up late at night.

He raised his head, looking surprised to see her. "Maggie," he said in his usual affable way. "What an unexpected pleasure! What brings you to my neck of the woods?"

A person could make the mistake of underestimating Teddy's laid-back, aging surfer-boy demeanor, but Maggie knew that LaCrosse was a tough negotiator and nobody's fool. She reached across the desk to firmly shake his hand. "Good to see you again, Teddy."

"I thought we were going to be talking later today."

"I was in town anyway," Maggie lied. "Could we chat now?"

"Sure, sure. I assume this is a business visit."

"It is."

He nodded toward the rear of the office. "Then you won't mind if Will sits in."

Maggie turned to see Will Stewart at the small kitchen counter, pouring a cup of coffee from a battered-looking pot.

She felt a jolt like an electric current turn her insides over. She hadn't been expecting Will to be here, and considering her suspicions, she certainly wasn't eager to speak to LaCrosse in front of him. She barely heard Teddy introduce Will as the project's chief architect, a fact she'd already learned from the Internet.

Will inclined his head. His quick, assessing gaze played over her face, but his eyes were without depth, like polished windows with the blinds down behind them. The smile he gave her, though. She remembered that. It was no more than a tight line of acknowledgment. "We've met," he said.

She wished she could think that he'd aged horribly in eight years, that somehow an overachieving lifestyle and corporate stress had whittled him down. But the truth was, the picture on her computer hadn't done him justice. He still had that vigorous, youthful strength about him. Not a touch of gray in his dark hair. Not one inch of flab at the waistline. His clothes only accentuated his power and grace, making Maggie wish she'd opted for her best suit instead of this too-casual skirt and blouse.

She turned back to Teddy. "If I've interrupted anything, perhaps we could—"

Teddy waved away the suggestion and motioned for her to take one of the vinyl-covered chairs in front of the desk. "No, no. You're here now. Sit."

He indicated Will should do the same. That put him awfully close to Maggie, but there wasn't much she could do about it. She lifted her chin a little. No way was she going to let him know his proximity bothered her.

"Will is involved in every phase of the project, of course, so there's nothing he can't hear," Teddy said. He gave Maggie a sharp look. "Tell me what's on your mind. You look a little flustered."

That was the last thing she wanted either man to think. "No," she said firmly. "I'm…I just drove up this morning. I'd like to find out where Sapphire Seas stands with this contract. Do we have it or not?"

Teddy tilted his head at her. "You don't waste any time, huh? Okay. Not."

Her heart swooped. Just as she'd feared. "You've signed with someone else?"

"Not yet, but you're out of the running, I'm afraid. I'm sorry. It's just a business decision. You understand that, don't you?"

"Of course. If that's what it really was. A business decision."

Teddy's brow puckered. "What are you getting at?"

Maggie's eyes flicked toward Will. He sat utterly still, but distant, as though he could hardly expend the energy to listen. It only strengthened her resolve. "I'm a businesswoman," she said, leaning slightly forward in her chair. "I can take bad news, Teddy. But I think I deserve complete honesty. I thought my bid on this project was fair—"

"Your bid was fine."

"Then my designs, perhaps. Did you want something different? You seemed to like what I showed you."

"I did."

"Then why isn't Sapphire Seas getting this job?"

Will spoke up for the first time. "Miss Tillman, this project isn't right for your company."

Maggie turned her head to give him a frank but carefully civil look. "I'd like to know why. And I'd like to hear that reason from Mr. LaCrosse, if you don't mind."

Teddy laughed, a loud, genuine sound of amusement that drew her attention. "That's one of the things I admire about you, Maggie. You're not afraid to speak up." He shook his head. "But it's not enough."

"Then what is?"

There was a moment's pause. She saw Teddy's glance cut to Will for an instant, but she refused to check his reaction or what signals he might be sending. Then Teddy crossed his arms, a silent indication that she wasn't going to like what he had to say. "I need a company with deeper pockets and a full-time crew," he told her. "Your guys are strictly job-to-job. You have equipment issues. That can create inconsistencies in production and quality."

Maggie shifted in frustration. "I told you what the company situation was when we first met and the measures I take to overcome challenges like that. That didn't seem to be a problem then. In fact, you said you admired my entrepreneurial efforts because that's how you'd gotten *your* start."

"Sapphire Seas is young. Too young for a job this size."

"What we lack in experience, we more than make up for in—"

"Maggie, this project is a huge investment for me, and I have to believe that an older, more experienced outfit like Coastal Communities will meet our needs more effectively."

"Why must you believe that?" Maggie asked, running out of patience. She jerked her hand out to indicate Will seated beside her. "Because *this* man advised you to go with Coastal?"

"As a matter of fact, I did," Will admitted quietly.

That nearly took Maggie's breath away. She hated that he sounded so sure of himself, so superior. Inside, her blood seethed, but she'd never let him see just how much he'd upset her. "I knew you would," she told him. "As soon as I saw your name attached to this, I knew you'd do everything you could to keep me from being involved. This isn't a business decision. This is your personal, petty revenge." She shook her head slowly. "It's not worthy of you, Will. In the old days, you'd never have done something so underhanded."

The solid power of her anger left her unable to go on. They stared at one another. At least until Teddy cleared his throat and spoke up. "Would one of you like to tell me what's going on here?"

Will looked at Teddy. "Miss Tillman and I—"

Maggie, her heart cold and hard as a jewel, couldn't take any more. "For God's sake," she snapped. "Considering the fact that we slept together for almost a year, you'd think you could call me Maggie."

She felt her cheeks go hot, but frankly, she was pleased to see that Will was momentarily speechless. Obviously annoyed as hell, but speechless.

Teddy raised a hand to catch their attention. "Hold on, you two. I love a good tussle, but let's keep the gloves on."

Maggie wasn't sure Will was listening. And she didn't much care, because she was perfectly willing to go toe-to-toe with him now, even though she could hear her own heartbeats drumming in her ears. Will swung toward her, clearly intending to…

Well, she didn't know what he intended, and she never found out.

At that moment, the construction trailer door was thrown wide, and a small, bustling tornado that turned into a little girl came barreling in. She headed straight for Will. When she got to his chair, she threw herself into his arms. The hard hat she wore, too big for her head, went flying, and a cascade of brown curls fell down her back.

"Daddy!" she cried. "Look! I got scared, and so did my arms."

Maggie stared, transfixed not by the fact that the girl's thin arms were covered in goose bumps, but by the realization that this child was evidently Will's daughter.

In all the scenarios she'd ever imagined for his future, a house bright and noisy with children had never been a consideration. Perhaps not even a wife. Silly, really, because Will, a handsome, successful man in his thirties, must surely have caught many a woman's eye.

She watched father and daughter interact, her mind straying into new and disturbing channels. A child. Family. Something she'd longed for once upon a time.

Some queer pang stabbed her heart, and for the life of her, Maggie couldn't explain it.

Or make it go away.

# *CHAPTER THREE*

JOHN DENVER, rest his soul, had once recorded a song about some days being diamonds and some being stone. Will Stewart thought this was definitely a stone day.

*Most definitely.*

The week had started out well enough. His sister, Lisa, seemed in a great mood lately, having met a new guy in her college English class. Quarterly returns on his investments were up. Yesterday, Jacobson had taken him to lunch and actually used the word *partner* when talking about Will's future at the firm. This morning he'd turned on the computer to find an e-mail from his stockbroker. And Amy, the one unpredictable component of his life, had managed to eat breakfast today without spilling a single drop on her clothes. Now *there* was a genuine miracle.

Then he'd made the mistake of stopping by the LaCrosse site, catching Teddy in the trailer as he spoke with his construction supervisor. Will should never have taken that offer of a cup of coffee, never stopped long enough to discuss how yesterday's press conference had gone.

If he hadn't, he might never have come face-to-face with Maggie Tillman.

A John Denver stone day for sure. And if things had gone downhill from that moment, they showed every indication of heading even further south right now.

He had to work hard not to stare at Maggie.

He couldn't argue that over the years he'd grown *more* curious about her rather than less. He knew the basics of her life—still living in Key West, unmarried, working. When he chose to use them, he had connections enough to find out that sort of thing.

But was she happy? What kind of woman had she turned into? Did she ever think of him? You couldn't get answers to those kinds of questions without digging a little deeper, and he had always refused to do that.

He mistrusted those rambling thoughts and was sometimes quite annoyed by them, as well. Old lovers weren't supposed to stick around and blight your mental landscape. He had wanted the end of his relationship with Maggie to be like a heavy door closing behind him, firmly locked and impenetrable.

Instead, here she was again, popping back into his life with all the fire and fury that was pure Maggie. Aware of her sitting stiffly beside him as he listened to his daughter chatter, Will didn't think for a minute she was done with arguing yet. Tenacious. Passionate. That had been Maggie, too, and she didn't look like she'd changed much over the years. He needed to keep that fact uppermost in his mind.

He needed not to panic.

But, most of all, he had to find the quickest way possible to get Amy out of this trailer.

Amy's words ran down to nothing as her interest was drawn to the stuffing peeking out of his chair arm. He loved her so much. Being a father was tough, time-consuming. But every moment he was with his daughter, Will felt as though he had trapped sunlight in his hands. How could you ever let anything mess with that?

He touched her cheek, drawing her gaze up. "So you liked the tour Aunt Lisa gave you?"

The child nodded. "It was kind of scary, though. My stomach felt funny when we went up in the elevator with no walls. Aunt Lisa says nobody ever fell out and got squished on the ground, but I said I bet it happens sometimes. I didn't like that part."

He smiled at her with tender amusement. His fault, probably, but Amy sometimes tended to be more fearful and cautious than the average seven-year-old. Lisa said he was overprotective, too restrictive with the child, but what was really wrong with that? The world was a tough place, and you had to look out for the people you loved.

The trailer door opened again, and this time it was his sister. They were going to have lunch today, but first, Will had wanted to talk to Teddy. Lisa had volunteered to keep Amy occupied while he was busy.

"Aunt Lisa shouldn't have taken you up in the elevator," he said.

Hearing Will's admonition as she came in, Lisa

grimaced at him. “Really, Will. Don’t you know that going up in an open elevator is the best part of visiting any construction site? Did you think she wanted to watch them pour concrete?”

As she approached, she removed the hard hat she wore so she could shake out her hair. His sister was going to be twenty-one in a few weeks, and Will couldn’t believe so much time had passed. She’d been ten when their parents had died. He could still clearly recall the fear that had clenched his gut when Ernie Becker, a family friend and the executor of the estate, had told him he was legally responsible for her. The same fear that had gripped him the day Amy had been placed into his arms.

Lisa, remembering her manners, gave Maggie a vague smile. “Hello. I’m sorry to interrupt.” Then she did a double take. “Oh, my gosh! *Maggie.* Is it you?”

Maggie turned farther in her chair. “Lisa?” Her eyes traveled up and down his sister. “I can’t believe it. Look how big you’ve grown!”

Lisa laughed. “Not too big, I hope. It’s so good to see you again. What have you been up to all these years? Where have you been?”

“I live in Key West now. But we must get together and catch up. I’d love to hear all about what you’ve been doing.”

Will felt Amy lean into him. She was always hesitant around strangers. The movement caught Maggie’s attention, and she smiled down at Amy. “And who are you?”

Nerve centers within Will had begun to register swift alarm when Amy had come into the trailer. Now they went into overdrive. He didn't want Maggie interacting with her. The woman could be mad at him, come up here to fight whatever battle she chose for the sake of her business. But he didn't want her within a hundred miles of his daughter.

"I'm Amy," the child said shyly.

"My daughter," Will added, though he supposed it was quite obvious.

"You're such a pretty girl." Maggie reached out to touch one of Amy's dangling curls. "Your hair's like mine. Just wavy enough to be a challenge. I'll bet your mommy has her hands full trying to get it to behave."

Amy wiggled against Will. "Aunt Lisa does my hair every morning."

"Does she?"

Maggie's eyes seemed glued to Amy's face, and Will felt a sudden tightness in his chest and a vague feeling of vulnerability. His fingers clumsily straightened the collar on his daughter's blouse. Then, fighting off panic, he stood and set the child away from him, guiding her toward Lisa. "Ladies, I hate to interrupt," he said in his calmest tone. "But Mr. LaCrosse and I still have business to discuss. Lisa, will you and Amy meet me at the restaurant at noon?"

Lisa agreed immediately and offered Maggie a quick goodbye. Much to Will's displeasure and chagrin, they made promises to be in touch. He suddenly wished that Lisa had not turned out to be such a good-natured, friendly young woman.

He watched them leave, and felt enough relief to melt his bones. No disaster in the making here. No danger.

He leaned against a beat-up file cabinet. Teddy was looking at him curiously, but Will managed something like a smile. "So. Where were we?" He turned toward Maggie. "Ah yes, I believe you were in the middle of an accusation."

A dangerous light kindled in Maggie's eyes again. Good, he thought. He wanted her mad and concentrating on him. Angry enough to keep her distance. So much safer that way.

She tapped the edge of the file she carried, and he saw her bite her lip, possibly trying to make up her mind as to the best approach. "Teddy, I'm sorry," she said at last. "I'm not trying to be difficult. I just want to be sure that the reasons you're going to sign with Coastal are legitimate. Not based unfairly on the history Will and I share."

Will opened his mouth to object, but Teddy cut him off with a raised hand. "Hold on, Willy-boy. Let her finish."

In a voice full of quiet, precise anger, Maggie said, "Eight years ago, Will and I…had a relationship. It ended badly and we haven't spoken since. Now I discover that you're going with Coastal Communities. I can't help but think that—on some level—the decision was made in their favor due to circumstances that are unrelated to my ability to carry out the job."

Teddy's eyes were guarded, but not hostile. "I would be very foolish to ignore the opinion of my chief architect."

Will spoke up. "I advised him against you for specific reasons that have nothing to do with our past. We've already talked about your lack of experience and that of your construction team. Frankly, knowing you as I do, I was also concerned about maturity. My firm can't afford to take chances—"

Maggie had gone rigid. Will knew he'd struck a nerve.

"How dare you talk to me about maturity?" she flashed out. "How mature is it to judge me after an eight-year gap? I was nineteen when we were together. You don't know me at all now. I've worked hard to develop Sapphire Seas into a respected operation I can be proud of." She swung a glance back to Teddy. "I'm not asking for a handout."

"Good, because you won't get one," Teddy replied.

As though sensing some small window of opportunity, Maggie leaned forward again. "If you'll reconsider, I can promise you results that will knock your socks off. I'm not talking about a few pretty aquarium backdrops, Teddy. I'm talking about living works of art. If you're not one hundred percent satisfied..." She opened her folder on the desk, turned it upside down so he could see it and jabbed a finger at the bottom of the page where a column of figures ended. "I'll eat my costs. *Every* one of them."

Will barely disguised a sharp breath. He knew

Teddy, and saving money always got him to sit up and take notice. Damage control was in order. He said quickly, "That's a ridiculous promise to make, and even suggesting it shows—"

"I like it," Teddy said.

Maggie blinked and then smiled, clearly thinking she'd won. "I'll even—"

Teddy held up a hand again. "Stop. Remember the salesman's creed. Once you get your yes, stop talking. You've made your point and caught my interest." He lifted a brow at Will, who managed to stifle any hint of emotion. "I don't know if what Maggie says is true or not, but as long as we've done business together, I've never known you to be unethical." He grinned. "But I've also never seen you this agitated, and that makes me curious as hell. So I'm asking you to reconsider your advice. Make sure your motives are legit. I'll abide by your decision, but I liked Maggie's designs a lot, and I want her to have a fair shot at this. Will you agree?"

The moment stretched interminable and a few seconds beyond. Finally, Will made a sound full of disgust. "This is a foolish waste of time. I'll admit it occurred to me that working with Maggie would be difficult given our history. But I advised you to go with Coastal for the right reasons. I don't reach conclusions based on personal prejudices."

Teddy laughed and gave him a smile that was wide and full of sly humor. "Son, take my word for it. Whatever happens in the bedroom always messes with what goes on in the brain."

## *CHAPTER FOUR*

AS SOON AS Maggie left the construction trailer, she called Zack. Her nerves still sang with tension from her confrontation with Will in front of Teddy LaCrosse, but at least she felt some small measure of relief that she hadn't been completely shot down. Sapphire Seas had a chance—a slim one, especially if Will refused to be fair and found fault at every turn, but a chance all the same.

She asked Zack to start lining up the oven team who would be responsible for pouring acrylic molds for the tanks. He might be terrible with paperwork, but her business partner had a real knack for handling her part-time construction crew.

"I heard Dick Iverson moved back to Wisconsin after the last hurricane, so he's out," Zack told her as she sat at one of the constant stream of traffic lights on Collins Avenue. "Are you coming back tonight? We can have dinner and talk about who else might be available."

"I think I'll stay a couple of days. There's a huge homebuilders' convention in town. Maybe I can drum up some business. Since you're coming up tomorrow to do the installation on the Blue Reef job, we could talk then."

"Okay," Zack said. "But if you show up at the Blue Reef, I'm putting you to work."

The Blue Reef Bar and Grill was one of their latest clients, an upscale watering hole that had contracted for a large bi-view tank that would separate the restaurant from the bar area. Nothing too difficult or exotic, and on those kinds of jobs Maggie seldom got involved in setting the end product in place.

"Fine," Maggie teased back. "I'll show you boys how it's *supposed* to be done."

Zack laughed. "Just don't run up a big hotel bill while you're there. No room service."

"I know what the budget will tolerate. I'm going to ask Alaina if I can stay at her place. In that big house of hers, she's bound to have room."

There was the slight hesitation that Maggie always got from Zack at the mention of her sister's name. Then he said easily, "All right. I'll talk to you tomorrow, then."

Although Zack couldn't see her, Maggie shook her head in disgust. Ten years had passed since he and Alaina had broken up—too long to let the heated, passionate turmoil of those young days still bother him. Alaina had been married for ages, presumably for keeps. Zack, on the other hand… He dated, but he never seemed interested in settling down.

What was he waiting for? Did he think Alaina would

change her mind? It seemed silly for a great guy like Zack Davidson to let an old love continue to affect him.

But as Maggie hung up from Zack and dialed her sister's number, she scolded herself. Who was she to tell people how they ought to deal with their emotions? Sometimes, didn't those early relationships do enough damage to last a lifetime? After all these years, coming face-to-face with Will Stewart had certainly set *her* blood on fire, hadn't it? Thank goodness, though, it had been for an entirely different reason than unrequited love.

Maggie was relieved when Alaina seemed delighted at the idea of having an unexpected visitor. It had been at least a year since they'd last seen one another, two since she'd visited her parents.

Years ago, when Maggie had left Miami for Key West, she'd been furious with all three of them, but she hadn't been able to stay angry at her sister for long. Alaina could seldom stand up to their parents, but she didn't have a mean bone in her body. She would have done anything for her younger sister, including raise Maggie's illegitimate baby as her own—an idea Connie and James Tillman had unbelievably considered the best solution for everyone.

A solution that Maggie had hotly refused to consider.

The moment Alaina opened the front door of her huge home in North Miami, Maggie found herself swallowed in a tight, welcoming hug. It surprised her a little. Alaina was reserved and not much of a "hugger."

Alaina had always been delicately beautiful, articulate and poised, everything that Maggie had never been and never *would* be. Just shy of thirty, she had an elegant sophistication now. She looked trim and spotless in white shorts, with long, bare legs that were sun-gilded to a rosy gold. There wasn't a blond hair out of place, in spite of the fact that she looked like she'd just come off the tennis court.

Maggie had to hide a secret grimace. Any time *she* had played tennis, it had strictly been baggy pants and sweat marks at the armpits of her T-shirt.

Alaina drew back, still holding Maggie's arms. "I've missed you so much!"

"You have?" Maggie replied in a stunned tone, without thinking. She wasn't used to this kind of effusive greeting from Alaina. Her sister tended to welcome you like a queen inviting a television crew into the palace.

"Of course," Alaina said. "Come on, I have your room all ready. It's Delia's day off, so the place is a mess, but a little clutter never used to bother you much. Close your eyes if you can't bear it."

Maggie kept her eyes open as she followed her sister through the house. She made a mental note to look up the word *clutter* in the dictionary when she got home. Alaina's definition must be an iced tea glass sweating on the coffee table without a coaster and a tennis racket tossed onto a chair. Everything else looked model-home perfect and boring—from the impressive baby grand piano placed artfully by the floor-to-ceiling windows, to a massive piece of modern sculpture that soared skyward in the foyer.

Maggie thought suddenly of her lumpy but comfortable couch at home, snagged at a neighbor's garage sale, and her mismatched dining chairs. Her apartment boasted the kind of decor that came from seldom having guests and never seeing your own home with fresh eyes. Compared to this place, it was a disaster.

Honestly, it was amazing that she and Alaina were actually sisters.

"Same old dump, I see," Maggie remarked.

Alaina smiled back over one shoulder. "It's awfully bland, isn't it? But Gil insisted we use a professional designer for the common areas. He feels a certain impression has to be maintained. The house has to *say* something about who he is."

"Oh, it does," Maggie replied.

She clamped her tongue between her teeth to keep from divulging more. She didn't like Alaina's husband, Gil. He might be a brilliant, prominent pediatric surgeon, but Maggie thought him overbearing and a complete snob. And the few times she'd been around him, he'd been so bossy with Alaina. Of course, that hardly differed from the way her parents had always treated her sister, but it seemed a little unfair that Alaina should have gone from one domineering household to another.

But...maybe Alaina, never much for taking chances or bucking authority, liked it that way.

She led Maggie down a long hallway. Finally, she came to a door, opened it, and stepped aside. "I redecorated the back bedrooms a few months ago. I hope you like yours. I don't care if it *is* all last year's colors."

Maggie had been about to make a playfully snarky remark about being stuck with "last year's colors," but when she stepped into the room, the beauty of it took her breath away. The furniture didn't match, but actually worked together instead of looking like a hodgepodge. Cream and rose hues, with a touch of green for accent. All the soft colors of a Victorian garden party. The curtains at the tall windows were real lace, billowing an invitation in the soft breeze.

Noting Maggie's silence, Alaina said, "Do you think it's too girly? Gil refuses to put any of his relatives in here."

Maggie turned to face her sister. "Al, it's gorgeous. You really did miss your calling. You shouldn't have let Mom and Dad talk you out of a degree in interior design."

Alaina shook her head. "That was just a silly dream. I didn't really have enough imagination to sustain that kind of career. So now I'm exactly who I should be."

Maggie frowned a little. And who was that?

She didn't know her sister all that well anymore. They had always been very different people, but as the years had gone by, the gap had widened. They certainly didn't have mutual friends and interests, or kids or husbands. Just their parents.

And Alaina knew better than to encourage *that* particular point of connection.

Maggie turned back to the room, feeling a tightness in her chest, regretting that she and her sister had become so distant. She made the sudden, impassioned decision that from now on she would try to rectify that, try harder to be a real friend to Alaina.

She rolled her weekender to the bed and hefted it on top. Alaina went into hostess mode, pointing out the bathroom and a basket of high-end toiletries that put Maggie's hotel freebies to shame. She promised to bring more hangers if Maggie needed them. Would she like scented ones?

Maggie had to laugh. "I don't think I'll need more. I usually drape my good clothes over a chair and ball up everything else in a corner."

"Even after all these years?" Alaina asked. "Mom would be horrified."

"It wouldn't be the first time I've shocked her. Or Dad, either."

"It doesn't have to be that way."

Maggie gave her sister a wry smile. "Don't start. That's just the way it is. We're pleasant to one another. I still love them. Didn't I come up for Dad's retirement party? We're just not destined to be close."

Alaina went to the windows and fiddled with the curtains while Maggie unzipped her bag. Somewhere in the distance she could hear wind chimes tinkling sweet notes.

"Are you going to stop by to see them?" Alaina asked, still intent on the drapes.

"I doubt it. I only need to stay a couple of days."

"Mom would probably like to see you. Since Dad's retired he doesn't have enough to do, and she says he drives her crazy."

"I can imagine," Maggie replied. It wasn't hard to picture her father trying to rearrange her mother's household chores or deciding on the spur of the moment to remodel the family room. "Maybe I'll swing by for an hour or two on my way out of town."

Maggie visited Connie and James Tillman mostly out of obligation now. She still considered herself a dutiful daughter. But when she came up to see them, their time together was deliberately brief. Her parents were better taken in small doses, and there was a coolness to all of their interactions, as though they were guests she'd only just met at a party and not the people who'd raised her.

She pulled a blouse out of her suitcase, shaking out the wrinkles. From the corner of her eye, she was aware of her sister turning from the window.

"I wish things could have been different," Alaina said suddenly.

"Different how?"

"You know. About the baby."

Maggie looked up. Alaina, never comfortable talking about unpleasant family history, seldom mentioned those early days when Maggie had discovered she was pregnant.

Her sister grimaced. "I wish I'd tried harder to make them see how wrong they were back then. It's true Gil and I were eager for kids, but letting Mom and

Dad persuade me to take your baby wasn't the answer. I should have told them no right away instead of allowing them to browbeat you for days."

Maggie let the blouse drop from her hands. She could hear the sudden anguish in her sister's voice. How long had Alaina been wanting to say this?

In dismay, Maggie said, "It wouldn't have mattered if they had gone on at me for a month. There was just no way I could bear to end up being *Aunt* Maggie, living on the outskirts of my own child's life. But I don't blame *you,* Al. At the time, they thought it was a perfectly sensible solution, and you couldn't have refused."

Their eyes met, and immediately Alaina's looked elsewhere, leaving a brief burn of barely concealed shame. "I know they hurt you," she said. "I should have taken your side. But I'm not a fighter and never have been. I don't like…confrontation. Arguing is so…"

"Fight phobia."

Alaina's gaze swung back to her. "What?"

Maggie gave her a small smile of understanding, hoping to lighten the mood. "Back in high school. That's what Zack used to call it when I'd complain because you wouldn't take a stand with me against Mom and Dad. Fight phobia."

Maggie came around the bed to go to her sister's side. Gently, she squeezed Alaina's arm and drew her closer. "It's all right. Everything worked out for the best."

"Did it?" Alaina asked, looking uncertain. "I want

a child so badly. I don't know how you reached that point where you could—" She colored suddenly. "I'm sorry. That came out wrong. I'm not judging you."

"You couldn't possibly judge me more harshly than I do myself sometimes." Maggie felt a sudden, tight thickness at the back of her throat. Talking about children—particularly the fact that she didn't have any—always made things difficult. Maybe it was time to change the subject. She touched Alaina's cheek. "Are you and Gil still trying for a baby?" she asked quickly, hoping that her sister wouldn't notice anything wrong with her voice.

"Not so much anymore. We've done everything the doctors say. But after nine years, you start to think…"

"Maybe you need to spice things up a bit. I hear the Internet has all kinds of Web sites where you can buy—"

"Mag!"

"Oh, good grief. How can sex make you blush after nine years of marriage?"

"There are some things that are just too personal to discuss."

Maggie waved that away. If she was really going to try to strengthen her relationship with Alaina, she might as well start now. "Between sisters? Nonsense. Ask me anything. I guarantee I'm long past the blushing stage, and very few things make me uncomfortable anymore."

Alaina gave her a searching look. "Do you ever think about your baby?"

Maggie blinked rapidly. She could not hold Alaina's gaze, not even for a second. Something inside her just couldn't manage it.

She had the quick vision of her daughter's face as the clinic's midwife had placed the baby in her arms. All red and unhappy and helpless as she wailed. And then gone, so suddenly. It had only been a moment. How could she explain to Alaina that such a tiny fragment of time still made her brain and her heart burn like brimstone?

"Every day of my life," Maggie said carefully. "I've second-guessed that decision from the moment I made it and wondered what my life would be like if I hadn't. What she might look like now, as a little girl."

The silence between them thickened, then Maggie straightened her spine, determined to be brisk. "But it's easier to find solutions when your stomach is full and you aren't sleeping in your car. When I showed up on Zack's doorstep, I honestly didn't know how I could manage with a baby. They need so much." She grimaced. "So I just made the best choice for her that I could. At least what I thought would be best."

"You should have gone to Will," Alaina said softly. "I always liked him. I think he would have helped you."

Maggie stepped away abruptly, returning to her suitcase. "Really, Al. You're too romantic to be believed. Will told me flat out that he hoped he'd never see me again. That the danger I exposed Lisa to was unforgivable. Do you honestly think he would have been thrilled by the idea of having a baby with a woman he despised? First he would have accused me of getting pregnant on purpose—which I didn't—"

"You were always so careless about keeping track—"

Maggie made a face at her, more comfortable to return to this testy camaraderie. "You don't have to point that out. I know. But I'm much better about it now, I assure you."

"Sorry."

"And then he would have been furious. Forced to share custody for the rest of his life with someone he hates? Never able to file me away in some compartment of his tidy little mind labeled Finished Business? Trust me, that definitely wasn't an option back then."

"I suppose we'll never know," Alaina said. "Isn't it funny how both of us, in our own way, always give in to fear?"

"What do you mean?"

"I'm always afraid of doing something that will disappoint someone. Mom and Dad. Gil. And you're frightened that people will think you can't manage your own life. That somehow they'll think you're weak. Too much pride, Maggie."

She didn't want to talk about this. She let Alaina take the blouse from her hands and slip it onto a padded hanger. Then she kicked off the heels she'd worn for the meeting with Teddy and began massaging one instep.

"What do you want to do about dinner?" she asked. "I feel like steak. Should I make a reservation for three at Maldanado's? Or is Gil still boycotting red meat?"

Alaina emerged from the closet, then headed for the door. "Gil's in Boston this week. He's giving a couple of speeches at a pediatricians' conference."

"I'm surprised you didn't go with him," Maggie said with a frown. "You love Boston."

Alaina shrugged. "Not this time. Now I'm going to fix us some lunch."

"Al…"

Alaina turned back.

"Why haven't you asked me about Zack? I've mentioned him twice now. Don't you want to know how he is?"

Her sister didn't miss a beat. "Okay. How is he?"

"He's great. Still the best friend a girl could ever have. And he's really my right arm when it comes to the business. I'm afraid I'm going to lose him next year."

"Lose him?" Alaina's brows rose. "Why?"

"He keeps talking about opening up his own shop. Nothing to do with aquariums, so I don't have to worry about competition. But his cabinetry work is so remarkable. I'm sure his talent has had a lot to do with the success of Sapphire Seas." She gave Alaina a curious glance. "Don't you want to know if he ever talks about you?"

Alaina bit her lower lip, and Maggie wondered if that was the only way she could keep it from trembling. Then she tilted her head back a little, all trace of discomfort gone. "No," she claimed succinctly. "Why would I? What we were in high school…what might have been…what difference does all that make now?"

Maggie grimaced. "Mom and Dad really did a number on both of us, didn't they? Trying to convince me that you could raise my child, until I just got fed up and ran away. Brainwashing you into thinking that Zack wasn't good enough. That you weren't head over heels in love with him."

"Maybe I wasn't." She sighed a little. "Like I said, it doesn't matter now. Eventually you have to leave behind all that foolishness."

"So you can become exactly who you're supposed to be," Maggie said, reciting Alaina's earlier words.

"That's right," Alaina replied. Then she frowned a little. "This is who I am now. I'm a married woman with a very successful husband who loves me. I have a beautiful home. Lots of friends. And parents who, unlike you, I get along with. What more do I need?"

"Sounds fantastic."

"It is. Now let me go fix lunch."

"Al?"

Again Alaina stopped, but this time there was a touch of exasperation in the look she gave Maggie. "What now?"

"You just said you were a married woman. How come you didn't preface that with the word *happily?*"

Alaina looked surprised and, for just a moment, Maggie thought her sister might actually give her hell for that question. Instead, she paused then shook her head. “Honestly, Maggie,” she said softly. “Now who’s being a silly romantic?”

## *CHAPTER FIVE*

BY TEN THE NEXT MORNING, Will had finally tracked down the Sapphire Seas crew at their current project—a bar and grill near Coconut Grove called the Blue Reef.

It had taken him the better part of an hour to get a name and address. The flunky in Key West who had answered the phone knew almost nothing and provided even less—until Will had told him that Sapphire Seas stood to lose a huge contract if he didn't get in touch with someone immediately.

Relieved that he wouldn't have to travel half the state to see Maggie's team in action, Will parked on the street and headed toward Blue Reef's front entrance. The place was closed, but he noted two large trucks parked near the wide double doors. He assumed they were rentals since neither of them carried the Sapphire Seas logo. The company bank account had probably never been flush enough to allow for that kind of heavy-duty equipment purchase. Understandable, but another clear sign that the infrastructure of Sapphire Seas didn't go very deep.

He resented having to make this outing. He wasn't

used to his recommendations being rejected or his motives questioned. Yes, Maggie had been his lover once, but he was confident that unfortunate fact had not influenced his vote against her company. It had been strictly a business decision, and the sooner he could prove that to Teddy, the sooner everything could get back to normal.

He drew a deeper breath, prepared not to like what he'd find inside, but resolving to be fair. He didn't doubt Maggie's passionate sincerity. He didn't doubt her determination to give it her best. She honestly believed Sapphire Seas could handle the LaCrosse project. Unfortunately, he simply couldn't share that conviction.

He made his way through the dining room and into the bar, a cavernous room that looked odd in bright daylight. The theme was tropical, of course. Lots of turquoise and sea-foam green, but not much excitement or imagination in the design. Will saw right away that the aquarium being installed between the bar and the restaurant was going to be a focal point, though it wasn't anywhere near the size Teddy wanted for his South Beach venture.

He negotiated past a pile of bubble wrap, two-by-fours, steel beams and cardboard sleeves to find a spot out of the way where he could observe the work. A couple of guys were positioning a large sump pump within sleek-looking mahogany cabinets. A third man was working on what looked like a filtration system. It fed into the tank, which right now was nothing more than a long, clear rectangular box with several viewing panels. Not a drop of water nor a single fish in sight.

He heard Maggie before he saw her. She'd evidently wedged herself inside the cabinet below the tank, and her voice rose eerily as she called out to one of her crew. "Alfredo, pass me a flashlight, will you? The standpipe for the overflow feels short down here."

Will watched her helper comply. He heard her mumble several things he didn't understand or couldn't make out. She was under the tank a full five minutes before she finally emerged, dusting off her jeans and scraping hair out of her eyes. She tossed the flashlight into a toolbox before turning to give the three men the thumbs-up.

"Fits like a glove," she said, and even from where he stood Will could hear the satisfaction in her tone. "I knew we could make it work if we shaved off a quarter inch. Listen, guys, if you're willing to skip lunch, we could have chem numbers by this afternoon so I can drop fish by midnight. That means you could be home by dinner. What do you say?"

Her team gave in with a minimum amount of complaint. Will couldn't catch every word, but he could tell Maggie knew how to deal with the guys. He remembered that about her. The maddening way she had of making a person want to agree to any request. The tilt of her grin. Her voice persuasive, as soft as flannel. How could any red-blooded man…

He turned away from those thoughts, away from memories of the past. He needed to stay focused on the task at hand. Look at Maggie's ability. Be objective. Be honest. Shut her out if that was the decision that was called for.

It ought to be easy. He'd already reviewed the company profit-and-loss statement she'd furnished Teddy with. For the past two years, Sapphire Seas had been operating on a shoestring budget, for God's sake.

One of the men saw him, looked at Maggie, then angled his chin in Will's direction. She turned immediately.

Surprise flitted across her features as she recognized him. Then everything about her became calm and precise as she walked toward him across the distance.

Someone who didn't know her might have missed it, but he recognized that battle-ready tension in her face. The image of how they were in those last horrible days before they'd split was just beneath the surface of Will's brain, and it wasn't hard to recall the look and feel of two people on the verge of making war.

Stopping in front of him, she crossed her arms. "I see you decided not to waste any time. You're here to check us out."

He nodded. "I want to get this settled as quickly as possible."

"I'm surprised you bothered to come at all."

The words were without inflection or force. She appeared not to care one way or the other if he was here to pass judgment, but Will wasn't fooled. Outwardly calm she might be, but inside he knew Maggie was wary and nervous, ready to go on the offensive. She was outgunned and outmatched, but she would face this meeting with every bit of her courage.

It was a character trait that he had admired.

It was a character trait he sometimes saw in their daughter, Amy.

"You didn't think I'd keep my word?" he asked, struggling not to sound irritated. Did she really have such a low opinion of him?

"Not really. Isn't your mind already made up?"

"If it is, it's up to you to change it."

"I'm not sure it wouldn't be a huge waste of time." She narrowed her eyes at him. "I dreamed about you last night."

He tried not to look stunned, unsure that he'd heard her properly. "Dreamed about me?"

"Yeah. You were sitting at the dinner table. Your daughter was telling you about the next school play she's going to be in. You were eating pork chops and pretending to listen. But the entire time you were trying to figure out how to send me packing as quickly as possible."

In spite of the fact that she'd mentioned Amy, he almost smiled at that. She thought she had him all figured out. He wondered how shocked she'd be if he told her the truth about their daughter. But that wasn't going to happen. *Ever,* if he could manage it. He shook his head.

She grimaced. "Are you telling me I'm wrong?"

"Yes, you're wrong. It was spaghetti last night, not pork chops."

She huffed out a short laugh with no humor in it and waved that away with an impatient hand. "Details. The outcome is the same. You'll do anything to keep me from getting this contract."

He sighed and gave her an intent look meant to convey that he was growing tired of trying to defend himself. "I can be a lot more objective about your ability if you'll stop trying to antagonize me at every turn."

"I guess I just don't trust you to be fair."

"Fine. I don't trust you to be competent. So show me I'm wrong. Walk me through your process. I'm here. Impress me."

He watched her jaw harden as she tossed a glance toward the bar. Two of her crew members were groaning as they struggled to settle a section of the tank onto the cabinetry.

Will caught Maggie's attention again. "Come on, Maggie. Be reasonable. The last time I saw you running a business, you were scraping algae and feeding guppies. You want me to let Teddy lay the contract in your lap? Then convince me that you're capable of handling something this big."

She gave him one last withering look, then nodded. "You're right," she said. "Let's get started, then. I've still got work to do."

She led him back to the bar area. While her guys continued to set the tanks in place, Maggie explained just what the Blue Reef job entailed. At first she was stiff and abrupt, obviously resentful of having to do this at all. He ignored the attitude and kept asking questions. When she realized he was genuinely interested in the answers, she loosened up.

Her features lost that pinch of suspicion. She forgot to be angry with him. She began to speak more animatedly as she warmed to the subject. From her briefcase she withdrew her designs, showing him calculations on everything from weight distribution to insulation that would minimize water temperature fluctuation. When he seemed receptive, she gave him a minilecture on the difference between glass and acrylic tanks and the benefits of chemically bonding joints instead of using silicone.

Through it all, one thing became glaringly apparent. She loved her work. She was earnest, confident and full of winning charm, and Will listened with something that felt oddly like envy. Lately, with the exception of the LaCrosse job, very few assignments he had handled for Jacobson and Duquette filled him with this kind of excitement.

Finally, Maggie wound down. She wrapped her arms around her waist and lifted her chin to look at him. "Well?"

"I think you've come a long way in eight years," he admitted.

He watched annoyance create a line between her brows. "But not far enough."

"I didn't say that. What you're doing here is impressive…"

"But?"

"But it's nowhere near the scope of Teddy's project."

She bit her lip, looking obviously disappointed. Then, as though irked that she'd shown any sign of weakness, she straightened. "I know what I'm doing, Will," she said. "I'll admit Sapphire Seas has never taken on something this big. But I know Coastal Communities. I've seen their work firsthand. Teddy's project is just money to them."

He smiled a little. "You aren't interested in money?"

"Of course I am. But throwing buckets of it at Coastal isn't going to work for Teddy. When we spoke, I realized what's important to him. He needs something different. This is his defining project. He's passionate about this restoration, and he deserves someone working for him who feels the same way."

He had to agree. "The one thing you never lacked was passion."

"I never saw that as a bad thing."

He grimaced. Ridiculous. Passion was lovely. But what about common sense and practicality? What about hard-boiled facts that clearly suggested Sapphire Seas would be biting off more than it could chew if Maggie got this job?

And yet, he didn't say a word.

"I can give Teddy what he wants," Maggie added. She tapped the underside of one of the aquariums that hadn't been set into place yet. "We paint the bottoms of our tanks black. Do you know why?"

"I haven't got a clue."

"It's to keep out any light. Fish aren't used to having light come up from below and I'm convinced it upsets them. We're the only company I know who does that. Coastal Communities certainly doesn't. They don't give a damn if the client ends up with stressed-out fish. In fact, the sooner their original stock dies off, the sooner they can sell you more. Those are the kinds of details I can bring to this job. If you'll just give me the chance."

He looked at her, thinking in that moment that he was about to do something completely idiotic. Even though a part of him was desperate to see her as far away from here as possible, he wanted to give her this chance. But there was such potential for danger in that.

And then, before he could even sort out his thoughts or any type of response, he watched frustration tighten her features. "I know what this is about," she said. "I can do this job. What I *can't* do is change anything that happened between us. Saying how sorry I am one more time about what that toad Huckabee did to Lisa isn't going to make any difference. Is it really going to keep you from giving me a fair shot at this contract?"

He made a low sound between his lips and faced her squarely. "I'm not asking for more apologies. And I definitely don't—"

A door slammed somewhere behind them, and they both turned toward the sound. A man about Will's age entered the bar. He looked vaguely familiar—tall and ruggedly fit—with hair so dark a black it looked like india ink.

He moved into the light, and Will suddenly recognized him, though he'd seen him only once, eight years ago. But long enough to leave quite an impression.

Three months after that last bitter argument, Will's private detective had located Maggie in Key West. Will had driven down, determined to speak to her. He'd been unnerved by their acrimonious parting. That wasn't how he normally handled things.

He was parked outside the address the investigator had given him only a few minutes when Maggie emerged. He followed her, watching her disappear into a medical clinic where she remained for more than an hour. When she came out, she was with *this* guy. They had embraced on the sidewalk, and then the man had placed his hand against Maggie's stomach, in the protective, proprietary way only someone who loves you could. In that moment, Will had seen the little bump of Maggie's belly, known that she was pregnant and suspected that he was the father.

After that, he'd been unable to do anything but watch as Maggie and her companion got into a beat-up sedan and drove off. Obviously she'd found a replacement for him, and Will was angry enough in those moments to leave her to him. Later, when he was clear-headed and calm, he had been able to make decisions, but none of them involved coming face-to-face with Maggie again. Or this man.

Now, as the newcomer talked with the crew, Will remembered the name his investigator had given him. Theodore Davidson. Her business partner. But was he still her lover?

He tried to make himself immune to curiosity about that. But even after all these years, he couldn't help the way his gut twisted—just a little—at the sight of the man who had stepped into his shoes so quickly.

Maggie was speaking, and he turned to look at her, indicating that he'd missed her words.

She pointed to Theodore Davidson. "I said, I think you ought to meet my partner. We've been together from the first. I can't imagine how I'd have managed without him."

"You're very enterprising. I'm sure you'd have found a way."

His tone must have been sharper, more sarcastic than he intended. Maggie looked at him warily, then waved a hand toward the little group at the bar. "Zack!" she called. "Come over when you finish. There's someone I want you to meet."

Will exhaled harshly, feeling suddenly as though he'd just descended into a fog. He definitely had no interest in meeting the guy who—

And then his brain tripped to a halt. *Zack*… No, that wasn't right.

Maggie had turned away from him, and he caught her arm. "Did you say Zack?"

She frowned at him. "Yes. Zack's my partner."

"I thought your partner's name was Theodore Davidson."

"Well…technically it is. Theodore Zachary Davidson. But he's always hated his first name and never uses it. No one calls him that. It's always been Zack."

She glanced down at her forearm, where his fingers lay. Will forced himself to loosen his grip. "What's wrong?" Maggie asked.

"When we… You used to talk about a guy named Zack who was in love with your sister. Someone she dumped right after high school. You said she was the love of his life, and that he never got over her."

"Right. Zack moved to Key West because he couldn't bear living in the same town as Alaina. Although he'd deny that if you asked him. What's—"

"*That* Zack is your partner?" Will asked carefully, inclining his head toward the guy. Part of him just couldn't believe he could have been wrong all those years ago. This man—a good friend instead of a lover? A ripple of shock started to run through his body all the way down to his toes. "But he's also Theodore Zachary Davidson."

"It shouldn't be that hard a concept to grasp."

"You'd think that, wouldn't you?" Will said, struggling to keep his voice sane.

TWENTY MINUTES LATER, when Will abruptly left the Blue Reef, Maggie went quickly to the restroom. Her face felt flushed, her stomach bloated, and her hands were actually shaking. It was a pathetic, childish reaction, but she couldn't stop any of it.

She splashed water on her cheeks, swallowed two aspirin and emerged from the restroom to find Zack waiting for her.

He took one look at her and shook his head. "Damn. The son of a bitch turned us down."

"No. Just the opposite. He said he'll talk to Teddy today and recommend that we get the contract." She blinked, realizing as she said the words out loud that it was really true. "Oh my God…" She threw herself into Zack's arms. "We did it, Zack! We really did it!"

"*You* did it," her partner said. "Alfredo told me that while I was out wrangling fish, you were in here giving the guy a college course on aquariums."

Maggie placed her fingertips over her mouth. "I still can't believe it. I was sure he was going to shoot me down any moment. I think at one point he intended to, but then he didn't. He really started listening. He didn't sneer. He didn't make jokes. He just…I don't know. It was all so strange."

"Who cares? We've got the job."

"I can't wait to get started." She nodded toward her team still working to set the tanks. "I told the fellows I wanted to drop fish tonight. Any problem with making that happen?"

"The truck from Tropic Beauties should be here by five."

"Good. I'll check them one last time tomorrow afternoon, then come on home. I promised Will that any alterations to the designs, any deviations from our schedule or the original plans would be run through him first."

Zack made a face at that news. "We don't need a babysitter."

"No, but it's his butt on the line with this project, so I didn't really mind making that concession."

"Okay," Zack acknowledged with a nod. He turned toward the guys, scanning the progress they'd made. "So where are we with this? Now what?"

*Now what?*

A foolish lump formed in Maggie's throat. *Now...everything.* A second look at her sketches for any changes that should be pitched to Teddy. A larger crew to pour acrylic and run the ovens. A loan from the bank to get some cash up front. So many things to take care of. But if she did this right, it would move Sapphire Seas to a whole new league. The thought was so wonderful. And absolutely terrifying.

And more than a small part of that terror came from the knowledge that she'd be interacting with Will once again. Maybe not often. Maybe not closely. But after all these years, how would she cope? How could she be around him and *not* think about the child they had created? And how foolish she'd been to give her up without ever letting him know.

Zack's hands descended on her shoulders, dragging her back to the present. He was one of the few people in this world who knew the circumstances of her child's birth. His eyes told her he had guessed just where her thoughts had taken her, that she wasn't concentrating on the job at all.

"No matter what," he said, "you're going to manage just fine, Mags. You can handle seeing this guy again. In fact, I think you can handle just about anything."

Maggie nodded. But in her heart, she felt none of Zack's confidence.

# *CHAPTER SIX*

THREE WEEKS LATER, Will sat at his home computer, reading the latest e-mail from Maggie. It was dated just this morning.

I've been rethinking the viewing panels behind check-in. Lots of guest traffic there. Suppose we bring them out to the floor or bridged them to the desks? If they're closer, the guest stays more involved. What do you think?
BTW, how's your shoulder? There's an herb I took a few years ago when I threw my back out hauling tanks. Something from the Kalahari Desert, I think. Check the health food store. Or maybe you should just stop playing racquetball? <g>
M.

Will smiled at the screen. He'd grown used to these breezy messages.

It had been three weeks since Sapphire Seas had won the contract for Teddy's project. They'd kept in contact through e-mails, texts and a few telephone calls, but he hadn't seen her.

At first, their communications had been all business, and Will was happy to keep them that way. The less he let Maggie back into his world, the better. Better for him. Better for Amy. Just better all around.

But he should have known that Maggie, outgoing and enthusiastic as ever, wouldn't be able to keep her notes stark and impersonal for long. She just wasn't built that way, no matter how angry she might have been with him initially.

Before the first week was up, she'd suggested some television program to him because it showcased artificial reefs. He'd watched it and e-mailed his impressions, then sent her a newspaper article he'd come across. Pretty soon, their business conversations began to end on a slightly more personal note—a discussion of books and movies and hobbies and reminders of the past they'd once shared. *Do you still like Tex-Mex ribs with hot sauce? Here's a great Internet site that says you can have them shipped right to your front door.*

The short messages back and forth remained light and friendly. Maggie occasionally asked after Lisa and Amy, but Will deflected any mention of family or just ignored it completely. Since she had returned to work in Key West, there was no chance that she and Amy would interact, and Will's relief was palpable. The situation felt controlled, safe, and he actually began to look forward to seeing an e-mail from Maggie in his in-box.

Now, halfway through composing his reply to her, Will stopped typing. He cocked his head, listening, certain that he'd heard whispering.

Amy.

He'd put her to bed half an hour ago, but he knew she was still awake. Tonight she had wanted to stay up until Lisa got home from her date, but Will had vetoed that. His decision had been met with a dark scowl and a pretty pout worthy of an Oscar.

He shut down the computer and rose, massaging his shoulder. It was just as sore as it had been first thing this morning. Maybe he'd take Maggie's advice and hit the health food store tomorrow.

He headed for Amy's room, which had once been Lisa's. When he'd first brought his daughter home, Lisa had been fourteen. He'd been sure he would have to answer a million questions about why he was suddenly introducing a baby into the house. But his sister had been amazingly receptive to the idea of becoming an aunt overnight.

Of course she'd been curious as hell how it had happened. But the tale Will had settled on—an old love affair that had foolishly flared to life again, a mistake made over good wine on a warm, sultry night—had seemed to satisfy Lisa, who was right at the age where the idea of making mad, passionate love could seem very romantic.

And when she tried to delve any deeper for details, Will slipped into embarrassed big-brother mode. Of course creating a baby with someone you didn't love was horrible. Of course he wished it hadn't happened. But he was responsible enough to do the right thing. Now, could they please not discuss it anymore?

Lisa, knowing Will's distaste for anything so dreadfully impulsive, and blessed with a nurturing spirit, had been quick to move beyond wondering where Amy had come from and right into mothering her. In days, she had fallen in love with the baby as much as Will had.

He nudged Amy's bedroom door open. With the nightlight to guide him, he sat down in the chair beside her bed and turned on the bedside lamp, the base a spiraling purple castle with glittery towers. Amy was firmly into fairy tales right now.

He saw that his daughter's eyes were squeezed tightly shut, faking a sound sleep. She had the creamiest complexion of any human he'd ever met, and her lips were parted as though relaxing into the gauzy pull of dreams. Just watching her, Will's heart felt loose in his chest.

He traced the line of her jaw with one finger. "Hey, little faker," he called softly. "How long can you pretend to be asleep?"

Amy's eyes popped open and she smiled. "Hi, Daddy."

"Why aren't you asleep?"

"I was trying." She lifted the edge of her blanket, revealing her favorite doll tucked tightly against her arm—some princess she'd gotten last Christmas, a blonde in a long white gown drizzled with embroidery and lace. "But she needed to talk to me."

Will gave the doll a forbidding look. "Tell Cinderella to save the chitchat for tomorrow. It's time for bed."

Amy gasped. "This isn't Cinderella. This is Princess Valentina, and she likes to do whatever she wants. And she can, 'cause she's a princess."

"Well, I'm the king of this castle, so she has to listen to me. The two of you should be asleep."

Amy brought the doll to her ear as though listening. "Princess Valentina says you have too many rules."

"Princess Valentina doesn't have school tomorrow. You do."

"I don't like school," Amy said quickly. "I don't want to go anymore."

Will looked at his daughter closely. He had discovered that one of the truly unnerving things about raising a child was his inability to know which moments to pay attention to and what would matter later on. Recently Amy had seemed restless at night. When he checked on her before he turned in, her covers often looked like a hurricane had blown through them. Was there some trouble brewing at school? But what kind of problem could first grade present?

"Why don't you want to go to school?"

Amy shrugged.

"That's not a good reason."

"It's the only one I got!" She pulled Princess Valentina from beneath the covers and began slowly twirling the doll over her chest. Ignoring him.

"Is it history?" Will ventured.

The princess stopped dancing as Amy's forehead puckered. "How do you know that?"

"Because Mrs. Proctor sent me an e-mail saying

you aren't doing too well, and that you didn't hand in your homework about George Washington."

"I told her what happened to it!"

Will shook his head at her, though he couldn't help smiling a little. The kid was so inventive sometimes. "Amy, did you really expect Mrs. Proctor to buy that aliens came down and stole it from you so they could study your brain power?"

Amy looked displeased and shook her finger at Princess Valentina. "I told you nobody would believe that." Will waited, and eventually the child turned toward him again. "I can't help it. History is hard, and Mrs. Proctor keeps talking about things that happened before I was born."

Will chuckled. "That's sort of what history is."

"I don't care. I don't like it."

"Why not? What occurred in the past helps us to understand who we are and where we came from."

"Well, it doesn't help me. And anyway, I don't even think I have one."

"Sure you do. Everyone has a past."

"Then how come you never talk about mine?" Amy asked. Her features were suddenly tight and filled with hurt. She looked like someone who had rummaged through a dark drawer and unexpectedly come across something sharp. "Jenny Allbright has pictures of when she was little all over her house. With aunts and uncles and her grandma. There's one of her sitting on her grandpa's lap with a parakeet pecking her face. She even has a picture of when she was a baby at the hospital. She knows where she was born and...and everything!"

"There are photos of you in this house. On my desk at work. What about the one of you and Lisa on the mantle?"

Amy barely drew breath, and the words fell out of her like a burden she'd been carrying. "But where are the ones of you and me and Mommy? Brandy Miller's mom was a famous swimmer, and she has a picture of her wearing her mom's medal. Did Mommy win any medals?"

"Amy—"

"When I went to Scott Balducci's birthday party, there was a big book on the table in front of the couch, and it had a bunch of pictures of his mom and dad at their wedding. It was really pretty, Daddy. His mom looked like Princess Valentina."

Will placed his hand on Amy's shoulder. He could feel her bones beneath his fingers, as fine and fragile as a shell. He cleared his throat, swallowing the faint coil of shock that had closed his windpipe. How could he make any headway in this conversation?

"Amy, stop. This is not the right time to discuss this. Maybe soon, but you have school tomorrow..."

"It's *never* a good time," Amy cried out. "Sometimes I don't think you even liked Mommy. She might be with us if you did."

Oh, hell. Where to go from here? Fall back on the few lies he'd already told her? More delaying tactics? "Sweetheart, I thought I explained it to you. Your mother has a very important job. She can't be with us. But she knows I love you very much and will always take good care of you." Quickly, he rose. "Now I want you to close your eyes and take deep breaths so you can fall asleep."

He didn't know if he was praying for relief or guidance, but when he heard the front doorbell ring, Will bent to place a kiss against Amy's forehead. Her eyes flew open again. It was an odd thing to feel cornered by your own child. "That's probably Aunt Lisa, forgetting her keys again," he said, then added more firmly, "I want you to go to sleep."

He didn't wait to see if she'd comply. Truthfully, he *escaped,* shutting her door behind him. Shutting out the look of vulnerability in his daughter's features, and that hunger for details, *any* details about her mother.

*Coward.*

For the past year, Amy had become more and more inquisitive about her mother. Obviously she'd been comparing notes with her little friends at school.

He hated lying to her. The same nonsense he'd spoon-fed to Lisa years ago burned in his throat, and there was no help for it now. Sooner or later he'd have to sit Amy down, talk everything out. Try to twist the fiction into making sense. But there was something unbearably abhorrent about deceiving a child who trusted you so completely.

Will's heart clenched when he thought about the circumstances that had brought him to this point and turned him into a fraud. Maggie—determined to cut him out of his daughter's life. In reality, determined to cut *herself* out, as well. Willing to hand Amy off to strangers. How had she been able to do that?

When he'd met with her at the Blue Reef job, her dedication to Sapphire Seas had been so obvious. It was one of the reasons why he'd finally had to concede that she should have the South Beach contract. But why couldn't she have shown that same commitment to their daughter?

He supposed he'd never know the answer to that. And a part of him wondered if he could ever forgive her for turning loose a treasure like Amy. Damn it! His daughter deserved better than his mountain of lies.

The doorbell rang again before he got to it. He swiped back the curtain along the side panel of the door, expecting to see Lisa and her new boyfriend, Charlie.

It wasn't his sister.

Instead of being safely in Key West, here on his doorstep stood Maggie.

*STUPID. STUPID. You should have called instead of showing up uninvited.*

Maggie balled her fists within her jacket. Unexpected company had always annoyed an organized planner like Will.

*What were you thinking?*

*I was thinking he wouldn't have let me come if I'd called him.*

*So? Why do you need to see him?*

No time to answer that because the front door was swinging open now. And anyway, she'd been asking herself that question for hours, all the way up from Key West. So far her brain had refused to cooperate and provide a logical explanation. Maybe there just wasn't one.

She smiled at Will, then pulled a small bottle out of her pocket so he could see it in the porch's pale light. "Devil's Claw," she told him.

He gave her a cool once-over. "I thought we'd gotten past the verbal abuse."

"Have you read your e-mail?" she asked, feeling a little relieved that he didn't seem completely displeased to see her. She dropped the container into his hand. "It's the herb I was telling you about. For your shoulder."

"You didn't have to make a special delivery."

She withdrew the long tube of designs she'd tucked under one arm. "Actually, I have some changes I want to suggest to Teddy for the lobby area, and I couldn't wait to show them to you to see what you think."

"Impulsive as ever."

She could have predicted that comment, but refused to let it bother her. What was wrong with being excited about your work? "May I come in?"

After the slightest hesitation, Will stepped aside to let her enter. He still lived in the house he'd inherited from his parents with its warm, friendly mix of fine furnishings and homey touches. She walked into the living room, feeling the strangeness of being in a place that she had known well at one time, but which now seemed unfamiliar.

"Do you want coffee?" he asked.

"I swore off caffeine years ago. A glass of water would be nice."

He nodded. He was barefoot, dressed in jeans and a navy sweatshirt. Maggie watched him head for the kitchen and thought that he still had one of the best rear ends of any man she'd ever met.

She settled on the couch and waited quietly for his return. She had been here hundreds of times during their months together, had sat snuggled against Will on this very sofa. Memories flooded in like rain, but she hated that the most prominent one was of the last legendary, sharp-tongued battle that had ended their relationship.

On the coffee table lay a box of crayons and some loose drawing paper. Evidently Will's daughter had been playing here. Maggie picked up the top picture. It depicted a little girl and a woman holding hands—Amy and her mom, perhaps. Next to the woman stood several purple elephants, easy to make out because of their curling trunks and big, floppy ears.

Maggie stared at the stick figure of the mother.

In all the conversations, e-mails and text messages that had passed between Miami and Key West the past three weeks, Will had never mentioned a wife, a divorce or even a custody battle. She suspected that was deliberate. He ignored any attempt she made to delve deeper into family matters, but Maggie couldn't help wanting to know. Who was Amy's mother? And was she still a part of Will's life?

She sat the crude drawing back on the stack, then

turned her attention to the other end of the table. Several architectural plans were anchored haphazardly on top of one another. She recognized the logo for Jacobson and Duquette, Will's firm, but none of these renderings appeared to be part of Teddy's South Beach project.

There were several schematics, variations of a large office building that rose four stories in a bustling downtown area. A stylized stone marker on the edge of the property indicated that the structure would be a new city hall for Hallandale Beach, a fast-growing community north of Miami. All of the designs were very contemporary, very sleek-looking, and Maggie wrinkled her nose in distaste. She couldn't say she cared for any of them.

Will returned and handed her a glass of water, then moved to a nearby chair. She took a sip and tapped the stack. "Hallandale Beach is getting a new city hall?"

"They've hired us to work up a few ideas. Purely on spec. No contract yet." When Maggie didn't say anything to that, he added, "You don't like them."

"I didn't say that."

"You didn't have to. I remember that look."

"Sorry. I guess it's just..."

"Just what? You can say it. You won't hurt my feelings. I've been struggling with this for two weeks. Can't seem to find the right mix. Everything I've tried feels wrong."

Maggie shuffled through the drawings. Will waited patiently as she looked at each carefully, and the silence made her stomach twist. She held up one of them. "I sort of like this version, with these triangular things."

"They're called step backs, and I've already killed that one as a possibility."

"Why?"

He rose and came to sit beside her on the couch so he could see the design from the same angle. "Because with the amount of sun we get here, it would need too many louvers or glass curtains to keep the interior temperatures down."

"But they give it such a graceful, open feel."

He smiled at her as though she were a simple child who didn't understand how things worked. "I'm not after graceful and open. This is city hall, not a hotel. It needs to be concise, authoritative…"

His attitude bothered her. Or maybe it was the fact that he was so close that she could see the slight shadow of tomorrow's beard along his jaw. She remembered what the feel of that had been like against her cheek. Rough, but oddly sexy. She gave him a sour look. "Just because it's a government building, just because everyone who goes there or works there is serious as a heart attack, that doesn't mean they want to be surrounded by sharp angles and sterile walls. What's wrong with giving it a bit of freedom, a little whimsy?"

"Whimsy," he repeated, his eyes full of skepticism. "At city hall."

"Well, maybe that's too frivolous a word. But you

know what I mean. In the old days, wasn't I always trying to get you to loosen up your ideas? Be a little less…structured?"

"And in the old days, wasn't I always telling you that free-flowing wasn't my style?"

"True." She made an exasperated sound as caution flew away like a bird let out of its cage. "Honestly, Will. Sometimes I'm amazed that we were *ever* a couple."

He stared at her, and then to her surprise, he glanced away. Maggie wanted to bite her tongue in half for making that statement. She supposed there hadn't really been a mood to kill between them, but it certainly didn't help to remind Will of how different they'd always been.

She took a quick drink of water, trying to think what to say next. She refused to look at him, certain she wouldn't like what she saw in his face.

Something moved at the limit of Maggie's vision. She turned her head. Will's daughter stood in the doorway that led to the bedrooms, peeking out at them in shy curiosity.

"Hi, there," Maggie said.

Will glanced over, too, and when he saw Amy, he frowned. "What are you doing up?"

As though she had been waiting to be noticed, the little girl trotted rapidly out into the living room. She came to the edge of the couch, looking at Maggie with wide eyes. She was dressed in pink pajamas covered in prancing ponies, and one hand tightly clutched a doll.

Maggie smiled at the girl and beckoned her closer. "Do you remember me?" she asked. "I'm Maggie."

Amy nodded, resting one bare foot on top of the other. "I remember."

The child stood near enough now that Maggie could see the sprinkling of freckles across her nose. "I'm sorry if I woke you," she said.

"It's okay." She lifted her hand to absently stroke the hair on her doll's head.

Maggie got a better glimpse of the toy. "Princess Valentina!"

"You know her?"

"Of course. Do you have Prince Willoughby, too?"

"Not yet."

Maggie felt Will's eyes on her and looked his way. "Zack's sister and her family stayed with me on their last vacation," she explained. "Her little girls were crazy for Princess Valentina, so I became quite an expert."

Will maintained the illusion of interest, but Maggie knew right away that something was wrong. He wasn't really listening. He seemed tense and unhappy with Amy. Maybe his daughter was a seasoned staller at bedtime, and Will, a stickler for rules, wouldn't have much patience with that. And yet, it felt like there was more.

Amy, on the other hand, seemed oblivious to her father's mood. Evidently, any reservations she'd had about approaching Maggie had vanished with the knowledge that here was another fan of Princess Valentina. The girl stretched out a finger to touch the golden links of the charm bracelet Maggie wore on her left wrist. "Your bracelet is pretty," she said, lifting one of the trinkets to examine it.

"You like it?" Maggie asked. She extended her hand, making a slow rotary motion with her arm that set the bangle flashing in the light. "I got this bracelet when I was about your age and have been collecting animals for it ever since. These are some of my favorites." She fingered one of the charms. "This is a penguin, and here's a lion. Do you know what this is?"

Amy squinted hard at the little figure. "A kangaroo?"

"That's right."

The child raised her eyes. "Can I put it on?"

Before Maggie could respond with a nod, Will said sharply, "No."

*Too* sharply in Maggie's opinion. Amy's cheeks had gone sunset pink, and her features clouded over with uncertainty. As though realizing he'd been too rough, Will rose, scooped Amy into his arms and planted a playful kiss against the side of her face. "Enough stalling, you little monkey. I want you to go to bed.

"I'll be right back," he told Maggie. Then he headed toward the bedrooms.

Amy peered at her from around his arm. "Good night," she called. "Will you come back and see me?"

"You bet," Maggie promised.

Kids were such funny, demanding, unpredictable creatures, but it must be wonderful to have them in your life. It was so odd to think of Will dealing with a daughter all these years. It left her feeling more curious than ever.

He returned in a very short time and gave Maggie a small smile before sitting down on the opposite end of the couch. "Sorry about that," he said. "We've had some issues lately about bedtime."

"No problem. I like kids."

He tilted his head at her. "Do you? I don't recall you ever saying so."

"I don't think it ever came up," Maggie said, feeling defensive.

He barely acknowledged that remark. Instead he asked, "What were those changes you wanted to show me?"

Maggie shifted on the sofa, knowing that she should leave well enough alone. Over the past few weeks, she and Will had reached a pleasant working truce, and she didn't want to ruin it. But there were answers she felt compelled to go after.

"Will," she began tentatively, forcing herself to ignore the crinkle of nerves that lay in the pit of her stomach. "I know there's been sort of an unspoken agreement between us not to discuss the past. But I can't help wondering..." She tipped forward until she could reach Amy's picture of her mother and the purple elephants. She held the drawing up for Will to see. "Besides being in this picture, where is Amy's mother?"

Unexpectedly, he didn't hesitate at all. "She's not part of our life," he said with that maddening casual air of his.

"I've gathered that. I'm sorry. I know it's really none of my business—"

"You're right. It's not."

She heard the bite in his voice but refused to run from it. "Amy's obviously your child. I can see the resemblance. But how did you end up with a daughter so soon after we broke up?"

He stood slowly with a rippling of muscles. The sharp, precise way he moved made her throat go dry. For a while, there might have been a universe between them.

Finally he said in a bland voice, "There's no mystery, really."

Maggie waited, giving him time.

He drew a deeper breath and turned toward her. "After you and I…ended things, I took Lisa out of town to get away from all the unpleasantness."

"I heard you went to Europe."

"Yes. Paris. We stayed with an old college friend of mine."

"A woman?"

Will nodded. "Seeing Tina again took me back to some wonderful times. One night we were feeling nostalgic, not thinking very clearly after working our way through a couple of bottles of wine. Things got out of hand." He stopped. "We ended up in bed together."

"I see. I suppose you must have been very eager to get me out of your system."

"Yes, I guess you could say that." He paused for a

minute, as though trying to figure out how best to proceed. He ran a hand through his hair, that old gesture Maggie found so adorable. "A few months later, Tina called to say she was pregnant," he went on at last. "She didn't want the baby. Her career was picking up steam, and she refused to consider coming here to live. Eventually I went back to Paris. When I came home again, I had Amy with me. And full custody."

Several beats passed. Then Maggie managed to say, "Instant fatherhood."

"It wasn't the way I would have chosen to do it, but I've never regretted having Amy in my life. Not for a moment."

Maggie felt a lump form in her throat. It served no purpose to wish things could have been different for them, that somehow they might have managed to avoid hurting one another so foolishly. But the truth was, everyone made awful bargains and wrong choices in their lives, and sometimes there was nothing you could do but deal with the consequences. Funny how the really tough, life-changing decisions for both she and Will had involved children.

Will's gaze was steady on her. Too steady.

"I wonder if she regrets that decision now," Maggie said. "Your friend Tina."

"That doesn't matter," he said evenly. The stillness of his body told her that he'd indulged her curiosity as much as he intended to tonight. "It's done. She was a fool to give up our child, but Amy's mine, and she doesn't miss having a mother in her life."

"How can you know that?"

"She has me, and her Aunt Lisa. She can't miss what she's never had."

# *CHAPTER SEVEN*

TWO DAYS LATER, Will left the house early. He headed for the Collins Avenue health club where he worked out several times a week, and where he had so recently pulled a shoulder muscle playing racquetball.

He had no intention of doing anything strenuous today, but he'd felt too restless to meet Ernie Becker at either of their offices. Instead, he sat waiting for his attorney and long-time family friend at one of the small café tables near the club's juice bar. He idly watched two middle-aged men fight it out on one of the glassed-in racquetball courts a few feet away.

In the pocket of his charcoal trousers he carried Maggie's gift from the other night—the bottle of Devil's Claw. He palmed it in his curled fingers again and again. So far the herb had offered little magic. His shoulder still hurt like hell. But then, after spending a couple of sleepless nights, there wasn't a single cell in his body that felt *right* anymore.

One of the club's "juice girls" passed by his table, and Will caught her eye. "Cindy, can I get the usual?"

The towering blonde with a body made for wearing

spandex nodded immediately. "Sure thing, Mr. Stewart. You want the protein booster pack in that?"

"Definitely," he said, and added under his breath, "I need all the help I can get."

Cindy went off to order his drink while Will pulled out the container of Devil's Claw and stared down at it. He wished he could view it for what it was probably meant to be—an innocent gesture on Maggie's part to help relieve the ache he'd complained about in one of his e-mails. All outward appearances suggested that, but then why was he tossing and turning at night, suddenly uncertain, feeling like a fool for believing that he could safely keep Maggie at arm's length? Everything she did, everything she said made him suspicious. And now, nothing about her visit felt innocent or friendly. God, this situation had him more paranoid than a pulp-fiction spy.

The chair beside him scraped back as Ernie Becker slid into it. "My boy," he said, placing a hand on Will's shoulder, "you look like a man who sees trouble coming."

"I think trouble is already here."

"Well, if it is, it's nothing that can't be dealt with. Tell me what has you so stirred up that you're getting me out of the house before I've even had breakfast."

Ernie Becker had been the Stewarts' attorney for years. He'd been a close friend of Will's father. He was godfather to both Will and Lisa, and since the deaths of Howard and Renee Stewart, the only family they had left, really.

Eight years ago, when Will had learned of Maggie's pregnancy, it had been "Uncle" Ernie he had turned to for help. The older man had arranged everything. And so, with Maggie back in Will's life now—however briefly that might be—it was Ernie Will had come to again for reassurance.

Cindy returned with Will's order, a nasty-looking high-energy drink filled with vitamins and minerals.

Ernie made a face as Will took a swallow. "I'll never understand how you can drink that stuff."

For a fifty-eight-year-old man who seldom bothered to exercise or eat properly, Ernie was in great shape. He credited his mother's side of the family with having fabulous genes.

"You get used to it," Will said.

"I'm not sure it's helping you any. You look like hell, son."

"Lisa and Amy pointed that out to me this morning. I haven't been sleeping well."

An understatement if ever there was one. For two nights Will had tried to bully his brain into unconsciousness, but nothing seemed to work. Instead, he kept replaying Maggie and Amy's conversation, searching his memory for suspicious looks or dawning comprehension in Maggie. He'd fretted over the lies he'd told her. Had he sounded sincere? Too slick? Had he brushed through the tale too quickly?

His head pounded with a thousand doubts.

Then last night, he'd finally gotten out of bed and tried to work himself into exhaustion by spending time with the Hallandale city hall designs. He made adjustments and forced himself to try out a couple of ideas without rejecting them immediately as inappropriate. In the end, he just stared at what he'd created. How irritating to discover that Maggie had been absolutely right. His designs *were* too straitlaced, and he *had* needed to loosen them up a bit. Damn her!

"What is it?" Ernie asked again. "What's wrong?"

"Maggie Tillman dropped by the house the night before last. Out of the blue. She brought some designs she wanted to show me, but she ended up having a conversation with Amy. Before she left, she asked me about Amy's mother."

"Oh." Ernie sat back in his chair. A few weeks ago Will had called Ernie to let him know that Maggie had shown up back in Miami, that they were going to be working together. Ernie hadn't found that to be too problematic. But what did he think now?

Will scratched a fingernail along the rim of his glass. "They only spoke for a few minutes, but I was going nuts trying to think of a way to end it. As it is, I'm not sure I handled it all that well."

"Do you think she suspects Amy is her daughter?"

"It's possible."

"What did you tell her about Amy's mother?"

"The same story we concocted seven years ago." Will grimaced. "As a liar, I try to keep things simple."

Ernie's brows shot up. "All things considered, I'm not sure your guilt is warranted. But regardless, that story about the old college friend happens to be very believable, so why wouldn't she buy it? You've said that Amy looks nothing like Maggie—"

"Physically, no," Will conceded. "But the older Amy gets, the more I see Maggie in her. The way she cares about animals. Her imagination." He smiled a little, caught in memories of his child at her most endearing moments. "Sometimes she'll duck her head and look at me, and I swear, it's like seeing Maggie standing there."

Ernie eyed Will shrewdly. "Listen to me. Since Maggie has resurfaced you've managed to keep them apart. Just continue to do more of the same. I think you're overreacting. She didn't want Amy seven years ago. Why should she be fretting about her now?"

"I don't think it's that simple," Will said with a frown. "And Maggie's going to be at Lisa's birthday party."

"How did that happen?"

"Lisa showed me her guest list this morning. She asked if she could add Maggie to it. I objected, and she accused me of holding a grudge because of what happened years ago."

"So let her think that and veto the invitation."

Will shook his head. "She's always claimed I have control issues, that I'm overprotective, but she knows I'm not usually small or petty. The longer I fought her on it, the more strangely she began to look at me. So I told her to invite whoever she wanted and walked out."

"Well...Maggie may not come. Or Amy could be in bed by the time she shows up at the party."

"I suppose," Will said with a deep sigh. "Maybe I'm

worrying for no reason. All I know is that I feel like I'm suffocating when they're in the same room together."

One of the players on the racquetball court banged violently against the back glass as he tried to return an errant ball, then slid helplessly down the wall. Will watched him mouth a curse as he picked himself up to rejoin his opponent.

*I know just how you feel, buddy.*

Ernie leaned in so that no one else could overhear his words. "Will, you've done nothing wrong. As the putative father in this case, you simply adopted your own child. It was legally and morally right. If the truth comes out—which is highly unlikely since it was a closed adoption—there's nothing this woman can do to make trouble for you."

Will straightened, tossing his napkin on the table. "I can live with whatever Maggie tries to do to me. But Amy...I've spent too many years making sure she feels loved even though her mother's not in the picture. If Maggie finds out Amy's hers and goes to court for custody... Hell, the truth is, what's Amy going to think if she discovers I've done nothing but lie to her from the very beginning?"

"That's not likely to happen," Ernie said in a stern tone that Will seldom heard the older man use. "Remember, Maggie Tillman didn't want that child. She gave her up freely so that she could get on with her life. With another man, if I recall correctly. As far as I'm concerned, she forfeited her parental rights."

Yes, she had, and Will needed to keep that in mind.

He'd do anything to make sure Amy suffered no harm. But still, there had been just a moment the other night—the tiniest flicker of time—when he'd felt a pang of regret that mother and daughter couldn't have shared more. Telling Amy about her ridiculously cluttered charm bracelet, Maggie had been very sweet and patient with the child. And Amy had seemed enchanted.

"Trust your old uncle," Ernie reassured. "What you did was right."

"It felt that way at the time." Will stared down at the table. Almost to himself he said, "But I'm not sure anymore. The man I thought was Maggie's lover back then turned out to be just a close friend, her business partner." His gaze connected with Ernie's. "What else could I have been wrong about?"

The attorney sat up as though his seat had suddenly given him an electric jolt. "Good God, Will. Don't tell me you're going soft on this woman again?"

"Of course not." The denial had come embarrassingly quickly. More calmly, he added, "I want to protect Amy. But I'm not looking to hurt Maggie. In spite of everything, there's still a part of me that..."

*That what?*

Will searched for the right words as if hunting for a trail out of an unfamiliar wood. None came. Finally he let the thought drift away. He couldn't bear to dwell on the *other* moments that had unnerved him during Maggie's visit. The faint, unmistakable vibration of sexual energy that ran through him when he watched her bend her head to listen to Amy's ramblings. The way her blond hair fell around her shoulders, as though it had lost some golden tussle with the wind. The soft planes of her cheekbones touched by lamplight.

He'd thought his mind had created a firewall Maggie couldn't break through, but evidently he'd been kidding himself. Maddening woman. She could still get to him, could still produce this secret inner upheaval. And he didn't have a clue what to do about it.

"I can see you're worried," Ernie was saying in his incisive lawyer's tone. "I'm sure there's no reason to be, but I'll tell you what I can do. I'll talk to a colleague of mine who specializes in adoption and custody cases. If Maggie *does* learn the truth and wants to make a fuss, he'll know how to shut her down. All right?"

Will nodded. "Thanks. I'd appreciate that."

"Leave it to me, son. Don't you worry about a thing. I won't let Maggie Tillman turn your life upside down again."

Once more Will nodded. But this time he couldn't help feeling that it was already way too late to keep that from happening.

MAGGIE SAT in the front passenger seat of Alaina's Mercedes, aimlessly watching the pastel-colored houses of North Miami Beach float past her window. It was a beautiful day. A perfect Saturday for going to the beach with your kids or in-line skating in the art deco district.

Too bad she'd allowed Alaina to talk her into spending all this precious free time with their parents.

She sighed heavily. Oh well, maybe a little jousting with Mom and Dad would keep her mind off…other problems.

It had been a week since she'd come up from Key West and landed on Will's doorstep. Since then, she'd been in a whirlwind of activity, but very little of it was turning out to be productive. Employee issues. Supplier holdups. Even an argument with Zack over some minor change she wanted to make to the tank designs. She wasn't at odds with Will, thank goodness. But maybe that was because she hadn't seen him since that night. And maybe that was a blessing.

Alaina reached across to give her arm a squeeze. "If you continue to look like that, you're going to spoil the whole day."

"Look like what?" Maggie asked.

"Like you want to squash someone. Or like someone has squashed *you.* Come on, sis. Play nice today. For my sake."

Maggie turned her head and gave Alaina a fake toothpaste-ad smile. "Better?"

"Great. Now you look like a grinning jack-o'-lantern. Mom and Dad are never going to buy that you wanted to come. That you were eager to see them."

Maggie laughed. "Are you completely naive? That ship has sailed. Mom and Dad know I'm not 'eager to see them'"—her fingers made commas in the air—"and they feel the same way about me. They're only marginally interested in what I'm up to. And I'm only marginally interested in telling them."

Alaina made a rude sound deep in her throat. "You're hopeless. I don't know why I continue trying to make things right between you guys."

"I'm not the only one who's hopeless," Maggie muttered. "You've never been able to leave well enough alone."

They were just passing an exit for the mall, and unexpectedly Alaina swung off the highway. She pulled into a vacant parking space, threw the gearshift into Park and turned in her seat to stare at Maggie. "What is *wrong* with you?" she asked harshly. "For the last two days you've been as agreeable as a bear caught in a beehive. This isn't just about spending time with Mom and Dad, is it?"

"It's nothing. Start the car. Dad will pitch a fit if we're late."

"Don't tell me it's nothing. I'm not stupid. You pick at your food. You seem distracted all the time. You're up at all hours of the night. Don't deny it. I've seen your bedroom light on."

Maggie faced her sister. "Look, Detective, there's nothing wrong that I can't handle."

"I didn't say you couldn't handle it. I just want to know what it is, and if there's anything I can do to help."

"Al, really..." Maggie began. Then she bit her lip, and fell silent. It would feel so good to unburden just a little. Since staying with Alaina off and on, she'd been trying to reconnect. But she wasn't used to having girlfriends and shoulders to cry on. Zack was usually the one she vented to. But maybe…

She made a sudden decision. Alaina had such a perfect life. If she wanted to see what it was like being Maggie, then why not give her a peek?

"All right," she said. "It's not just the prospect of spending time with Mom and Dad. It's *everything.* It's the possibility that I have bad stock going belly-up in the tanks we installed in Coconut Grove. It's cost overruns that I'm barely covering with the loan I took out and employees who don't show up to pour molds. It's my designs getting turned down by some cheapskate who thinks he knows more than me, and the convention center saying I can't pass out the business flyers I paid a fortune for because I didn't make some cut-off time. It's the prospect of working side by side with a former lover who—"

No. Better not go down that particular path. Things were difficult enough right now without having to chew over the fact that she couldn't seem to stop dreaming of Will in all sorts of immodest positions that had nothing to do with business. Practical Alaina would tell her to snap out of it. Great advice. If only it were that easy.

"It just hasn't been a good week," Maggie finished up.

Alaina stretched out a hand to capture hers. "I'm so sorry. Life stinks sometimes, doesn't it?"

"It certainly seems to lately. But I'm dealing with it. Not very gracefully, perhaps."

"Is there anything I can do? Name it and I'll try to help."

Maggie grimaced. Sweet, but her sister wasn't the tough-as-nails type who could take on real trouble. And in spite of this sudden confession, Maggie prided herself on being able to handle anything life dished out. She'd been doing it for years, hadn't she? "Just keep me from going off on Mom and Dad today," she told Alaina. "I don't need that on top of everything else."

FORTY-FIVE MINUTES LATER, Maggie had one heck of a headache.

You'd think that going to a family barbecue might be innocent and safe, maybe even fun. *If* her parents had invited any other guests. More people would certainly mean fewer chances to get deep into conversations that could go awry.

Unfortunately, the Tillmans weren't fond of big parties. It came down to the two of them and their children, with Alaina trying hard to make sure everyone got along, and Maggie doing her best to look happy to be there.

Seated in one of the chaise longues out by the pool, Maggie watched her sister help their mother lay the picnic table. Alaina, at least, seemed to have settled in just fine. No surprise there. Maggie, however, wanted to poke her own eyes out with the long fork her father was using to turn the steaks he had going on the grill.

Already she'd endured a host of challenges from her mother about her outfit, her hair, even her shoes, which were going to destroy her instep someday. Who in their right mind wore stiletto pumps to a barbecue? Connie Tillman had admonished her to stand up straighter, put on more sunscreen and stop chopping the carrots for the salad so big. Her father hadn't had a go at Maggie yet, but she knew it was coming. She thrummed with tension just wondering what moment he'd choose.

Maggie swung her legs over the edge of the lounger. "Might as well get this over with," she said under her breath.

She headed for the grill where her father was waving away a column of smoke with a huge oven mitt. Her heels sunk into the plush grass, and she swore under her breath. Damn her mother for being right about the shoes.

Hands wedged on the back of her waist, she stared down at the sizzling meat as though it were going to sit up and do a tap dance. Her father didn't say a word.

Just to fill the space between them, she said, "Those look good. Make mine rare, please."

James Tillman jabbed his fork in the air to proclaim, "No rare meat at this restaurant. Too dangerous."

Boom. In an instant Maggie was at odds with her father. Surely that had to be a new family record. But she was determined not to ruin the day, if only for Alaina's sake. "Okay. As rare as you're willing to go, then."

He stopped maneuvering the steaks, and his eyes traveled over her. Maggie barely resisted the temptation to jerk to attention. "You need some meat on your bones," her father said at last. "How often do you sit down and actually eat something that doesn't come out of a paper sack?"

"At least once a month. I'm fine, Dad. If I weighed two pounds more, you'd say I was getting chunky."

"You look tired."

"I'm in bed early every night." No point in sharing with him that she might be in bed by ten, but she was seldom asleep by midnight.

"I see you're still biting your nails."

Somehow she resisted the temptation to whip her hand behind her back. "Because I still have frustrations in my life and that's the way I deal with them. Anything else you want to know?"

"I'm merely a concerned father asking questions."

Maggie knew James Tillman would rather chop off a limb than admit he was out of line. She frowned. Shook her head at him. "So why do your questions always sound like an interrogation from a police sergeant?"

"Oh dear," Alaina said, surfacing out of the blue to hand her father his favorite platter. "Are you two fighting already?"

"We aren't fighting," James replied. "We're discussing."

Alaina looked immediately contrite. She turned

her attention to Maggie. "Mom wants flowers on the table, and I volunteered you to help her."

This was a fairly obvious ploy. Maggie was as much an expert at arranging flowers as she was decorating a house. But clearly her sister thought she needed rescuing. Maggie nodded and hurried off before her father found one more thing about her that didn't measure up to his standards.

First, though, she made a detour for her purse. She hadn't been foolish enough to forget the aspirin.

IN THE END, Maggie had to admit that the day didn't turn out a complete and miserable failure. The food was good and plentiful, and once it was on the table everyone seemed to settle in and relax a bit.

Alaina, the eternal peacemaker, did her darnedest to see that conversation moved from one pleasant topic to another. They all took care not to fall into the dangerous traps—all the places where there could not and never would be agreement. In between, they reminisced about the old days. Fun family vacations and a special Christmas. A sweet memory here, a worn, beloved joke told there.

It wasn't *all* bad, Maggie thought.

And then, disaster.

She was alone, carting leftovers out to Alaina's car while her sister helped their mother take measurements for new drapes she planned for the living room. Her father was at the curb, setting out trash for tomorrow's pickup. He had always been a stickler about getting garbage out of the house as soon as possible.

As Maggie shut the car door, her father turned toward her, dusting imaginary grime from his hands. "I suppose you won't want to hear this, or even discuss it, but I'm going to say it anyway."

Maggie's gut clenched. "Say what, Dad?"

"Why haven't you come to me?"

For a retired CPA who liked everything to march in obvious, uncomplicated columns, her father still enjoyed being cryptic. "Come to you for what?"

"Money. A gift. A loan. Call it whatever you want."

"Why would I do that?"

"Don't pretend with me. Your sister told me you're barely making ends meet."

Maggie had already started to move back toward the house. Now she twisted around. "What?" she said on a harsh rush of breath.

Her father's features were solemn as he ignored her horrified reaction. "Tell me how much you need to get you through, and I'll write a check."

He reached in the back pocket of his shorts and withdrew his checkbook and pen. Obviously he'd been waiting for the opportunity to pull Maggie aside like this.

She caught her father's hand. "Dad, I don't need your money, and I don't want it. Alaina had no right—"

"Stop standing on pride. It won't do a darned thing for you. I'm your father. I'll always be willing to get you out of a jam."

Maggie rubbed the space between her brows. What a miserable end to the day. She wanted to scream. But mostly, she wanted to strangle Alaina, who surely *should* have known to keep her mouth shut about the problems Maggie had shared with her earlier.

She stroked her hand down her father's arm. It wasn't his fault, really. He had always been this way and wasn't about to change now. "I'm not *in* a jam," she said quietly, calmly. "Yes, things are tight right now. But I'm perfectly capable of managing my business and paying my employees. I don't want your money."

"You'd rather dig a deeper hole for yourself than turn to your father?"

"Dad, please. Don't make me sorry I came here today."

"Why do you always fight me when I try to help?" James Tillman grumbled.

"Why do you always treat me like a child who needs your charity? I'm a grown woman running my own company. I've worked hard for years to get where I am. Why can't you respect that?"

"Making fish tanks? That isn't a real business."

"How would you know? You've never bothered to find out what I do. You've never come down to Key West to see. No, I'm not drawing a regular paycheck. No, I'm not going to some office in a three-piece suit every day. But that doesn't mean I'm not making a life for myself, that what I do has no value."

"Your mother and I only want what's best for you."

"No, you don't," Maggie said. "You just want me to be like Alaina."

"What's that supposed to mean?"

"You know what it means. You want a sweet, obedient daughter who doesn't ask questions or make waves. A daughter who has never embarrassed you by unexpectedly coming up pregnant without—" Maggie stopped, swiping hair out of her eyes. No point in going down that line of logic. "I'm sorry. I know you want someone who just does whatever you say, and that's not me, I'm afraid. It never will be."

"That isn't what I want, but what's wrong with having common sense and knowing when to accept help? Your sister has a fairly good head on her shoulders. She has enough sense to know that her parents only want to keep her from making the same mistakes they did."

"What's wrong with making a few mistakes?" Maggie complained. "That's how we're supposed to learn and grow and become real people. Instead, you've always tried to keep Alaina and me in some sort of glass bubble where nothing could ever touch us. But that's not living, Dad. That's just being some sort of…of doll, or robot—"

"Don't be ridiculous."

"It isn't ridiculous. It's the truth."

"The only thing your mother and I have tried to do is guide the two of you through tough times. What's wrong with that? We're older. We've had more experience. Children *should* be able to benefit from the things their parents have been through."

"Neither of you offer guidance. Mostly it's a hard push. You pressured Alaina to give up Zack because he wasn't good enough for her, and she caved. Now look. She's married to Gil, who—" She stopped. No telling what her father really thought of Alaina's husband, and she didn't want to fight with him over *that* guy. Better to stick with her own grievances. "You tried to pressure me about letting Alaina raise my baby, and—"

Her father snorted his disgust. "There's no point trying to talk to you about this." He waved his hands in a dismissing motion. "So don't take my money. File for bankruptcy if you need to. When you're left with pride and an empty bank account, maybe you'll realize that all I've ever tried to do is help you."

## *CHAPTER EIGHT*

MAGGIE WANTED SO BADLY to hang on to her anger, to not lash out. And she tried. She really did.

On the return trip to Alaina's house she fought hard to let the nastiness of that conversation with her father just slide right off her back. And in a way, that wasn't what had her all stirred up. Her father had never been any different. But Alaina. She felt betrayed by her sister, whom she'd begun to confide in and trust.

By the time Alaina pulled into the driveway of her swank, ridiculously huge home and cut the engine, it all came spilling out of Maggie like a volcanic eruption.

"How could you?" she asked in a low tone. She stared out the windshield, afraid to make eye contact with her sister. "How could you tell Dad my personal problems? You know what I said was confidential. How could you sabotage me like that?"

Her sister had reached to withdraw the keys from the ignition. Now she let her hand fall back into her lap as she turned to look at Maggie. "I'm not sure what you mean."

"You know perfectly well what I mean."

Caught, Alaina settled back in her seat. "I didn't intend to," she said in almost a low moan. "I wasn't thinking. It slipped out, and I knew right away it was a mistake."

Maggie swung to face her. "Did it just slip out? Or did you tell Dad deliberately, knowing he'd go into I've-got-to-save-my-idiot-daughter mode."

Alaina gasped. "I would never do that on purpose. It just—"

"Al, I'm trying not to reach over and throttle you right now. Don't make it worse by lying to me. You know Dad. You know he thinks I'm weak and foolish and irresponsible. Why did you want him to think I'm a failure as well?"

"I didn't—"

"Just tell me why."

"I don't know—"

"Yes, you do," Maggie said firmly. She gave her sister's arm a hard shake. "Maybe you can't bear to admit it to yourself, but I think there's a part of you that's very comfortable with me being the one who's always in the doghouse. As much as you *pretend* to want things to be better between Mom and Dad and me, you secretly *like* being the favorite, and you don't want anything to change that."

"That's not true!"

"I think it is. All our lives, Mom and Dad have been drawing comparisons between us, making us compete. And in spite of the fact that you haven't liked it any more than I have, I think there's a part of you that's fine with it as long as you continue to come out on top." Her sister started to shake her head again, but Maggie cut her off. "Earlier, when I told you all those things that are going wrong for me right now—just how thrilled were you?"

"That's a horrible thing to say!"

"I know. And I hate believing it because I've tried really hard the past few weeks to build our relationship. We're sisters. We should be there for one another. But honestly, Al, don't you ever get tired of being the perfect overachiever? Doesn't it get lonely on that pedestal where everyone's put you?"

"I don't want to fight with you."

Maggie released her hold, falling back against her seat. They were never going to understand one another. Never. "Of course you don't want to fight," she murmured. "You never do."

To her surprise, Alaina, who had been about to open her door, jerked around to face Maggie once more. "Do you think it's easy being the golden child?" she snapped. "Let me tell you, it's not. Everyone expects so much. Do you know how many times I gave up what *I* wanted out of life because it wasn't the future Mom and Dad had in mind for me? When we were kids, I learned pretty quick that I didn't dare disappoint. You've thumbed your nose at them all your life, but how could I?"

"You care too much about what they think."

"Maybe so, but with Mom and Dad it's always been easier to just give in than to battle with them all the time." Her hand flashed out toward the house in front of them. "It's all been the same with Gil. Do you think there's one thing I do that doesn't take into consideration what he wants? What he expects? Sometimes I rebel a little, but there's always a price to pay for it." Her fingers clutched the steering wheel so hard that her knuckles stood out in white ridges. Her mouth flattened. "God, Maggie, you have no idea how much I hate my life."

She looked so weary that a little of the steam went out of Maggie's anger. "Then change it," she said. "You don't have to—"

"You make it sound so simple, but it's not. You get to be the free-as-a-bird Maggie Tillman, doing whatever the hell you want, while I turn myself into a Stepford wife and daughter just to keep everyone happy. And does it do any good? Is Gil even around half the time—"

She broke off suddenly, as though shocked by her own words. They sat there in frazzled silence for a moment. Alaina was breathing hard, seemingly filled with as much misery as Maggie.

Finally, Maggie reached over to take her sister's hand. "Al…"

Alaina pushed her fingers away. Her eyes were bright, shining with the possibility of tears. "Maybe I did do what you say. If I did, I'm sorry. I just know one thing. Being perfect isn't all it's cracked up to be."

Before Maggie could say anything to that, Alaina jumped out of the car and hurried into the house.

Maggie remained in her seat, feeling numb.

What a mess. What a damned mess.

But how fitting, in a way. It seemed logical that in a week where everything seemed to be going wrong, she should fight with Alaina and end up knocking down that fragile, tiny bridge that had been built between them.

WILL ZIGZAGGED through traffic on the Venetian Causeway, heading toward the LaCrosse construction site on the beach. On such a beautiful, star-filled Saturday night, there were plenty of fun, interesting things to do in Miami, but he didn't feel like doing any of them.

No hot date. No guys' night out at a sports bar watching basketball and drinking beer. Lisa had taken Amy to see the latest Disney movie at the multiplex, so even a little father-daughter time was lost to him this evening. Sitting around, listening to the quiet, shadowed rhythms of the house held no appeal. He felt...edgy.

He had a moment's curiosity about what Maggie might be doing right now. They hadn't spoken in days, though there was no need to, really.

This past week he'd dealt more with her partner, Zack Davidson. Will had discovered that during this part of the job, the "molders"—the Sapphire Seas construction crew—were responsible for reinforcing the floors that would hold the weight of the tanks. They seemed a competent lot, but when Will passed through the lobby portion of the building where they worked, he couldn't help it. He was disappointed not to see Maggie with them.

Since talking to Ernie Becker a few days ago, his nerve endings had finally stopped snapping every time Maggie's name came up. Ernie was thorough, completely trustworthy. If he said Will had nothing to worry about, then he meant it. No matter what, facts were facts. Will was still Amy's father, and Maggie had freely given their daughter away. No getting around that.

The South Beach construction site was large enough to have its own security shack. Frank, the guard on duty, motioned Will past the gates before he even had a chance to wave his ID badge at the man. Of course, Frank was used to seeing him come and go at all hours.

He parked near the hotel's front entrance. With most of the other building exteriors complete, the structure was going up fast now. The area hummed with activity during the day, but at the moment, everything was quiet and looked pretty deserted. The emergency lighting gave it a ghostly feel, but Will was so used to walking construction jobs that he hardly noticed.

He headed into the lobby. The last of the glass had been installed more than a week ago. Drywall was up and primed for paint. It would be ready for the furniture-and-fixtures phase soon. Huge rolls of carpet and padding were piled in one corner. In front of him, several large crates filled with designer chandeliers were stacked like giant building blocks.

As he moved around a haphazard stack of lumber,

he heard voices coming from where the front desk would be installed. He stopped.

No. Not *voices. A* voice.

Someone else was in here. And he knew right away who it was.

*Maggie.*

"Honestly, you're such an idiot, Maggie. That's just what I'd expect from you. Why didn't you give it more thought? How long have you been doing this now? You know better."

There was no response to those echoing queries, and Will didn't expect one. He knew Maggie was alone.

When they'd been a couple, he'd come to understand her pretty well, all the quirks and peccadilloes that had made her the fascinating creature she was. Most of the time, Maggie handled trouble like a real trouper. But when stressed to the max, she talked to herself. Scolded her decisions. Vocalized problems instead of silently churning them over and over in her head. When he'd asked her once about the habit, she'd told him that saying the words out loud seemed to help somehow. He'd laughed at that, but never questioned her again. He supposed everyone had a different way of handling the tough stuff.

"If you suggest any more changes at this stage of the game, Teddy's going to fire you," she went on. "And Zack will go ballistic."

Will listened and chewed the inside of his cheek. He knew how easy it would be to just back out of the building silently. Go home. If Maggie was worried about the job, she wouldn't want to share those uncertainties with him. Not with the guy who had once told her that she couldn't handle this contract.

On the other hand… If she had run into problems, didn't he, as the chief architect, have a right to know about them? If it was something serious, something that jeopardized this project…

He should talk to her. Definitely.

It hit him out of the blue then. Just like that. No warning, no deep thinking and absolutely no possibility of misunderstanding.

He knew damned well that, whatever swivet Maggie had worked herself into, it could easily be sorted out in the morning. He could call her, ask her to come to his office or meet her at Teddy's. There, issues could be hacked up into manageable pieces. With plenty of people around to help keep it impersonal and professional and safe.

But that *wasn't* what he wanted. What he really wanted in this minute, was *not* to miss this opportunity to be with to Maggie alone. Talk to her. Antagonize her and make her laugh. To share and remember the easy friendship and deep closeness of their old relationship.

There had been warmth there. An exciting and yet strangely comfortable pattern. Damn it, he'd missed that. And with Amy safely out of the picture at the moment, he told himself that there wasn't any reason he couldn't indulge a little.

He took a few steps forward, around a couple of sawhorses that still held freshly cut timber. He listened to Maggie berate herself as the knowledge of what he was about to do settled in his gut.

She never failed to surprise him. He didn't find her standing in the middle of the lobby, but instead, she was seated on the bare floor in front of the desk area. She looked very lost and forlorn there in the poor light. As Will approached, he could see that she wore a sundress in sherbet colors and that the flowing skirt had been yanked up to her thighs.

She flopped back to lie flat on the floor, drew her knees up, and covered her eyes with her arms. "What a mess you've made of everything," she grumbled. "What the heck are you going to do now?"

Even if he hadn't been determined to join her, Will knew that curiosity had killed all sense of caution within him. He came up silently beside her, cocking his head so he could see her prone form better. He couldn't help noting that the sundress, held up by thin straps and tight at the waist, only emphasized the sharp temptation of her figure.

She sighed, still completely unaware of him. "Wait until Will finds out," she mumbled behind her arms. "After he finishes saying, 'I told you this job was too big for you,' about twenty times, he'll feed you into the nearest shredder. Then he'll paste all the pieces together and turn you into one of his stupid ties."

He stood over her, deciding he'd better divulge his presence quickly before he heard more bad things about himself. But before he could speak, Maggie must have sensed she was no longer alone. She uncrossed her arms and opened her eyes. She blinked up at him, and for once, Will suspected she was totally shocked.

"Why do you hate my ties?" he asked mildly.

Her lips parted, and he knew she struggled to find words. All he was aware of, though, was the blotchy look around her eyes. Sometime recently she'd been crying. His second surprise. The Maggie he remembered seldom found refuge in tears.

Still flat on her back, she said, "I hate your ties because they're boring and unimaginative."

"Ah." He crossed his arms. "Problems?"

"A few," she replied. Then she added quickly, "Nothing I can't handle."

He shook his head at her. "Try again. This is me, Maggie. I know you, or at least I used to. You always talked to yourself when you were stressed." He frowned. "Why are you lying on the floor?"

She sat up. "Two reasons. Come down here and I'll show you the first one." When he hesitated, she made a disparaging sound. "For heaven's sake, you're not exactly dressed for a dinner party. A little sawdust won't kill you."

He conceded. When he'd taken off in the car this evening he'd already changed into a worn, comfortable running outfit of gym pants and a sweatshirt. He lowered himself beside her.

"Okay," he said. "So what's the big problem?"

She motioned toward the far wall where the front desk counters would soon be placed, and where her own crew had already reinforced the floor. "Look straight ahead. What do you see?"

Nothing out of the ordinary, thought Will. The aquariums had been dropped into place, massive walls of continuous viewing panels that would look spectacular once they were filled with living reefs and tropical fish. Zack had told him that, starting Monday, the filtration systems would be mounted, and the week after that, his custom cabinetry would add the finishing touches to the construction part of the contract.

"Everything I'm supposed to see. Pretty soon we'll have the front desks installed, then the granite tops. Behind them, your tanks, which will be awe-inspiring and phantasmagorical. I believe that was your description of them."

"They will be. But guess who's not going to notice them one bit?"

"Who?"

"Little kids! The very people who should enjoy them the most. The perspective is all off. The tanks sit too low. Unless a child is on his father's shoulders, all he's going to see is a wall of wood counters. From down here, you can see the problem clearly. The 'wow factor' is going to be a big, fat nothing for them."

"So take the viewing panels higher."

"I can't. We'd have to redo the weight distribution for the floor. Why don't you make the front desks lower?"

"Too late for that, I'm afraid. And not very practical. What about the platforms the tanks sit on?"

Maggie rested her elbows on her bare knees, then cradled her head in her palm.

"Zack's already cut the wood. He'll kill me if I ask him to change the specifications now. And I don't want to add..."

She let the sentence trail away, but Will knew what she'd been thinking. Making adjustments at this stage would mean a bigger outlay of funds if they had to use more wood. Funds that Sapphire Seas probably didn't have to spare.

"I understand," Will said. "But there are ways we could get the tanks raised a bit without using high-end materials. Have Zack call me. I'll tell him *I* want to make the alterations. I'll bet between the two of us, we can come up with a solution."

Maggie's back went straight. She frowned at him. "Are you sure?"

Her lack of confidence stabbed him a little. "For Pete's sake, Maggie, I'm an architect. I know how to build things."

"No, I didn't mean it that way. I mean, are you sure you don't *mind* modifying the plans again? I know I've been changing a lot of things all along, but I only want to make it better."

"Will it wow the kids the way you want it to and make you happy?"

"Yes."

"Then we can do it."

She looked at him as though he'd suddenly grown another head. He didn't like it much. He wasn't trying to make her miserable. And anyway, a great end product for Teddy was best for everyone. Right?

"Thank you," she said in a subdued voice.

"You're welcome," he replied. "Now what else do we have to deal with?"

"I'm stuck."

"On what?"

"Not *on* what. *By* what?"

She moved the hem of her flowing skirt aside, and Will saw an open-toed shoe wedged in the floor boards they'd been sitting on. A ridiculously high heel. For the first time, Will realized that one of Maggie's feet was bare when she wiggled her toes for his benefit.

"My shoe got caught," she explained. "I can't pry it loose."

"Good God," Will said with a laugh. "Who wears high heels to a construction site?"

"Did my father pay you to ask that?" she accused, giving the shoe a hard yank. A petal from one of the artificial flowers on the toe came off in her hand. "Now look what you made me do!"

"Hold on a minute. Let me try."

"Be careful," she said, placing her hand over his as he took a firm hold of the heel. "I might have gotten them at the thrift shop, but they're still Manolo Blahniks."

"So?"

"Maybe that doesn't matter to you, but it matters to me."

He gave her a pained look, but he had to admit, he was enjoying this. He felt her warmth beside him, and the soft, tender scent of her made his mind buzz. Was it an accident that the blue in her sundress was only a shade lighter than her eyes?

Adding a little pressure, he rocked the shoe back and forth while Maggie hung over him as though he were a surgeon at the operating table. She gasped when the heel popped loose at last.

"Here you go, Cinderella," he said, dangling the shoe by its ankle strap.

She snatched it out of his hand before he could offer to replace it on her foot himself. Once she slipped it on, she stuck both of her legs straight out, wiggling the toes that were no longer bare.

"Thanks," she said. "Aren't they great?"

They certainly were. Two of the prettiest legs he'd seen in a long time. Shapely. Tanned. Even after all these years, he remembered how sexy they could feel wrapped around his hips.

"So…" he said, clearing his throat to give himself a moment to find his equilibrium. "How about we get up off this floor and go find a Denny's? We can sort out the rest of your problems over coffee."

"I don't have any other problems."

"I'm betting you do." He hadn't forgotten that trace of tears in her eyes when he'd first joined her. Now he touched a fingertip to her cheek. "You never were much of a crier," he said softly. "Maybe that's why it's so obvious when you do. Care to tell me about it? I don't believe it's the issue with the tanks or a pair of silly shoes."

Her brows drew together, and she looked away. Will waited, beginning to wish he'd never started this, never come into her orbit tonight. He was being driven by something completely untrustworthy—pure emotion—and where could it lead? But he wasn't going to leave her. He just couldn't. Not now.

She rubbed at her throat, as if a secret were buried right there, above her collarbone. He thought she might try to deny the truth of his words, but when she spoke, there was nothing in her voice except raw honesty.

"I had a fight with my sister," she said slowly. "I was so upset, I just started walking from her house. Eventually I hailed a cab and came here because I thought it might help to think about something else for a while."

"So that's why I didn't see your car outside," he said almost to himself. He turned his head to look at her more sharply. "Was it an argument that can be fixed?"

"I don't know. I'd rather talk things out, but Alaina likes to ignore unpleasantness in the hopes it will just go away and be forgotten. I might have to give it a couple of days and then see how she is."

"Can you tell me what the fight was about?"

She'd lowered her gaze, so that all that soft blond hair screened her face from his view. "Our relationship with Mom and Dad, of course. We spent the day with them today, and it wasn't too bad until Dad started in on me." She tossed her head, offering him a knowing grimace. "You remember how well I used to get along with them? Nothing's changed, I'm afraid."

"I think *you've* changed."

For the briefest of moments, Maggie looked so completely stunned by that comment that something curled in Will's chest. Then she shook her head matter-of-factly. "Not in any way that matters to them." She sighed. "Honestly, I do try, but they're impossible. There doesn't seem to be any statute of limitations on driving your kids crazy."

"I thought you were the one who didn't care what they thought."

"I don't."

"Maggie." She stared at him, and the silence lasted a few intense seconds. Strands of her hair lay against her cheek, and Will reached out to sweep them back behind her ear. "You don't have to work so hard to prove yourself to them. I've seen you in action these past weeks. You're a very competent, smart businesswoman."

She blinked, evidently startled by his words. Finally she said, "Thank you for that."

He shrugged. "I wouldn't say it if I hadn't discovered that it's true." Then, seeing the frown that suddenly creased her brow, he asked, "What's the matter?"

"You're being awfully agreeable tonight."

He had to laugh. "Oh, no! There goes my reputation."

"You know what I mean. All things considered…" She smiled at him. "I like you this way. It reminds me of how things used to be between us."

"Me, too," he replied quietly. His hand came up to the bright curls at the side of her face. "Hold still. You have wood shavings in your hair."

She started to shake her head to dislodge them, but stopped when his fingers sifted deeper. He had always loved her hair. The silky feel of it against his skin. The way it could lie against her back like a veil. Even after all these years, the memory of that pale golden mass fanned against his bare chest was suddenly there, sliding into his mind with such frightening clarity that his heart gave a little kick.

His movements were thorough, unhurried, and he was aware of Maggie sitting silently, waiting, with her breath moving inward with slow care.

His gaze crossed hers, and as though she had fallen into his same cushiony lack of resistance, Maggie turned her head until her cheek rested against his hand. His blood pumped in slow surges as she moved farther still, letting her lips touch his palm.

He put his against her hair. It was impossible not to. Impossible.

In another moment, their mouths met in a kiss. He fully intended it to be tender, gentle, but something flooded up from within his body and overwhelmed him. Overwhelmed Maggie, too, evidently, because her response was quick and enthusiastic. She kissed him back, and when his tongue slid against hers, a soft, lost sound escaped from her throat.

He wasn't doing much better. *God, I'm drowning*

*here,* he thought. But how could he stop now? He remembered this. The deep, satisfying kiss of a woman who used to be very good at it.

And still was.

"Mr. Stewart?" a male voice called out, echoing loudly in the room. "You in here?"

As though a great, smothering wave of panic hit her, Maggie jerked away. Will pulled back, as well, though he felt uncertain what there was to defend himself against. A beam from a flashlight bounced around the walls insanely, as though chasing an unseen enemy.

"In here, Frank," he called to the security guard, though he could not take his eyes off Maggie's mouth.

Frank came into the lobby, looking uncertain, eyes wide with curiosity. "I was just making my rounds," he explained. "I heard something and thought I'd better make sure it was you instead of a couple of kids up to some mischief." Will narrowed his eyes as Frank played the flashlight over him, then Maggie. "Hope I didn't disturb you."

"Not at all," Maggie said smoothly. They both rose, and she brushed a few flecks of sawdust off her skirt. "We're all done here, aren't we, Will?"

What could he say to that?

He thought fleetingly of telling Frank to go take a hike, leave them alone. But he canceled that impulse and nodded instead. "Yes, we're done."

## *CHAPTER NINE*

ALAINA HAD ALWAYS BEEN an early riser, but the next morning, long after she heard Maggie's car roar out of the driveway, she remained in bed, thinking.

She couldn't come up with a single good reason to get up. Not one.

In the early years of her marriage, she and Gil had often slept late on the weekend. They had lain in bed, drinking some ridiculously fancy blend of coffee and reading the newspaper to one another in those quiet lulls between the irresistible desire to make love. Those had been blissful days. Like living in a golden bubble of passion and safety and contentment.

She turned over on her side, stretching out her hand to run fingers down the cool, silky sheets where Gil used to be. A month ago, he'd left their king-sized bed for the one in the spare bedroom. He claimed that lately he'd been sleeping poorly, that he didn't want to wake her when he rose in the middle of the night.

Alaina had accepted that excuse, even though she knew deep inside that it was a lie. Gil had no interest in sleeping with her anymore, and no interest in doing anything else, either. In the last six months, her husband had faded to become a visitor in their marriage, a cameo performer with very few scenes.

She wondered where he was this very minute. Unable to bear admitting the truth, even to herself, Alaina had repeated to Maggie the story Gil had told her. While at the Boston conference, he had reconnected with a college buddy. Now they had joined two other old roommates for a two-week camping trip to Montana.

Another lie, she was sure. Hospitals were rich breeding grounds for gossip, and recently, more than one vicious rumor had been whispered loud enough in Alaina's presence. Gil's new nurse practitioner was pretty, single and eager to make points with her boss.

Alaina knew that in spite of Gil's talent, intelligence and good looks, her husband had a fragile ego that needed lots of attention. He'd strayed once before in their marriage—with promises that it would never happen again. But Alaina saw it so easily in her mind—Gil and his attractive nurse sequestered in some luxurious resort. Massages and expensive bottles of wine and long walks on a starlit beach. All the delights that had been missing from their relationship for so long.

She was too much of a coward to investigate, of course, to confirm any of the malice that touched her by way of sympathetic smiles and eyebrows that soared in polite disbelief. She knew people thought she was blind or stupid or both, but she told herself that she had to trust Gil to keep his word. She didn't want to be one of those shrewish wives who constantly fretted over infidelity.

Now, it shocked and depressed her to realize the truth. The love in her marriage had disappeared piece by piece, layers carved away over the years until her heart felt like no more than a hollow drum. If her husband's new nurse had taken over all the parts Alaina had been used to playing, the hopelessly sad part of it was, she wasn't sure she cared all that much.

With a disgusted groan, she fell back against her pillow. Her heart gave a small, sad drop when she thought of her marriage. It was failing, and sooner or later, she knew she would have to do something about it.

*Why not today, Al? What are you waiting for?*

She was such a coward. About everything. Every situation. Every relationship. She was so determined to avoid unpleasantness, so desperate to please, that she ended up pleasing no one. Least of all, herself. She had the backbone of a sponge, and she was sick of it.

But how did you change the habits of a lifetime?

One step at a time. One little step.

With a growl of determination, Alaina threw back the covers and slipped out of bed. She knew one place to start.

Maggie.

After spending a sleepless night replaying in her head yesterday's argument, Alaina knew her sister had been right. Whether intentionally or not, she had sabotaged Maggie. She'd known how their father would react. And the realization that she could do such a thing horrified her.

Having a better relationship with Maggie had looked so promising. Was she really going to let it slip away because she couldn't bear to face her own imperfections? Right now she couldn't do anything about her marriage, but she could do something about her sister.

Traffic was light on Sunday, and she reached the LaCrosse South Beach construction site in no time. As expected, the place seemed empty, but she'd heard Maggie tell their mother that she intended to work today. Her sister was a lot of things, but lazy wasn't one of them.

The guard on duty signed her in, then suggested she go directly to the construction trailer. Someone there would probably be able to tell her where to find Maggie.

She was halfway up the wooden steps when the trailer's door swung open and a man came out so suddenly that she was forced to grab the railing to keep her footing.

"Sorry," he said. "I wasn't paying attention."

"That's all right," Alaina replied automatically. "I shouldn't have..."

She stopped.

*Zack.*

It had been so long since she'd seen him. He had none of Gil's slick good looks. The years had etched imperfections in his features. He looked older, scruffier, with a delicate calligraphy of lines around his eyes. But she'd have recognized him anywhere.

Decades of social skills left her. She could do nothing but stare at him. He didn't seem any better off. He frowned, searching her face, as though trying to quickly assimilate the impossible. That after all this time, Alaina Tillman could be standing here in front of him.

"Alaina...?"

She wished suddenly that she'd taken more trouble with her appearance. When you ran into old boyfriends, who didn't want to look their best? In this unforgiving morning light, she knew it must be obvious just how much time had gone by, time she could never recover.

Then she breathed in the ocean air as if it were smelling salts. She wasn't about to let her new determination desert her so soon. She didn't have to be perfect for Zack. She didn't have to be perfect for anyone.

The silence between them had dragged on too long.

"Hi, Zack," she said with a smile, desperate to seem calm and breezy, while inside her brain buzzed and her stomach had swooped into a bottomless swan dive. "I...I was looking for Maggie."

He held a tightly rolled tube of blueprints and used them to motion toward a cluster of nearly completed buildings. "She's working over at the main lobby. It's not hard to find."

The fact that he seemed disinterested in escorting her dropped her confidence a couple of points. So did the way his jaw compressed over and over again.

She did her best to ignore it. "Could you take me there?" she asked.

After another excruciating silence, he nodded. "You probably shouldn't be roaming the property on your own, anyway. Not without a hard hat."

"I'd appreciate that."

How polite and impersonal they sounded. She wondered what he was thinking. Zack had always been so open and easygoing. She remembered the morning she'd told him that they couldn't see each other anymore. No way to misinterpret his thoughts and feelings *that* day.

He went down the stairs and started off through a maze of construction equipment. His long strides were hurried, as if he couldn't wait to be done with this favor. Alaina did her best to keep up with him.

"How have you been?" she asked, trying to open a real dialogue between them.

"Fine."

"You look well."

"So do you."

"Thanks. I don't know why I should be so surprised to see you. Maggie could never do this job without you. She says you're indispensable."

"Maggie exaggerates."

It was the most disheartening conversation she'd had in ages. Even Gil was usually more communicative than this. But how could she expect anything more when she'd hurt him so badly?

Only a hour ago, she'd been filled with new resolve

to change her life. To stop hiding behind her fears. This was an opportunity. A chance to make things right. She mustn't let it get away from her.

They had reached a stack of portable storage units, and just beyond them sat a huge yellow forklift. Before Zack could lead her around it, Alaina called out, "Zack, stop."

He didn't look at her. Instead, he pointed toward a nearby building. "You'll find Maggie through that door."

When it seemed he might leave her, she caught the sleeve of his shirt. "Just stop. Please."

He turned. Waited. His mouth tightened as he pushed air from flared nostrils. He had a strong face, full of character, but she couldn't find any welcome there.

Choking on nervous tension, Alaina said quietly, "It's good to see you, Zack. Really."

He shifted impatiently. "I'm sorry, I have work to do."

"I don't want to keep you from it. But I just… It feels strange to see you today, when I've been reflecting so much lately about the past. After ten years, don't you think we could have more to say to one another than just hello?"

He crossed his arms. "Frankly, I'm not sure *any* conversation is wise."

"We meant a lot to each other once." She swallowed. Hard. Was she delusional to imagine she could repair the damage between them? Unwilling to be discouraged by Zack's attitude of complete rejection, she added, "I guess I'd like to say that I've missed you. And I wonder if perhaps you've missed me, too. Just a little."

"Maggie keeps me posted. I know all about the big house and the fancy boat and the charitable work that gets you pretty plaques and lots of nice write-ups in the paper. I hear your prominent husband makes anything possible for you. Sounds like you've got a wonderful life. Congratulations."

His tone of voice, those words, made her shiver. His eyes were as sharp and hard as chips of ice.

"Oh my God," she said. "You really do hate me. I didn't want to believe that was possible, but it's true, isn't it?"

"No. I try not to spend any energy thinking about you at all. A crazy teenage crush that ends badly isn't a very solid foundation for hatred. You grow up. You get over things."

"How odd. I said almost the very same words to Maggie not long ago. But I'm not sure anymore if that's the case. And I wouldn't call what we had a crush."

He shuffled his feet, clearly wanting to be gone. She couldn't have stopped him. But he paused.

"It doesn't matter what words you use," he said. "It was over a long time ago."

That came out bitter enough to make her flinch. "This is so horrible," she told him, trembling inside. "I've often imagined how it would be if we ever saw one another again. This isn't the way it all played out in my head."

"How did you expect it to go, Al? You'd have to be one hell of a cockeyed optimist to think we could ever..." He shook his head, then straightened. "It's nice to run into you again. Maybe we'll see each other in another ten years. Why can't you leave it at that? You have what you wanted out of life."

"What I wanted..." she repeated absently. A cold, hollow feeling had settled in the place where all her new confidence had once been. "I suppose it does seem that way, doesn't it? I know for a long time I've been trying to force myself to believe that. But it's not true, and I'm not sure it ever was. I was so confused back then..."

"Well, you must have figured it out eventually. You let your mom and dad convince you not to do something foolish, like marrying me. If you went on to college, you just might do better than a nineteen-year-old kid who had no money, very few prospects and no particular goals. So you dumped me. And you found that better life, didn't you? Good job. Now what the hell do you want from me?"

She pressed her fingers to her cheeks. They were as hot as if she had a raging fever. "I don't know. I guess I'm just trying to make sense of things." She dropped her hands and stared up at him. It was so hard to explain. But she felt desperate to try, and right now, pride seemed like a useless, forgotten luxury. "Zack, my life is filled with so many holes these days. I'm just trying to figure out how to fill them with something meaningful."

"Learn to accept. That's what I've done."

"Please. Can't we—"

A wave of anger moved across his brow as he reached out to grab her arm and give it a rough shake. "Don't you get it? We can't be friends. We can't *be* anything." He turned her loose. With only a touch less exasperation, he said, "I'm sorry if you're in the throes of some personal crisis. If you're unhappy, if you're trying to figure out what needs to change in your world, then find a therapist in the phone book. Write 'Dear Abby.' Consult a palm reader if you think it will help. Just don't expect me to solve your problems anymore, because I'm out of the knight-in-shining-armour business, and I have no intention of being pulled back in. Got it?"

Her throat felt so dry that it hurt to swallow. She nodded and managed to say, "You've made yourself very clear."

"Good," he replied. "Now I have to go. Can you find your way from here?"

Find her way…? What a joke.

## *CHAPTER TEN*

"COME ON, Maggie, drink up. This is a party. Not a funeral."

Maggie, who had been standing poolside at the Grand Beach Hotel, sipping a rum and Coke and watching the crowd, turned to find Lisa Stewart standing beside her.

She wore a long, flowing gown of bright colors that made her seem very adult. In her hand was a tropical cocktail with a parade of fruit stuck along the rim.

She clinked her drink against Maggie's. "Having a good time?"

Maggie nodded. A few days ago, Lisa had called to invite her to her twenty-first birthday party. Will had rented a huge banquet room in the hotel. There was an open bar, a steel drum band playing under a thatched roof and enough vivid lanterns overhead to give everything a lovely glow. According to the embossed card Maggie had been handed upon arrival, there would be dinner and dancing until eleven, fireworks at midnight and a final toast to Lisa. Then she and five close friends were going to go upstairs to spend the night before leaving tomorrow on a cruise to the Caribbean.

"Thank you for inviting me," Maggie said.

"I'm glad you could come. I'm sorry we haven't had much time to get together and catch up. But maybe after I come back."

"That would be nice."

Lisa motioned toward her with her glass, and a little of the ruby liquid splashed over her fingers. "You look very pretty tonight."

Maggie thanked her, though she felt a little dowdy compared to some of the other guests. Her gauzy, one-shoulder dress in swirling greens and blues had been pulled quickly off the rack in Macy's. She refused to spend a lot of time thinking about what Will might like to see her in. This wasn't a date.

Still, she couldn't help scanning the crowd for him. She'd arrived late, and they'd spoken briefly as he and Lisa greeted the guests who came into the banquet hall–turned–tropical paradise. Since then, she hadn't seen him.

She wondered if he minded that Lisa had asked her. But then, if that was true, why had he been so understanding the other night? Why had he kissed her?

She still couldn't figure out how that had happened, but she couldn't honestly say she was sorry about it. Being held by Will again—that had felt so good, so right. You could almost imagine…

She shook herself mentally. No sense in reading too much into it. She'd been vulnerable; he'd been kind. It was only a few moments. It didn't change anything. And although she'd been here almost an hour, Will certainly hadn't made any effort to seek her out.

But he must be busy tonight. With his penchant for organization, he was probably making sure everything went off without a hitch.

A sudden thought occurred to her, and she turned toward Lisa. "Did your brother bring a date tonight?"

Lisa laughed. "I guess we're going to skip the part where you try to get me to tell you if Will is seeing anyone." She winked. "That's what I always liked about you, Maggie. No beating around the bush. No, Will's here on his own. I don't think he's had a steady girlfriend in at least six months. As for a *serious* relationship…well…I think you were the last one."

Maggie doubted that, but said nothing. She took another sip of her drink, and let her attention wander. The pool was one of those free-form extravaganzas made to look like a lagoon. The water's rippling surface grabbed the moonlight, shredding it into thousands of shimmering strands.

"I wish the two of you would patch things up," Lisa said. "I always thought you were perfect for one another. You really bring Will out of himself. He needs someone who can keep him from being so serious all the time."

"I think your brother might disagree. He seems perfectly happy to stay the way he is."

"Yes, you would definitely make him a great wife," Lisa went on. "And what about motherhood? Have you ever thought about a child? Will's a wonderful father, but you'd make a terrific mother for Amy."

Maggie held up a forestalling hand. "Whoa. I'm not in the market for a husband and an instant daughter. I can't even keep plants alive."

"Don't you want a family?"

Maggie lowered her gaze, staring into the fizzing swirl of her drink.

*Family.* The word vibrated in her mind like a single note plucked on a violin. Funny how what was deep inside always surfaced, no matter how hidden. Of course she sometimes dreamed of having a husband and kids to fill a home with love instead of the bleak loneliness she often felt in her apartment. But the older she got, the farther away that fantasy seemed. Unattainable as catching the tip end of a rainbow.

Deliberately she let the silence spin out. Lisa was tipsy enough that she wouldn't necessarily think it odd if Maggie didn't answer a direct question.

The girl took another swallow from her glass, then spread her arms wide to encompass the party before her. "So what do you think?"

"Your brother outdid himself. I think he loves you very much."

"I know," Lisa said with a grin. "He can drive me crazy sometimes. He's still just as uptight as he ever was, but he means well." She coerced the cherry out of her drink and dropped it into her mouth. "There's a buffet set up in the Flagler Room. Help yourself. I'd better go. Will insists I make the rounds and mingle with everyone." She scrunched up her nose, looking young again. "Always have to do the right thing, you know?"

She floated away, grabbed another tropical concoction from a passing waiter and very soon melted into a small group of young men and women who seemed intent on starting a limbo contest. Watching them, Maggie felt about a hundred years old.

Determined not to take root in one place, she wandered around the pool. She listened to the buzz of other people's conversations, falling into ones she thought might be interesting, slipping politely away from others that were not. It was odd attending a party where she knew so few of the guests; it was like being adrift in a small boat.

Eventually, she made her way to the Flagler Room. When all else failed, there was always food, though it was nine o'clock and by now nearly everyone had eaten.

She rounded a corner and came into a wide hallway that led into the banquet room. No one seemed to be around, and she thought she might have the place to herself.

Until she spotted Will and his daughter in a corner behind a trio of low ficus trees.

She spent several long seconds studying him. Just as earlier, her reaction was swift and intense. And probably foolish. But it couldn't be helped. A good-looking man in a tuxedo always took her breath away, and Will had the whole package. Sophistication. Charm. Pure sex appeal.

He looked up suddenly. She couldn't help it. His brief

smile made heat pool in her stomach, then run along her veins like lava. So much for trying not to overreact.

As she approached them, however, Maggie became aware that she'd come upon a father-daughter disagreement. Even if Amy's puckered brow and flattened mouth hadn't spoken volumes, Will's body language clearly indicated trouble. He seemed to be exercising deliberate patience and restraint.

Amy saw her and jumped off her chair to run forward.

"Hi, Maggie!" the little girl said in an exclamation of such pure delight that Maggie felt beguiled.

"Hi."

"That's a pretty dress. You look like a mermaid."

"Thanks." Maggie reached out to finger the peach taffeta that Amy wore. "I like yours, too."

"It has birds on it."

"So I see."

"Amy..." Will said softly.

The child turned her head to look at her father so sharply that the dark curls rippling around her temples danced. "*Please,* Daddy..."

"Sorry, sweetie, I've already let you stay up long past your bedtime. You have to go home now with Mrs. Melnick. You aren't going to miss much, I promise."

"But the fireworks will be the best part," Amy said with a fierce scowl, determined to have her way. "I want to see them."

Maggie couldn't help sympathizing. A memory of what it felt like to be young and powerless came to her, but she remained silent, watching the two of them find their way through this dispute.

Will pushed a wayward strand of his daughter's hair back from her face. The girl responded by turning her body away from him.

"Amy, don't be like this," Will said in a reasonable tone. "You can't stay. You love spending the night with Mrs. Melnick, and she loves having you. She's going to be here any minute. You don't want to hurt her feelings, do you?"

The girl remained mutinously silent.

Will held out his hand to her. "Enough stalling. Let's go."

As though struck by sudden inspiration, Amy's head jerked up and she looked at Maggie. "Are you staying for the fireworks?" she asked.

"I…I don't know." Maggie cut a glance at Will, hoping for guidance. She had to remember that as much as she might fantasize about having a child of her own, she knew nothing about raising one. But Will wasn't offering any help. His gaze was on a lineup of wineglasses that stood in red-stained battalions on a nearby table. She watched his jaw clench, doubting if he really saw them.

"Daddy won't let me," Amy went on.

"He won't?"

"No. He never lets me do anything fun."

"Oh, brother," Will muttered, giving his daughter his full attention once more. "I can't believe I'm hearing this."

"Aunt Lisa says your dominoing, and it's true."

He huffed out a short laugh, but Maggie noticed the slightest trace of pink bloom along his cheekbones. "That's *domineering,* and I'm afraid you'll just have to live with it."

Sensing she was losing ground, Amy swung back to Maggie again. "Tell him I should get to stay for the fireworks. I'll go home with Mrs. Melnick right after they're over, and I promise not to be cranky tomorrow." When Maggie said nothing, she added desperately, "I *love* fireworks. It's just not fair that everyone gets to see them but me."

"Well…" Maggie began. She wasn't sure how to respond. To her it seemed like no big deal. One late night. What was so disastrous about that? Will had been awfully strict with Lisa, too, she recalled.

Then, just as quickly, she remembered how her own lack of discipline and common sense had once wreaked havoc in Will's life. Maybe this didn't have nearly the potential for danger, but encouraging Amy when it plainly went against her father's wishes would be a huge mistake.

She shook her head. "Sorry, Amy," she said, crushing back every bit of sympathy she had for the child and feeling like a wicked witch. "I don't think I should get into the middle of an argument between you and your dad. If he says you need to go home, then you need to go home."

"But—"

Will reached down and took his daughter's hand. "Say good night to Maggie, Amy."

Looking stunned and thwarted, Amy said her goodbyes. Father and daughter trooped down the hallway, heading for the hotel's front entrance.

AN HOUR AND A HALF LATER, Maggie wondered why she didn't just give the valet her parking ticket and go home. She'd eaten everything in sight, including two desserts. She'd mingled as much as she could stand and danced a couple of times with one of the partners from Will's firm. She'd even allowed Charlie, Lisa's boyfriend, to coax her into a conga line. Now she sat at one of the patio tables by the pool, drinking soda and wondering if she should take some aspirin for her headache.

Yes, she should call it a night. The party, a success by most standards, had been a dud as far as Maggie was concerned.

Her source of irritation? She'd had almost no face time with Will. She didn't know if that was deliberate or merely the efforts of a host determined to keep the fun going for *all* the guests, but she felt cheated somehow. As though an opportunity had slipped away.

What opportunity she'd been thinking of was way beyond figuring out. But, darn, it wasn't often she wore makeup and bothered with anything fancier than jeans and a T-shirt. Was it so wrong to wish Will had spent more than a few quick moments with her? It didn't have to be anything major. Just chatting about something other than aquariums and square footage and delivery schedules.

But tonight, it just didn't seem to be in the cards.

About the time she decided to head out, Lisa slid into the chair next to her. A few hours of drinking had left the young woman a little worse for wear. Her smile was lopsided, and she kept pulling on one strap of her dress, which slid down her arm with every move she made.

She gave Maggie a silly grin, lifting her glass in salute. "I love being twenty-one. And I love this punch, don't you?"

Maggie hadn't had any of the sweet stuff, and the couple of drinks she'd enjoyed over the course of the evening had barely made a dent in her judgment.

"How's my lady doin'?"

Charlie slumped down next to them. Lisa's boyfriend didn't look any better off. "I'm completely plowed," Will's sister responded with a giggle. She smacked Charlie on the knee as she turned back to Maggie. "Thanks to lover boy here adding a little 'something extra' to the punch bowl. Good thing Will's made sure the hotel holds some rooms open for the guests who can't make it home."

Charlie nodded, though no one had really asked him a question. "Of course, tonight stiff-shirt Will might have to stay here himself."

Maggie glanced at him. She didn't really enjoy talking to drunks, and she wondered how soon she'd be able to leave them sprawled around the table. "Why do you say that?"

The young man wagged his finger back and forth between himself and Lisa. "Because we've been handing him so many glasses of punch for the last hour that he can't be feeling any pain. I'll bet the reason he's not here right now is because he's passed out in some planter." He winked at Maggie. "We should call Security."

Maggie frowned at Lisa. "Do you think it's a good idea to get your brother smashed?"

Lisa cocked her head, seeming to give this serious consideration. "Maybe not, but just once I'd like to see him loose as a goose. I want him to let his hair down and act like a regular guy instead of the all-knowing, all-seeing big brother. I've waited twenty-one years for it, and I think it's long past time."

"He's not likely to appreciate your efforts."

"Who cares?" Lisa said, waving her hand wildly to dismiss that comment. "By the time he sobers up, we'll be on a big, fancy boat in the middle of the Caribbean."

Charlie let out an excited whoop and crashed his glass against Lisa's. "To the Bahamas, babe!"

Maggie's eyes swept the pool area. No Will. Just lots of people who seemed determined to bring in the fireworks with rowdy good cheer. "Lisa, I'm not sure…" Maggie began, then realized that Will's sister was completely absorbed in blowing air down the front of her dress. No point in trying to reason with her. She caught the girl's arm to draw her attention. "Do you know where Will is?"

"He's a big boy, Maggie. He'll be fine."

"I think he headed down to the beach," Charlie offered. "We ought to follow him. He said he felt like skinny-dipping, and *that's* something we won't want to miss."

Maggie's mouth fell open. *Skinny-dipping? Oh, God.*

Will *must* be drunk. He'd never in his wildest days do something like that. He'd never been a prude with her; if anything, he could be brazenly sexual. But this… He had a natural reserve and dignity. He hated people who behaved like asses in public. If anyone saw him splashing in the waves without a stitch on…

He'd be humiliated. And then, when he sobered up, he'd be furious with Lisa and her idiot boyfriend for playing such a prank.

Maggie rose from the table suddenly. "Maybe I'd better go and check on him."

"Why?" Lisa asked with a goofy frown. "It'll do him good to relax. And if he actually takes a dip in his birthday suit, the cold water will sober him up. So there's no danger."

"His ability to swim isn't what worries me."

# *CHAPTER ELEVEN*

THE TRANQUILITY of the beach was a welcome change after the crowded gaiety around the hotel pool. Long before she left the path that spilled into a sandy clearing, Maggie could hear the waves of the Atlantic. There were no lights on the shore, but she didn't need them. Overhead, the moon seemed huge, an oval spotlight one sliver short of full.

"Will," she called softly as she reached the edge of the manicured hotel lawn. "Will, are you here?"

No answer.

She slipped off her shoes, set them down where she could find them later, then stepped onto the warm sand. Almost immediately she bit back a curse as she tripped over a necklace of floats some fisherman had left lying among the dunes.

Clutching her toe, she hopped a few steps, flinging sand everywhere. She couldn't make out any footprints to follow. Maybe this was a fool's errand. "Will," she called again more forcefully. "If you're out here, answer me, damn you."

Nothing.

The breeze fanned Maggie's body like a caress and sent her hair in a windblown tangle. She squinted toward the water, but saw no pale male body churning through the surf in the moonlight. That was a good sign, wasn't it?

"Will?"

"Lisa?" A quiet voice drifted toward Maggie.

"Will, where are you?" Maggie replied quickly.

She scanned the darkness. Near the edge of the hotel property, there were wide banks of thick mangroves. They diffused angry tides that sometimes washed ashore during storm season. She trudged along the beach in the direction of Will's voice.

"Lisa?"

"No, it's Maggie. Where are you?"

"Over here."

She reached the bushes, and suddenly she saw him just beyond. He was seated on a swing that the hotel had hung from the sturdy limb of an Australian pine. His tie was loose. Other than that, he was fully clothed.

Thank goodness.

She came to a halt in front of him, feeling such relief that she said the first thing that came into her head. "You're not naked!"

He'd been bent over, resting his elbows on his knees, but now he straightened. He gave her a curious look. "No, I'm not. Did you want me to be?"

"No, of course not," she replied quickly. "It's just...Lisa and Charlie said you might be out here skinny-dipping. I guess they thought you were looped enough to throw caution to the wind."

His mouth twisted, clearly offended. "Will Stewart does not get publicly drunk. And to get me to swim in the buff, I'd have to do more than throw caution to the wind. I'd have to toss out every lick of sense I have." He patted the seat beside him. "Sit down. Tell me what motivated you to come down and look for me."

Maggie's pulse had just begun to settle. She wasn't sure sitting close to Will—in the moonlight—would be a good idea. "I came because I thought you might need a little help."

Will laughed. "My savior."

"What are you doing out here?"

"Escaping."

"Oh. Then you aren't looking for company, and since you're obviously fine, I'll just go back to the party."

She turned on her heel as much as the thick sand would allow, then began striding toward the hotel. Will was beside her in a moment, pulling her up against him by catching her arm.

"Hold on," he said. "Who says I don't want company? Stay and enjoy the stars with me. They're beautiful tonight, aren't they?"

She flipped a minuscule glance skyward. "Very nice."

A bemused smile touched his lips. His gaze fused with hers as he deliberately let his hand skim her jaw. His fingers drifted lower, along the side of her neck. She had missed the chance to walk away, and he knew it. "I guessed what Lisa and Charlie were trying to do, passing me drink after drink. You were very sweet to want to save me."

"I'm not sure you deserve saving."

Uneasiness crossed his features, though he never took his eyes off her throat. "According to the women in my family, I do. You heard Amy earlier. She thinks I'm a tyrant. And Lisa's always lecturing me about being too uptight, too repressed."

"She's just in a hurry to grow up. Turning twenty-one makes you feel empowered. You think you know everything."

"All the same, I'm a little tired of hearing about every way I've been found lacking. The two of them make me feel old."

"You're not old. You're…mature."

His expression told her just what he thought of that comment. "Oh, hell. I'm becoming my father. As much as I loved him, he was so traditional. Boring, even." He touched her bared shoulder lightly. His mouth widened into one of those smiles that a woman knows is meant only for her. "Tell me something. Do you think I'm boring?"

"No."

"Too controlled?"

Uh-oh. This was tricky ground. "I think…you're not very spontaneous."

"Not true." He shifted suddenly. Her hip bone melted against his. She gasped, and his smile stretched wider. "I'm having very spontaneous ideas right this minute. Want to guess what they are?"

"No. I—"

He dropped his mouth to the spot just below her ear, nuzzling gently, as though she were made of silk. His lips made her shiver. "How's that for doing the first thing that comes to mind?" he whispered with lethal softness against her hair.

"I…can't complain."

"Good. How about this?"

His tongue flicked against her ear, leaving her trembling again with expectation and longing. He was so near she could feel his heat, smell that soap and male scent of him that threatened to reach right in and yank her foolish libido to attention. This was the stuff of pure fantasy, and how was she supposed to ignore a temptation like that?

Maybe she wasn't.

She turned her head, catching his lower lip with her teeth to nip lightly. "Yeah," she encouraged him. "That's really…that's really innovative."

"You inspire me. You always have."

"I can't believe that fifteen minutes ago I was going home."

"Don't. Stay here with me."

Will slipped the strap of her gown down her arm, planting a line of kisses along her bared flesh. She moaned her approval. "You mean, stay the night at the hotel?"

He nodded imperceptibly. "I have rooms set aside. We can take one. What do you say?"

"I didn't come prepared."

He chuckled and lifted his head to meet her eyes. His twinkled in the moonlight. "Of course you didn't. But since when has that ever bothered you? Come on, I know we're totally wrong for each other, but there's no point in denying what we've both felt for days. We're still attracted to one another."

With a sudden clarity that stole her breath, Maggie stopped and gave him a sharper glance. "Is that what you really think?" she asked. "We're wrong for one another?"

Will wasn't paying much attention and didn't seem to notice that she'd stiffened. "Uh-huh. Completely. We always have been, but at the moment, I don't care."

She felt a soft thud in the pit of her stomach as his words touched a raw nerve deep inside her. "Well...I think I do," she said, pushing away from him. Her gaze swept the star-studded sky as she wondered how she could have been so stupid. All that lovely yearning and anticipation. Gone in the blink of an eye. She felt hollow. No, gouged out. "I had a lovely time tonight, Will. But I think I'll head home now."

He frowned. "Maggie?"

She wasn't going to wait for him to connect the dots. She whirled before he could say anything more, wiggling her fingers over her shoulder. "Good night."

WILL SAT IN A CHAIR in front of Amy's classroom door and frowned, willing it to look better instead of the potential disaster it appeared to be.

When he'd agreed to join the school committee

with all the other parents, to help his daughter decorate one of the school's doors for the annual Spring Fling celebration, he hadn't expected it to get so complicated. Really, how hard could it be to throw up a roll of brown paper, slap on some paint, and then glue on some fussy seasonal symbols—a few flowers and birds? Maybe a bunny or two.

In every design class in college, Will had aced his tests. His creations, though a little traditional, had still received top marks for innovation, scope and practical use of materials.

So how come he couldn't seem to make a simple tulip out of construction paper? How come his trees looked more like melting lollipops than palms? What had happened to quality glue that stuck to paper instead of the person using it?

Amy, seated on the floor in front of him, came up on her knees to check his work. He'd been fiddling with a trio of sunflowers for…oh, about half an hour.

She looked up at him as though she'd just realized she was working with a chimp. "That's no good, Daddy. They have to be poofy-er." She threw her arms out to make ever-widening circles. "And bigger."

Poofy-er. Bigger.

The problem, Will decided, was Amy.

Why couldn't he have a child who didn't care a thing about art? Some unimaginative slug who would have been more than happy with your basic store-bought decorations.

But not Amy, bless her creative little heart. She'd

told him she wanted their door to be the best one in the whole school. With lots of stuff on it. And she knew just what would take it over the top.

Glitter.

There was so much of the shiny sparkles on the door, the floor, on Amy, on *him,* that a stranger wandering past might have thought he'd gone through some wormhole in the universe and landed in Vegas. A very messy Vegas.

Will's stomach growled. He looked at his watch, using a fingernail to scratch away a blob of glue. Nearly dinnertime. The project had begun at four o'clock. They should have been finished by now.

Oh, well. What could you do when you had a inventive diva in your family who wouldn't settle for simple or fast results? Maybe Amy got her interest in art from him, or—he had to grudgingly admit—possibly even from Maggie.

He glanced down the hallway. Earlier, at every door there had been mothers with their kids, all of them working on this project so it would be finished by tomorrow. There was only one parent and child left now, a woman a few classrooms down who had to keep calling her son back to help her. The boy had spent more time running up and down the corridor than working with his mom.

Occasionally, a few of the women had come by to offer advice and opinions. They seemed to find it amusing that he was the only guy, and a couple had actually commented on it. One of them had even flirted with him.

He supposed it *was* odd to be the only father, but he'd long ago made up his mind that Amy would have his full attention and support when it came to things like this. Recitals, Christmas pageants, soccer games. Whatever she wanted to be involved in.

He just hoped they weren't all going to involve glitter.

"How about this?" he asked, holding up the sunflower he'd cut out of yellow paper. "Poofy enough?"

His daughter eyed it critically. She had a huge streak of blue paint across her chin. "It's okay," she said. "When's Aunt Lisa gonna get back from the boat?"

"The day after tomorrow. Why?"

"She makes really good sunflowers."

*Little brat. People pay me good money for my designs.* Will hid an inward smile. At least until Amy asked her next question.

"Do you know how to make a horse?"

"Why?" he asked suspiciously.

Amy pointed to one corner of the door. "I think it would be pretty if we put a horse and wagon over here, and then filled it with flowers."

He shook his head at her, holding up the "okay" sunflower. "I can barely manage these. You're on your own, Picasso."

"Who's Picasso?"

"An artist who didn't believe in a lot of poofy stuff, and who still made lots of money. Can we pick up the pace? I think the glue is starting to make me woozy."

Letting his eyes roll, he reeled dramatically in his chair. Amy giggled and went back to taping birds in the palm trees he had made earlier.

He stroked his hand down her thin back for a moment, just to connect with her. They really ought to get a move on. But when he was around Amy, he couldn't help it. He lost his loneliness, forgot the problems of the day and found new reasons to feel lucky and blessed. She was the best thing that had ever happened to him.

He supposed he had Maggie to thank for that. All the things that were so delightful about her had turned up one by one in Amy's personality. Sure, his daughter could be a real pill sometimes, like the other night when she'd dug in her heels about the fireworks, but she had a naturally sunny, upbeat disposition that came straight by way of Maggie's genes.

Maggie might have made a pretty good mother if she'd allowed herself half a chance. But she hadn't, and Will wasn't sure he could ever completely forgive her for deciding to give up their child.

The problem was, he was having a hell of a time seeing Maggie as immature, dishonest and self-absorbed. As foolish as she might have been eight years ago, he'd seen no signs of that since she'd gotten the LaCrosse job. The night he'd kissed her in the darkened lobby, he'd meant it when he'd told her that she'd changed. She hadn't lost any of the things that had attracted him to her in the first place, but she *was* different.

Of course, it didn't help that his mind kept drifting back to that Saturday, and the temptations he'd come smack up against on the night of Lisa's party. He still wasn't sure just what had possessed him to behave that way. He hadn't been drinking, and pulling Maggie into his arms had Bad Idea written all over it.

But what the hell?

That was where he had wanted to be at that moment, and that was where he wanted to be right now. Back in her arms. He had an intense longing to see her mouth really smiling again, the guarding of her emotions coming down as she looked into his eyes in the moonlight.

*Right this minute.* A frisson of excitement slid through him as he thought of her, and he hated that. How could you feel that way about a woman you supposedly wanted nothing to do with?

He became aware of movement down the hallway. The last team had finished and were carting supplies out to their car. Just to be polite, Will walked down to their door. It never hurt to see what the competition was up to.

He stood with his arms crossed as he examined their artwork. Something to do with April showers, maybe? If all those blue blobs were raindrops.

Mother and son eventually returned. The boy charged past to join Amy, while his mom came up beside Will. He'd met her once, briefly, and thought her name was Jennifer Lundquist. She had pretty mink-brown hair and the luscious feminine appeal of a rich candy bar.

He favored her with a friendly nod. "I like the umbrellas," he said as he pointed with his half-finished sunflower. "I *assume* they're umbrellas."

"They are," she replied, grinning. "I painted them. Which is why they're the only thing you can recognize. Brad's a wiz in math, but he can't draw a straight line with a ruler." She squinted down the corridor where Brad and Amy were laughing over something. "How's your door coming along?"

"That depends on how you feel about glitter. Amy swears it all makes sense, but I still can't figure out our theme."

"You may be overthinking it."

"Could be," Will said with a rueful shake of his head. He rolled a kink out of his neck. "And who would have guessed this was such hard work?"

Jennifer tossed him a sympathetic look. "You're an awfully good sport to come out for this sort of thing. None of the other fathers would be caught dead drawing hearts and flowers with their kids, including my husband." She looked at him curiously. "Of course, I've heard about your situation, and I don't suppose you have much choice right now."

Will stopped staring at the door and turned to face her. "My situation?"

"With your wife."

"My wife?" He frowned. Damn, he sounded like a parrot. He gave the Lundquist woman a small smile, trying to coax open pathways between them. "I'm sorry. What have you heard about my wife?"

Jennifer bit her lip, perhaps afraid she'd spoken out of turn. "I hope there's no problem with word getting around," she said quickly. "When Brad and I were coming here today, he said that you'd be helping Amy with the door instead of her mother. He told me that your wife will be in Africa for two years, tagging elephants. For scientific research purposes, I think he said."

"Elephants."

She nodded. "I think it's a very noble cause. Quite brave, too. But I suppose it will leave you in a bit of a lurch for a while. For things like this, I mean. Being a single parent, even for a little while, can be very stressful."

"Yes, it can," Will agreed, hanging on to the edge of his endurance. He wondered if he looked half as poleaxed as he felt. Just to confirm what he already knew in his gut, he said, "Mrs. Lundquist, where did Brad hear the story about my wife?"

"Why, from Amy, of course."

FORTY-FIVE MINUTES LATER, they had completed their door. As Will had promised earlier, they were seated at Amy's favorite beachside diner, waiting for burgers and fries to be delivered to their table.

She was happily sucking on a strawberry milkshake and coloring the paper place mat. She sat there, completely oblivious, while Will stared across the table at her. How could the Fates have given him a child who could look like a perfect angel and be such a clever little con artist all at the same time?

A mother in Africa tagging elephants. God help him.

Unexpectedly, he felt a miserable laugh tickle his throat, then chastised himself internally for daring to find this situation the least bit funny. Clearly, any hope he had of raising a daughter who could be president of the United States in two thousand and something had gone right out the window. Americans didn't elect pathological liars. Well, if they did, they didn't know it when they cast their vote.

The question was, what should he do about it? No, make that *two* questions. Why had she felt compelled to tell such an outrageous tale?

Unable to wait any longer, Will reached across the table to still his daughter's hand. "Amy, before our burgers come, I want to talk to you."

She looked up, her eyes wide because she knew that tone. The serious-Daddy voice that said there might be stormy seas ahead. "Am I in trouble?"

"I don't know. Did you do something that you think would get you in trouble?"

She scrunched up her nose. "Are you mad because we used so much glitter and now it's in your hair?"

He resisted the temptation to run his fingers over his scalp. Glitter was a mere annoyance compared to lying. "It's not about the glitter," he said calmly. "It's about fibbing. About you making up stories and deceiving people."

"I di—"

He held up his hand. "Before you tell another lie,

stop. I want you to think about your answer. I want you to tell me the truth instead of the first thing that pops into your head. I love you very much, and part of the reason I do is because I feel I can trust you to always be honest. So if you're not, it will hurt me a lot." He lowered his head, giving her a sharpened look. "Do you understand?"

She nodded.

"Good. Now, did you tell Brad Lundquist that your mother is in Africa tagging elephants? That she'll be gone for two years?"

"Yes."

"Did you tell anyone else that?"

"A couple of kids," Amy replied. She skated her nearly empty milkshake glass around in a small circle on the tabletop. "And Miss Shawbeck."

"Your math teacher?"

"Uh-huh. 'Cause she likes animals."

"You told all these people this story when you know it's not true?"

"You don't know it's not true. It could be."

He sensed she was beginning to feel stubborn and gave her a sterner look. "No, it couldn't. I've never told you anything like that about your mother."

"Maybe she doesn't exactly tag them, but I asked you once, and you said she likes animals."

"There's a big difference between liking animals and being a research scientist who works with wild elephants."

"Elephants are animals!" she cried with a sudden

spark of anger that made one or two heads in the diner turn in their direction.

"Amy…" He stopped. He felt weary, battered, but he willed himself not to lose control. It didn't entirely work. "Just tell me why. Why would you tell such lies?"

"'Cause…"

"Because why?"

"I don't know."

"Think about it. Tell me why."

"I just thought…" There was a betraying wobble to her voice. She screwed up her mouth, as though to control it, the picture of misery. She pretended a sudden curiosity for the ketchup bottle.

He tugged it out of her hands and set it aside. "You thought what?"

A flash of anger lit her eyes for the briefest of moments. She looked sullen, determined. She knew they'd reached showdown time. "All the other kids talk about the things their parents do. It's not cool stuff. It's just…things. But I never have stories about Mom 'cause you won't tell me. You keep everything secret."

He refused to let that accusation knock him off balance. "That isn't true," he said calmly, though his throat threatened to close as tight as a vise. "I've told you that your mother can't be with us. I've explained that there are reasons for that. They aren't secrets. I've just never felt that it's been the right time to tell you everything. It's…complicated, and I've wanted to be sure you were old enough to understand."

"I don't know what that means," Amy complained, looking frustrated and confused. "At first, I thought Mommy must be like a secret agent or something. Or maybe an astronaut who lives on the space station. But I don't really like astronauts. And then I go, she probably loves animals just like me! I'd try to help them. Like going to Africa."

"To tag them."

"Uh-huh." Her mouth softened into a wistful smile, absurdly charming. "I didn't really think about it being a lie, Daddy. I just thought…maybe it could be true."

"Amy…"

Will broke off as the waitress came to their booth with their dinner. He settled back and let the woman distribute plates, sensing the futility of further discussion. Amy was reaching for the ketchup again, already having lost interest in the conversation.

Besides, how much more could he say? He could tell her there could be no more lies. He could threaten punishment if there were. He could even promise a long talk sometime about her mother, though what he should say he still didn't know after all these years.

What he couldn't do was give his little girl what she seemed to want most in the world.

A mommy.

## *CHAPTER TWELVE*

THE FOLLOWING SATURDAY, Maggie was at the construction site when she got a call from Lisa Stewart. She and Amy were at the Miami Seaquarium and wanted to know if Maggie would be interested in meeting them inside the park.

The invitation surprised her, and when she hesitated, Lisa said, "Don't say no. You can't work around the clock. Besides, Amy is especially keen for you to join us since she knows you like animals as much as she does. Here, hold on a minute."

The next thing Maggie knew, Amy was on the phone. "Can you come?" she asked in that breathless little-girl voice. "Lisa says you know all about fish. And there are dolphins, Maggie. Do you know about dolphins?"

"I do," she replied, unable to resist smiling. "But I—"

Lisa was suddenly back on the line. "Meet us at eleven o'clock by the entrance to the main aquarium. We'll wait to do anything major until you get here. Just come. It'll be fun. Besides, don't you want to see my pictures from the birthday cruise?"

It did sound like fun, and a lot more interesting than anything she'd been able to accomplish so far today. Zack had been out of sorts lately, and all morning Maggie had been trying not to argue with him. Maybe she needed a break.

When she told Zack, he made shooing movements with his hands. "Great! Go! You're driving me crazy. Just don't come back with any more suggestions for changes. I'll talk to you tonight."

As she jumped into her car, she wondered if Zack's bad mood had anything to do with being in the same city as Alaina. Maybe he worried that he'd run into her, that they'd actually have to talk to one another.

Which seemed a shame, because if anyone needed someone to talk to, she suspected it was Alaina. Something wasn't right in her sister's marriage. Gil had been a no-show for weeks now, and that cock-and-bull story about a camping trip in Montana was almost laughable. As if a plastic-perfect pretty boy like Gil would ever sleep anywhere but at a five-star hotel.

She'd tried to chat with Alaina about the situation, but her sister wasn't around much lately, and when she was, she ignored Maggie's less-than-skillful hints. At least they'd made up. After that argument in the car, Alaina had apologized the next day. Twice. They'd hugged. Cried a little. They'd both promised to continue working on their relationship. That was the end of it.

At least Maggie had hope for the two of them. When

this job was over and she went back to Key West, they might actually have forged a better friendship.

Of course, the thought of returning to Key West made her think of Will. That night on the beach. His mouth had certainly worked havoc on her poor, scrambled senses. He had drawn her to a place without restraints or regrets. Yeah, all systems had been go, no doubt about it.

Only then he'd completely shut down the launch, turning her off with that remark about them being "wrong for one another."

Okay, so maybe they were, and always had been.

But knowing that didn't curb the sexual tension that had started to tighten between them weeks ago. Hot, panting, immovable desire. They ought to just give themselves over to whatever would happen and be done with it. Better that than this hopeless, confusing, sexual fencing that seemed determined to slice them up into little pieces every time they were together.

She pulled into the parking lot of the Seaquarium. As she forked over the price of admission, she realized how much she was looking forward to this outing. She loved aquariums. She couldn't wait to share a little of her knowledge with Amy, who seemed fascinated by all creatures. The kid was such a charmer, the kind of child who made Maggie's heart clench with longing for things she couldn't even name.

The park was crowded. With guide map in hand, Maggie slalomed pass a group of Japanese tourists, wound her way around the congestion near the killer whale stadium and slipped through a knot of teenagers who seemed more interested in each other than anything they might find here.

The air was scented with the smells of freshly made popcorn and hot dogs. Above one of the outdoor restaurants, several gulls hung on currents of air, hoping to steal a treat.

She spotted Lisa and Amy standing by the aquarium. They saw her and waved a welcome.

"You came!" Amy said excitedly.

"Too good an offer to pass up," Maggie replied. She glanced at Lisa. "Thanks for inviting me. So, what should we do first?" She motioned toward the huge, circular building that descended below pavement level by way of a carpeted ramp. "Have you been inside yet?"

The crowd moved around them, trying to maneuver toward the cool, dark entrance. Maggie was about to suggest that they get out of the flow of tourist traffic when someone pushed lightly past her shoulder and stopped in front of her, leaving her staring at a broad, masculine back.

"Okay, water for everyone," the guy said. "Now what?"

Maggie stepped sideways so she could see Lisa and Amy and the man who was passing around bottles. For just the briefest of moments, Maggie prayed that she'd discover that it was Charlie, Lisa's boyfriend, who'd joined them. No such luck, of course. It was Will.

Somehow he got the message that they were now a quartet instead of a threesome, because he turned slightly to face her. If he was shocked, she couldn't see it. He smiled at her, in his usual pose of complete control.

"Where did *you* come from?" he asked.

"I got invited," Maggie managed to say over the paralyzed knot in her throat.

A quiet, as bewildered and potent as any silence could be, descended. His gaze continued to snag hers, and she would have bet good money that their thoughts matched. Awkward. *Very* awkward, considering the way they'd left things the other night.

Lisa coughed. "I phoned her right after I called you to come and join us. I figured if anyone would love being here, it would be Maggie." She gave her brother an innocent look. "Right?"

Will stared at his sister as though he had lost his place in the conversation. Then he said quickly, "Right. Good idea." He indicated the main aquarium entrance with one hand. "Shall we go in?"

They trooped off, filtering into the crowd. Lisa took Amy's hand, leaving Maggie to keep Will company almost shoulder-to-shoulder. Neither of them said a thing to one another as they entered the building. After the heat outside, the dark, cool environment around them was a welcome contrast. Or maybe it was just that it was nice to have something else to focus on.

They came to a trio of viewing panels. Inside were

dozens of small tropical fish darting this way and that—yellow-tailed damsels. Maggie let Lisa and Amy get a little ahead of them. Then she leaned closer to Will.

"I'm sorry if my being here messes up any plans you've made."

He turned to look at her, finding her eyes in the dim light. "No, not a bit. I'm sorry if I seemed less than welcoming. It's just—I wasn't expecting you." Before Maggie could respond, Amy called him over, eager to share her excitement. As he moved away, Will said, "Let's just enjoy the day, shall we?"

And surprisingly, they did.

They watched divers feed the fish in the big tank. They got up close to the sharks, stroked stingrays and handled starfish as big as dinner plates. They fed the rowdy crowd favorites—the seals—whom you couldn't help laughing at. Amy was picked out of a small audience to help a trainer teach a walrus to sing. By the time the afternoon was nearly over, they'd covered almost all of the park and were just about out of energy.

Finally, only one thing remained—feeding the dolphins. Her feet beginning to ache, Maggie sat at a café bistro table and waited for her three companions to buy a few cups of small fish for the animals.

The dolphins were one of the park's most popular exhibits. Checking them out might take Amy a while, but Maggie didn't mind. It had been a lovely day, full of the kind of good fun she remembered sharing as a child with her parents and Alaina. Things had been so simple then. Why couldn't life have stayed that way?

She watched Will emerge from the crowd, then head toward her table. She experienced one squeeze to her heart before smiling up at him as he pulled out the chair beside her.

Honestly, she was pathetic. He'd done nothing all day but be kind, a real gentleman. So how come she found herself wishing he'd look at her, just once, with that same sexy, jaw-dropping grin he'd used at the beach? Yep. Pathetic.

He relaxed as much as an iron patio chair would allow. "Lisa's going to feed the dolphins with Amy. We may have quite a wait."

"I'm fine," Maggie said, closing her eyes as she lifted her face skyward. "The sun feels good."

She remained silent, enjoying the break, savoring the sights and sounds of the park around her. Giggling, hyper children. Parents barely exercising control as they called instructions. She supposed they felt harried, worn out, but Maggie envied them that loving interaction. She'd seldom had that in her own family, and it seemed quite possible she'd never have it in the future.

Feeling that Will's silence had gone on a little too long, she opened her eyes to see if he was still seated at the table. He was. And he was looking at *her.*

There was something warmer in his eyes, the mere hint that maybe he was glad she was there after all. Oh, no. Those were dangerous thoughts she had no business thinking. She pulled away from them, letting her brain lose focus. The brilliant afternoon light picked out the brightest colors—the green of the landscape, red and yellow flower beds nearby, the blue reflection of water—and beat them to a sparkling blend. Yes, it really was turning out to be a wonderful day. Concentrate on that, she told herself.

"You look like you're having fun," Will said.

"I am. Aren't you?"

"Yes. You know what's in play here, don't you? With Lisa and Amy doing their best to throw us together."

"Uh-huh. Matchmaking. The question is, was this planned by Lisa or Amy? I'm thinking Lisa."

Will took a sip from his water bottle. "I don't know. Amy can be very devious sometimes. And lately, she's been so fixated..." He frowned, as though he definitely didn't want to consider what else Amy had been up to lately. "No, you're right. It's got to be Lisa. She thinks she's in love with Charlie, and it's made her want romance for everyone."

"I have to admit, hearing that is a huge relief."

"Relief?" Will cocked his head at her. "What do you mean?"

Maggie shifted in her chair. She wished suddenly that she hadn't said that, but almost immediately she refused to yield to the temptation to change the topic. No, better just to say it. "After what happened...with that jackass exposing himself to Lisa, I've always worried that it would scar her somehow. That she'd be afraid of men, or...I know the therapist said she'd be fine, but..."

"I understand. I was concerned about that, too. I think that's why I was so over-the-top about it." His eyes met hers for a moment. "With us, I mean. I just couldn't seem to get past it. But eventually, you realize that things like this happen and it doesn't have to be the end of the world."

"I'm so sorry for my part in it, Will. I would have done anything to keep Lisa from being hurt. It just never occurred to me—"

He reached out and placed his hand over hers on the table. "Maggie, stop. You've apologized. Lisa is fine. We should have put this behind us long ago."

His words caught her off guard, though not as much as they would have a few weeks ago. They shared a smile, a gossamer-thin thread of connection.

She was still assessing their conversation when Amy came charging out of the crowd, skidding to a stop in front of the table. Her eyes were so bright with excitement that Maggie couldn't help grinning. "They're so pretty!" the girl cried. "I touched one when I gave it a fish. Will you come and take pictures of all of us?"

"Sure."

She and Will rose, exchanging a look as Amy ran back to the dolphins. "I wish I had half her energy," Maggie said.

"Trust me, keeping up with her is like trying to lasso a cyclone."

But so wonderful, Maggie mused. *Do you know how lucky you are to have her in your life?* And then, just as quickly came the most wrenching thought of all. Where was *her* daughter right now?

They joined Lisa. Amy, eager to participate but barely tall enough to see over the edge of the pool, lifted her arms to her father. "Hold me up, Daddy! Hold me up!"

Will swung his daughter into his arms. Clutching her tightly, he tilted her over the parapet so that she could dangle a bait fish to one of the dolphins bobbing nearby. Several others, spotting an easy handout, churned the crystal-blue water of the tank and chattered their unique call.

Lisa, recognizing a photo op, stepped back so that she could snap pictures of father and daughter. She clicked off several, dancing around them like a professional photographer.

Maggie touched her arm. "Why don't I take some of the three of you?" she suggested.

"Thanks," Lisa said. "Snap as many as you like. Then I'll take some with you."

She handed over the digital camera. It required a minimum amount of instruction. The three Stewarts grouped together by the feeding pool. Amy, wanting a dolphin in the picture, extended her thin arm so a fish could be dropped into the open mouth of one of the playful creatures.

Maggie took a series of photos quickly, pleased by how good they looked when she reviewed them. She moved in for a close-up. "Amy," she called. "Over here. Show me a big smile."

The child complied, and Maggie pressed the shutter.

"Did you get the dolphin?" Amy asked.

"I sure did."

She tilted the screen away from the sun, cupping her hand to shield it against the brightness. The pictures were great, full of fun and brilliant color. Not bad, she thought. Will might want to frame one or two.

She smiled at the last one she'd taken. With that calendar-worthy handsomeness of his, Will looked particularly hunky. Lisa had a model's smile and eyes. And Amy…Amy was adorable. Caught in midgiggle as she mugged for the camera.

It was the kind of captured moment that parents loved. Even her own mom and dad's family room walls were plastered with shots like this. She and Alaina as kids, carefree and innocent in their childhood, just the way Amy—

Maggie frowned down at the camera. Something clicked within her as clearly as if she had pressed the shutter. A fierce sense of shock went through her and ice chilled her stomach like a glacier. This picture of Amy… It looked so much like… No, it couldn't be…

Her brain was processing so many possibilities, Maggie half expected it to short out. She couldn't take her eyes off the image of Amy, laughing, reaching to connect with the dolphin, her eyes wide with excitement.

The hair color was wrong. So many features were Will's. But that chin. The way her mouth twisted in amusement.

In this particular picture… *Amy looks just like me at that age.*

## *CHAPTER THIRTEEN*

"HONEY, JUST TELL ME what you're looking for, and maybe I can help," Connie Tillman said from the doorway.

Maggie stood in the middle of her parents' spare room, the one where things that couldn't be relegated to the hot garage got stashed. Mementoes from the past, wrapping paper, the best Christmas decorations. At her feet, and lined up across the day bed, were boxes and boxes of family photos. Six months ago, her mother had decided to sort them all into albums, but it was still a work in progress.

Surveying the mess, Maggie realized that this mission might not be as easy as she'd hoped.

"It's just a picture of me," she said as she stepped over a tower of boxes. "Remember when we went to Orlando that summer it rained so much? How old was I? Six or seven?"

"Eight, I think. Which picture, Maggie? We took so many."

Feeling a little desperate and wishing that her mother would just leave her alone to search, Maggie cleared a space to sit down. She needed to find that snapshot from her youth. Before the digital image of Amy she had filed away in her mind disappeared completely.

"We went to Sea World," she explained. "Alaina and I were feeding the animals. Seals, I think."

Connie bent to retrieve a box marked Vacations. "Try this one. Why do you want to see those old snaps now? You never used to like to look at them."

That was certainly true. She'd always shied away from poring over family photos, especially those of herself. In any she'd ever seen, Alaina had always come off better. Who wanted to be reminded of cowlicks and crooked teeth and summers spent fighting acne? All the things that had never seemed to plague her gorgeous sister.

Maggie didn't want to tell her mother that, though. She shrugged as she lifted off the lid. "Guess I'm getting nostalgic in my old age."

Quickly she flipped through the processing packages while her mother came to join her on the bed. The shot Maggie wanted had to be here somewhere. But where?

Her mother was hunting through one of the other boxes. "Remember your cousin Celia's wedding?" she said, handing Maggie a print from the ceremony where Alaina and Maggie had been bridesmaids. "I loved those dresses."

"Uh-huh," Maggie replied absently. She didn't have to glance at the outfits to recall hers clearly. "I looked like Babe the Blue Ox."

"Oh, look. Here's your great-aunt Jane. I'd forgotten your father brought the camera to her sixtieth birthday party."

Frustrated, Maggie slid one carton off her lap and picked up another. What if what she suspected was true? What if the resemblance was undeniable? What then?

Her mother tried to hand her a snapshot of her great-aunt. "Mom, please try to focus," Maggie said. "Sea World. Me and Alaina."

Unfortunately, when her mother was in full family-appreciation mode, there was no stopping her. She held the picture at arm's length, smiling. "Your father insisted on taking so many of her. He can be such a sweet, sentimental sap sometimes."

Maggie was aggravated enough that she couldn't help a snort of disbelief. "Sweet and sentimental? Are you sure we're talking about Dad?"

"Maggie! Honestly, sometimes I don't think you understand your father at all."

"I think I understand him all too well," she muttered. Her father had been raised in a military household, served in the Marines and, as a CPA, had thought numbers were far more interesting than people. You couldn't get more straight-arrow in life than that. "Strict, no-nonsense, by-the-book James Tillman," she said. "That pretty much sums him up, doesn't it?" She eyeballed a box labeled First Days. "What are these?"

"All the first days of school for you and Alaina.

And no, that doesn't sum up your father." She rose from the bed. "Let me show you something."

Her mother bent to dig through the stack of boxes on the floor. If what she had in mind was a walk down memory lane, Maggie definitely wasn't interested. She wished her father would come home from the driving range and whisk his wife out of here. "Mom…"

"It will only take a minute." Finding what she searched for, Connie came back to the day bed, sat down beside Maggie and handed her a slightly faded Polaroid of children lined up outside a brick town house. "Do you know who these people are?"

Maggie had seen very few pictures of her father's family. Her grandparents had died years ago, and his three younger brothers were spread out across the country. She handed back the photo. "I'm guessing Dad?"

"Yes, along with his brothers." Her mother pointed to each boy. "There's Uncle Jack and Thomas and the youngest boy, Steven." Then she indicated a small bundle in her father's arms—clearly a baby. "Do you know who this is?" Connie Tillman asked, and when Maggie shook her head, she added, "It's your Aunt Pauline."

Distracted momentarily from her task, Maggie said, "I didn't realize Dad had any sisters."

"That's because no one in the family talks about Pauline very much. Certainly not your father."

"Why not?"

"She died when she was two. Drowned in a neighbor's pool."

"How horrible."

"It was. And even more so because your father blamed himself for the accident." Seeing Maggie's surprise, she went on. "He was the oldest child—ten at the time. He was supposed to be watching her. But he was having so much fun with the other kids, and he thought she was secure in her swim ring. By the time he realized that she had slipped out of it and gone under, it was too late."

"But he was just a kid himself."

"I know. But your Uncle Jack told me your father never got over it. Especially since your grandmother always thought it was his fault, too. Although she never came right out and said it."

Fascinated, Maggie turned to look at her mother. "I don't remember Grandma very well, but surely she wouldn't lay that kind of guilt on her own child."

A weak smile played across her mother's lips. "Parents do terrible things when they're grieving."

"Why are you telling me these things now?"

Her mother reached out to take Maggie's hand. "Honey, for a long time this family has been...splintered. I've certainly had my share of arguments with you—most of them foolish, I'm sure. But the way you and your father are...I know he can be bossy and demanding and hard on people."

Unable to deny it, Maggie kept quiet.

"From the time you were little, you've defied him,

questioned his authority. I swear, if he said it was night outside, you'd say it was day. You two have always been at odds with one another."

Maggie nodded agreement at that statement, though she couldn't ever recall her mother acknowledging that her father might have faults. "After getting an angel like Alaina, you two must have been ready to tear your hair out when I showed up."

"You were always a handful," Connie said. "Flitting from one interest to another. Messy. Boisterous. Your father used to beg you to stop slamming doors and leaving lights on, but it never did one bit of good."

"I get it, Mom. I was a terrible kid."

"You weren't terrible. You were just…challenging. But I want you to understand something. It didn't mean we loved you any less. It just meant we had a more difficult time…connecting with you. Particularly your father."

"I'm not sure Dad ever *wanted* to connect with me."

"He tried. He *still* tries. I'm no expert, and I'd never say this to him, but I think that the reason he so often doesn't succeed is because…he's afraid. And he lets that fear blind him to his own behavior."

"Afraid?" Maggie said with another frown. "Of what?"

"Of failing you and your sister when you need him most. Alaina never required much guidance. She welcomed our help. But you—not you. All your life you've rushed headlong into things. No matter how many times we counseled you to look before you leaped, you didn't. You always jumped in with both feet. Sometimes everything was fine, and sometimes…it was pure disaster."

"I never meant to make things hard for either one of you, Mom. I just wanted to be my own person."

"Of course you did! Nothing wrong with that. But your father—I don't think he'll ever see you and Alaina as adults. You'll always be his little girls. You need his protection. His help. He couldn't save his sister, but he'll never let you down if he can prevent it. Even if it means he oversteps sometimes, sticking his nose in where it's not wanted or welcome."

"I'm a big girl. I don't make near the mistakes I used to."

"No, thank goodness. But the next time he starts to drive you crazy, will you remember what I've told you? You're just that little girl he wants to save."

Maggie picked up one of the pictures in the carton she held, pretending to find interest in it. For some reason, she couldn't look into her mother's face. "Back when I found out I was pregnant," she began cautiously, "why did Dad push so hard for me to give the baby to Alaina to raise? Did he really think I would be so completely hopeless as a mother?"

Connie reached out to push hair from Maggie's shoulder with a gentle touch. "Whether you'd have been a good mother or not never entered into it. Your father and I took the news very hard. It was inconceivable that one of our children would make that kind of mistake. It was embarrassing, and I know your father considered it a flaw on our part, as well. That we'd somehow failed to raise you to know better—"

The phone rang, cutting off her mother in midsentence. She rose quickly. "That will be your father, telling me he's on his way home."

Maggie watched her leave the room. Her mother had given her so much to think about. But right now, all she could seem to focus on was finding that photo. Alone at last, she rummaged through another box. Almost immediately she saw the pictures from the family's Sea World vacation. She sorted through them with shaking fingers.

Her breath stalled in her lungs as she found the one she searched for. It was just the way she remembered it. The clothes were dated. The hairstyles different. But the picture of her feeding a seal, laughing into the camera lens, her jaw thrust forward in that I-have-the-world-by-the-tail attitude…

In this one shot she and Amy could have been twins.

It wasn't a coincidence. It wasn't her imagination. Maggie ran her finger down the photograph of herself. It had to be true.

Amy was her daughter.

WITH THE PICTURE tucked safely in her purse, Maggie left her parents' house and went straight to Zack's hotel. She knocked on his room door and felt a huge sense of relief when he opened it. She didn't think she could have hung out patiently in the lobby, waiting for his return.

Obviously not expecting her, he frowned. "What's wrong?"

Zack was the only one she'd ever confided in eight years ago. He'd helped her get through the worst days of her pregnancy, gone with her to every clinic appointment and arranged for an attorney to handle the adoption of her baby. Back then, she'd been so desperate to get her life back on track as quickly as possible that she hadn't asked many questions. But now she needed help getting some answers.

Such as how Will might have ended up adopting their daughter.

To say she was still reeling was an understatement. When she was finally able to catch her breath, she said, "I need to talk to you. About my baby."

He stood back so she could enter. She settled into the desk chair, then rose again almost immediately. She couldn't sit. She was hard-pressed to remain calm at all.

Sensing her distress, Zack said, "What is it? What about the baby?"

No point in a slow buildup. "I think Amy Stewart, Will's little girl, might be my child."

He jerked. "What?"

"I know it sounds crazy, but just hear me out."

Since Zack had never seen Amy, Maggie told him about when she'd first met the girl, how they'd established a friendship, the ways they were similar, the story Will had told her about the child's mother, as many details as she could remember.

She explained about today—the pictures she'd taken at the Seaquarium's dolphin pool. That sudden, overwhelming sense of seeing herself in Amy. The need to confirm her suspicions as soon as possible by unearthing that photo of herself. She showed him the old snapshot, though obviously there was no way he could validate her suspicions since he had nothing to compare it to. She tried to keep it all coherent, reasonable.

It was a huge disappointment when Zack handed her back the photo with a somewhat skeptical look. "And based on how this picture stacks up against the one you took today with Lisa's camera—one picture that you might not even be remembering correctly—you think Will Stewart somehow adopted your child."

"Our child," she amended, feeling so frustrated she could have wept. "I know it sounds bizarre, but it's still possible, isn't it? He was my lover. Somehow he found out I was pregnant and managed to be the one to adopt her. I don't know how, but there has to be some way to find out the truth."

"You do remember that it was a closed adoption? That both the attorney and the birthing center assured you that the records would be sealed for everyone's protection."

She grimaced as she settled on the edge of the king-sized bed. "I realize that. But there has to be something I can do." She stretched her arms out pleadingly. "Help me, Zack."

"Mags, I can see that you're worked up about this, but—"

She jumped up, feeling her face flame. "Worked up? You don't know the half of it. I've spent years wondering where my child is. How she is. And beating myself up for making such a stupid decision. Now, to think that she might have been with Will all these years." She raised one hand, counting fingers. "I've been *four* hours away, Zack. Four. Do you know how many times I could have seen her, the things I could have known about her? The milestones we might have shared?"

Her dearest friend seemed determined not to be as rattled as she was. She tried to remember that it was one of the strengths she loved about him. He gave her a hard glance. "So you think you can come in now and take her back?" he asked in a calm voice. "Is that what you want?"

"I don't know what I want yet. Right now I'm just looking for some answers."

"You don't think you'll get them if you ask Will?"

"Maybe," Maggie replied quickly. Then just as quickly, she said, "No. If she is our child, he obviously didn't want me included in Amy's life from the very beginning. No reason to think he'd feel differently now." She sighed, trying to pull herself together. But how could she do that when the more she thought about this, the more of a mess she felt? "After I got the picture from Mom and Dad's, I almost drove over to his place. I wanted to confront him. But that was just a knee-jerk reaction. So I came here instead."

"I think that was a good idea," Zack told her. "If, by some chance, she isn't your daughter, do you really want Will to know you were pregnant and gave up his child? What can of worms will that open up?"

She hadn't even thought about that. Raking a hand through her hair, she covered her face with her fingers. "I'm so confused about what I should do."

"Have you considered the possibility that you should just leave well enough alone? Yes, she might be your kid. But the decision you made back then was the right one at the time. It may *still* be the right one."

"It *wasn't* the right decision. I knew it two seconds after that baby was taken out of my arms. It was the wrong solution then, and it's still wrong now. I live with that every day, Zack."

"Okay, maybe it was. But it's still the reality you may have to live with."

She brought her hands down, piercing him with a sharp look. "You aren't making this any easier."

"You want easy, or you want the truth? I think it's only sensible to point out a few things. You *did* give the baby up, Mags. If Will is a good father, do you have the right to make trouble now when Amy seems to be in a happy home? You want to fight Will in court?"

"No, of course not. I don't want it to come to that. I can't do that to Amy. No matter how I feel about Will, he seems to be doing a great job. Maybe a little strict at times, but Amy appears to be a contented, well-adjusted child. I could never do anything to upset that."

Zack sighed heavily. “Are you sure you haven’t got this all wrong?”

She wanted to strangle him. “No! I’m not sure of anything. That’s the problem. I’ve tried to figure it out dozens of times. One moment I’m thinking…how come Amy’s mom has never been in the picture? Will told me she didn’t want Amy, but that could certainly be a lie. Then the next minute, I’m wondering if this is just me, jumping to the wrong conclusion that Amy’s my daughter because I’d *like* it to be that way. Am I imagining this resemblance because I’ve always secretly longed for a child of my own?”

“That’s entirely possible, you know.”

She collapsed in the desk chair again, bringing one palm to her forehead. “God, I’m going crazy trying to reason it out.”

Zack came to kneel in front of her. He pushed her hand away from her brow so that he could meet her eyes. “Listen to me,” he told her. “There are some basic answers we can get. The Internet must have information about the rights of birth mothers and closed adoptions. It doesn’t mean you have to act on them, but at least we can find out what your chances are. We can start there.”

“But—”

He squeezed her arm. “Mags. Amy isn’t going anywhere. You don’t think her father knows that you suspect anything?”

“No. It’s ironic. Today we had a really good time. We got along well. It was just like the old days.”

"Fine. Keep it nice and friendly." He stretched to retrieve her purse from the bed where she'd tossed it, then placed it in her lap. "I want you to go home and get some rest. You look beat. Tomorrow we have a big day ahead of us and I need you to be focused on the job. But I promise, we can find out where you can go from here. Agreed?" When she didn't respond at first, he gave her forearm another squeeze, harder this time. "*Maggie.* Agreed?"

"All right," she said, feeling drained. The war of logic versus emotion had left her numb, helpless. From her hunched-over position she glanced up to find Zack's eyes full of sympathy. "I just know it in my gut, Zack. Amy is my child."

His mouth formed a half smile. "Unfortunately, if it comes to it, I don't think your gut can be used as evidence in court."

## *CHAPTER FOURTEEN*

THE NEXT MORNING, Alaina was alone in the house. Maggie had left unexpectedly early for the construction site, and Delia, the housekeeper, had yet to arrive. When the phone rang, Alaina, feeling lonely and isolated, had hoped it would be Gil, telling her when he'd be home.

Instead, it was her credit card company, looking for information.

"I don't understand," Alaina said to the representative on the line, a sweet-voiced woman named Caroline. "Are you saying that you think my card has been stolen?"

"We certainly hope not, ma'am. It's simply our policy to contact clients when we see certain purchasing patterns. In the past couple of days, there's been a great deal of activity on your card, some of it for rather large luxury items. We just want to make sure that there's nothing amiss. Do you have your card handy, ma'am?"

Alaina found her purse and pulled out her wallet. "It's right here. I haven't used it in days."

"And your husband's card?"

"I assume he has it, or he would have called you to report it lost or stolen."

"Just a moment, please." On the other end of the phone, Alaina heard the clicking of keys on a computer keyboard. At last, the woman said, "The charges we're concerned about are all from the Hilton Head Island area."

"Hilton Head? My husband and I haven't been there since our honeymoon. I can't imagine…"

She put the brake on her tongue as a drowning sensation of despair suddenly overwhelmed her. Oh, no, no, no, she thought. Could her world really collapse with one phone call? She wanted to hang up. Pretend they'd been disconnected. But something kept her on the line.

"Ma'am?"

"Yes, I'm sorry. Could you…could you tell me what was purchased?"

"Let's see. A diamond bracelet from Island Fantasy Jewelers. About a thousand dollars for clothes at a shop called A Pretty New You. A full day of spa treatments from a resort named—"

Alaina barely heard the rest. She felt the enormity of it inside her breast, the reality that Gil was not camping in Montana with college buddies after all. Here it was at last. The truth of her marriage revealed by a kindly stranger who had no idea what this conversation had set in motion.

Pride, however, prevented Alaina from sharing her humiliation with the woman, no matter how kind Caroline sounded. Through a quiver of suppressed tears, she said, "There's no need to go on. I think I know.... My husband has been up there for a few days playing golf, but as soon as he comes home we'll be celebrating my birthday. He knows I've been wanting that necklace, and I suppose you've just spoiled his surprise."

There was an extended silence. Right away Alaina realized her mistake. Caroline had told her that a *bracelet* had been purchased, not a necklace.

The woman was diplomatic enough not to point that out, and Alaina was grateful for the consideration. "I'm so sorry," Caroline said. "I hope you understand that we're only interested in protecting your card."

"Of course," Alaina replied. "I appreciate the company's vigilance."

They spent a few more minutes talking. Caroline seemed eager to move on to special offers and customer service issues. Alaina wondered if the woman was aware of what she'd done. How often did she inadvertently expose cheating husbands to their wives? But Alaina's shell of composure was cracking now, and she couldn't get off the telephone quickly enough.

Hanging up at last, she sat on the couch, unable to move. She stared out the front window, watching the leafy green morning leave spots like golden dollars on the front lawn. Her mind began to go around on a familiar track.

*What now? What now?*

*Leave.*

The idea shot through Alaina with enough force to make her flinch. Immediately she rose and went to the closet where her luggage was stored. Removing all four pieces, she took them back to her bedroom, then lined them up on her bed.

She tossed things into the suitcases with no rhyme or reason to what she chose. She knew she wasn't thinking, only reacting, but she just couldn't bear to give it any more thought right now. She had no idea when, or if, Gil would come home, but she didn't intend to be here. Until she could figure out what to do, she'd stay with her parents.

When the bags were fully packed, she trudged them out to the foyer. She'd have to leave a note for Delia. Call Maggie. What else?

The front doorbell sounded, making Alaina jump. When she answered it, she was surprised to find Zack on the step. After their spectacularly unsuccessful meeting the other day, she hadn't expected to see him again.

He didn't bother with pleasantries. "I need to talk to you."

Given what had just happened, she wasn't feeling particularly sociable, either. She crossed her arms as her brows lifted. "Has it been ten years already? I thought you didn't want to talk to me again for at least that long." When he didn't rise to that, she added, "I'm sort of busy right now."

"This won't take a minute."

He looked so serious. She lost her inclination to

be difficult. "Fine," she said, stepping aside so he could enter.

Naturally, he caught sight of her luggage. "You going someplace?"

"I hope so." She tilted her head at him. "What can I do for you?"

"I want to ask you a question, and if you've ever been honest with me about anything, don't lie to me. Don't try to cover. Just tell me the truth."

She couldn't even put a name to all the turmoil inside her, but the way Zack looked at her, the tone of his voice, caught her interest. "What do you want to know?"

"Eight years ago, when Maggie was pregnant, you and your parents tried to talk her into letting you raise the baby. She refused and came to me because she felt she had no place else to go."

Remembering that time, Alaina had to swallow hard. She was still ashamed of the part she'd played in her parents' solution to Maggie's dilemma. "I never—"

Zack put up a hand to stop her. "I'm not here to discuss the right or wrong of that idea. I just want to know one thing. When Maggie put her baby up for adoption, did your parents interfere?"

"Interfere?"

"Did they try to involve themselves in the adoption in any way? I know they were pretty pissed off when she wouldn't let them tell her how to live her life, but how determined were they to control the situation?"

"They didn't even know where Maggie was until

after she'd had the baby and told them she'd given her away. How *could* they have done anything?"

"Your parents are very enterprising. Particularly your father. And he doesn't like being thwarted."

"You make Dad sound far worse than he is."

"Come on, Al," Zack said, giving her a tough look. "Stop being defensive and just answer me. Your parents had a lot to do with breaking up the two of us, so let's not pretend that they aren't manipulative. Maggie gave birth at a clinic that takes the baby from the mother almost immediately. The adoption was arranged months before that. Is it possible your parents found out where she was, what she intended to do and—"

"No. Nothing like that happened. I would have known. And there's no way I'd have been involved and not said something to Maggie." She shook her head at him. "My God, how terrible do you think I am?"

Zack looked at her from under his lashes. When he spoke, he sounded less accusatory. "I'm sorry. I'm just trying to get a better understanding of what might have happened back then."

"Why? What's all this about?"

Even before he spoke, his body language told her he wasn't going to reveal much. "You can imagine how Maggie has struggled with the decisions she made. I'm just trying to help her find some information but I can't discuss it any more than that."

Alaina's throat spasmed as tears welled in her eyes. She had always thought herself a master of control, but right now she felt herself spinning wildly. When

Zack frowned at her, she said, "You've always been such a good friend to Maggie. Far better than I've ever been, and I'm her sister."

She bit her lip to keep an anguished cry from escaping. Life was so difficult. Here she stood, ready to walk out on her husband, her world shattered. But was Maggie any better off? Maybe not.

As though he sensed something was wrong, Zack was suddenly in front of her. He cupped her shoulders in his hands. "Hey," he said gently. "What's going on here?"

She straightened and gulped, but she could barely draw breath. "It's so impossible, isn't it? Do any of us make right decisions? Do all your best plans eventually blow up in your face?"

"Not always."

Zack pulled her to him stiffly, as though he hadn't wanted to but could not deny her need. She brought her head against his chest. The scent of soap, the scratch of his work shirt, the sound of his heart beating fast in her ear, all of it brought a strange sense of peace. Stretching her arms around Zack's back, she hiccuped away a sob. It felt so good just to be held like this. To pretend that you were cherished, even for a moment.

Neither of them moved for a long time. Alaina wanted to be strong enough to bury her feelings, but she knew it was hopeless. The fear and misery seemed to be pouring out of her under his warm touch.

His fingers brushed her cheek, lingering there. It had been so long, so long…

But when she felt Zack's lips against her temple, something within Alaina stuttered to a halt. She knew where this could lead, but was it right? Was it fair to either of them? Given her current situation, how could she allow herself to act—

"Alaina," Zack said as she began to pull away.

"I'm sorry," she whispered.

Surprisingly, when she looked into Zack's eyes, she saw no anger. He seemed calmly accepting, as though he'd known all along she would be the one to stop this.

"I have to get back to the job site," he told her. "Will you be all right?"

Feeling incredibly awkward, Alaina nodded. She moved toward the front door, eager to put distance between them. He took the hint, and in another minute, she closed the door behind him.

She looked down at the litter of luggage at her feet. Was she really going to walk out of this house, walk out on Gil without ever knowing the real truth? Was it possible there was some legitimate explanation he could offer? And if the worst was confirmed, if he had taken his new nurse to Hilton Head, shouldn't they talk it out? It would be so horrible, but... She hated that her natural inclination to run from trouble had kicked in once again.

She sank down on the bench that sat against one wall of the foyer. "Are you ever going to stop being a coward, Al?" she asked aloud.

But the house remained silent, offering no answers.

THEY WERE BUSY at the construction site, struggling to put the finishing touches on the tanks, sanding down imperfections in the cabinets. That wasn't a bad thing, Maggie thought. It helped to keep her mind focused on the job instead of Amy. Still, she couldn't wait for the day to end, and by the time five o'clock rolled around, she was already heading for her car.

Zack stopped her as she dug through her purse. "Where are you going? I thought we could have dinner and discuss a few things."

"I can't right now. I have an errand to run. Then I want to go by Will's place."

"Are you sure that's wise?"

"No. But I'm tired of talking or thinking. I want to…do something."

"Like what?"

"I just want to look at Amy a little closer. Maybe I'm imagining there's a resemblance."

"Is that what this is really all about?" he asked, looking skeptical. "You've said that Amy doesn't take after you, and seeing her one more time isn't going to confirm anything."

She found her keys and looked at her friend squarely. Trying to fool Zack almost never worked. "All right, maybe that's a poor excuse. The truth is, if she *is* my daughter, I just want to be with her. I want to spend every moment I can getting to know her better." She bit her lip. "Is that so wrong?"

He shook his head at her. "Maggie, you're just torturing yourself."

"No, I'm not," she said firmly as she unlocked her car door. "The torture has been spending the last seven years without her."

She swung out of the parking lot before he could say anything more. Before he could offer advice that made perfect sense, but that she was going to completely ignore. She knew there were a dozen better ways she could handle this situation. Methodical. Organized. Sensible. But she didn't feel up to being any of those things right now.

All she really felt like was seeing Amy.

She went to Al's house. Her sister had left a note on the kitchen counter saying she'd be out of town for a couple of days, and frankly, Maggie was glad to have the place to herself. She didn't want to make small talk with anyone.

After a quick shower, she changed into a turquoise-blue sundress and sandals. She headed for the mall. It didn't take her long to find exactly what she was looking for. Then she drove to Will's house.

When he opened the front door, she offered a big smile.

He looked taller than ever in jeans and a forest-green polo shirt. He smiled back at her. "Hi. What's up?"

*Tell me the truth. Is Amy my child?*

No. No way could she go there.

Now that she was actually here, she felt unbelievably tongue-tied. She didn't have a clue what was going to come out of her mouth, but hadn't she always been good at improvising?

"A couple of things," she said. "First, I thought I'd drop by to let you know we're going to run water into the tanks tomorrow. Once the chem numbers settle, we'll start slowly introducing stock."

Will nodded. "Zack told me that a couple of days ago."

Okay. Not her best, most innovative performance. She shrugged her shoulders. "Oh. Well…I guess I could have saved myself the trip." She lifted the small gift bag she held in one hand. "I do have one other thing, though. May I come in?"

He ushered her into the living room. No one else seemed to be around. The TV was off, and she heard no sound coming from the other rooms. Had she lost this golden opportunity?

Before she lost her nerve, she said, "I have a present for Amy."

He looked at her with shrewd curiosity. "I'm afraid you've just missed her. Lisa's taken her to a friend's house for a sleepover. Her first, actually."

Her heart sank. Everything—*everything*—inside her screamed in frustration. It wasn't fair. All she'd wanted to do was spend some time with the child. Excuses to do so wouldn't come very often. But what could she say without making Will suspicious?

As calmly as she could she asked, "Is she old enough for that sort of thing?"

"According to her and Lisa, she is." He pointed to the bag she held. "So what's the present?"

"Oh." Maggie rescued the slim box from the tissue in the bag. She lifted the lid, showing Will the bracelet she'd bought at the jewelry store in the mall. One golden charm lay along the links—a leaping dolphin. She looked up at Will, hoping he wouldn't think it too much or too odd that she should give such a thing to Amy. "She admired mine so much, I thought she might like one of her own."

He seemed accepting of the gesture, though Maggie couldn't help wondering what he really thought. If Amy *was* her child, he had to know this was her very first gift from her mother. How did he feel about that?

"Very pretty," he said at last.

"I know it might seem a little extravagant," she said nervously. "But over the years, as she attaches more charms, she'll need a good quality bracelet to hold them."

He smiled at her. "She'll love it. It's a wonderful thought, Maggie."

"I think she'll like the dolphin, but animals may not be the only things she decides to add over the years." She let her fingers glide over the golden chain. "I'm sure she'll have lots of wonderful experiences she'll want to commemorate."

The words came out as pleasant, mild conversation. But inside, her heart felt as though it was breaking at that moment. If Amy was hers, but Maggie couldn't find a way to be part of her life, would she ever *see* any of her daughter's wonderful memories captured on this bracelet?

She cleared her throat to swallow past the lump that was suddenly there. She put the lid back on the box and returned it to the gift bag.

"I'd like to give it to her in person," she said, trying to regroup. "If it's all right with you, I'll just hang on to it until the next time I see her."

"Of course. Though it might be a while."

Why is that? she wanted to ask, but didn't dare. If Will was actively trying to keep her away from Amy, she didn't want him to know she was on to him.

"Would you like to stay for dinner?" he asked unexpectedly. "After she drops off Amy, Lisa's going to a concert with some friends, so I'm on my own tonight. I was going to grill a steak, but there's enough for two."

She supposed Will might feel safe with Amy clearly out of the picture for the evening. She accepted the invitation eagerly.

Maybe she was dreaming all this up. Maybe there was absolutely no reason for him to worry about her presence. No subterfuge. Just her foolish imagination working overtime as it sometimes did. Her child could be out in the world someplace, being raised by *two* loving parents.

And still just as inaccessible to Maggie.

Will went to the kitchen to get iced tea for the both of them. There really was no accounting for how depressed Maggie felt inside. It wasn't as though she suddenly couldn't deal with the idea of having put her daughter up for adoption. She'd known perfectly well how difficult it would be to accept that, and over the years that decision hadn't settled any better on her. She'd told herself she'd done right by her baby, but now, if somehow her child had ended up with Will, how was she ever supposed to get past wanting to have some involvement with her? It was just…

She felt as if her brain were going to explode.

*Stop. Stop!*

Sighing, she took a turn around the room while she waited for Will to come back. On one end of the couch, she saw a file folder with the Jacobson and Duquette logo on it.

"Still struggling with the Hallandale city hall design?" she said, loud enough for Will to hear. Even talking about miscellaneous work projects would be better than allowing her mind to wander into more dangerous scenarios. She felt so fractured inside, with every nerve ending zinging.

"As a matter of fact, no," Will called back to her. "We've gone to contract."

In another moment he reappeared in the living room with the drinks. He handed one to her. She took the tea and raised it to him. "Congratulations, then."

After they'd both taken a swallow, he said, "I should thank you. You were right. Once I loosened up a little and stopped thinking everything had to be so damned practical, I was able to give them something they could buy into."

She clinked her glass against his. "Here's to being impractical."

A tiny frown line marred his brow. "Maggie, is something wrong? You seem very…tense."

"No, everything's fine."

"Will you be glad when the LaCrosse project is over?"

"Not really. It was an enormous challenge, but I've enjoyed it."

He took another sip of tea. "I suppose you'll be going back to Key West soon."

"Yes."

She didn't really want to think about heading home, either. In spite of what Will might or might not have done seven years ago, Maggie couldn't deny that she was still very drawn to him. Even in this moment.

The fireplace mantle was nearby, and she went over to it to admire the pictures lined up there. Photographs of Will's parents, young and full of life. Lisa in a prom dress. Amy wearing a Christmas sweater, holding a stuffed dog. There was snow on the ground.

Maggie ran a fingertip down the image. When and where had this been taken? It killed her to know that there must be dozens of places Amy had been, things she'd seen and giggled over and loved. So many times without Maggie.

"Do you have other jobs lined up?" Will asked her from across the room.

"A few," Maggie replied absently, her hand still toying with the frame. "Nothing as big as Teddy's, of course, but enough to keep us busy for a while."

"I'm sure you'll do well. Sapphire Seas is innovative and thorough. It's been great working with you."

Maggie turned to him, frowning a little. She'd been so fixated on Amy's picture that she wasn't sure she'd heard right. "What?"

Will set his iced tea glass on the coffee table and came toward her. When they were face-to-face he smiled. "I said, it's been great working with you, and insane as this sounds, I'm going to miss you, Maggie."

The words caught her off guard. "Really?"

"Yes. Really." He laughed a little. "Don't look so surprised. "

"Can't help it. I guess in spite of everything, we did know how to get past our anger, didn't we? How mature and sensible we've been. We could be poster kids for Dr. Phil."

She watched a smile skim across his lips briefly, and when it disappeared she was almost disappointed. Wanting was instinctive and overwhelming, she supposed, and right now, Will's nearness had set up a chemical reaction in her blood.

"I wouldn't go as far as that," he said. "But for the most part, we did manage to keep it sane."

"I don't feel very sane right now. I feel…undone. In so many ways you can't imagine." She shook her head. "I've made some bad decisions in my life. Really bad. I never thought I'd be the kind of person who would have regrets, but I do." She fixed her gaze on him. "I was so foolish to let you chase me off, Will. I should have fought harder for what I wanted."

He reached out, stroking his fingers along the underside of her jaw. Everywhere he touched, she tingled. "Stay. Stay here tonight," he said in a soft voice. "You realize, don't you, that all the old magic is still there between us?" When she nodded minutely, he added, "Let's do something about it."

"I'm not sure that's a good idea. As you pointed out very clearly at Lisa's party, we're completely unsuited to one another."

He swayed forward until a kiss, like a cool little snowflake, floated against her cheek. "Opposites attract, remember? And we're about as opposite as two people can get."

She was glad he couldn't hear the quick, cowardly tripping of her heart. "What happened to being sane and sensible?" she pursued doggedly, like a lesson she had learned by rote.

"Dr. Phil will have to find someone new for his poster."

He took a step closer, removed the drink from her fingers and placed it on the mantle. She stood still and dazed, as though she might shatter. The fear of letting go, all the unshed tears waiting for a break in her control, all those worries over Amy—she knew she had to bear them alone, locked up inside her, until she choked to death. But it was so hard, so hard when Will was this close. Her body was incapable of abandoning him, of walking away.

A craving for more of him, all of him, roared into her head, blocking out everything else. But in the moment when she was sure he would have pulled her into his arms, they both heard a key in the front door lock. Will swore lightly as they broke apart, leaving desire in cinders.

Lisa entered, smiling broadly at them, but she didn't seem at all suspicious about what they'd been up to, even though Maggie was certain she had that slightly flushed look of a woman about to have terrific sex.

"Hi!" Lisa said. "This is a nice surprise."

"I just came by to give Will an update on the job."

"I thought you were on your way to the concert," Will added.

"I was. But Charlie called, and he wants to go, too, so he's going to come over to pick me up." The younger woman's eyes went back and forth between them, and sudden curiosity bloomed in her glance. "I hope I'm not interrupting anything."

Knowing that she had to get out of Will's place fast if she was going to make it out at all, Maggie quickly retrieved her purse and Amy's gift from the couch. "Not at all," she said to Lisa. "I was just on my way."

Will followed her to the door. She stood on the stoop, smiling up at him, though what there was to smile about she couldn't imagine. "I'll talk to you tomorrow."

He shook his head at her. "Maggie, don't. Stay here," he said in a low voice.

But she had already turned and begun heading for her car.

# CHAPTER FIFTEEN

HANK PRICE, the owner of the Blue Reef Bar and Grill, pointed toward the aquarium Maggie and her crew had installed only weeks ago. "You can't tell me that's normal."

First thing this morning, Price had called her, hot under the collar because another one of his fish—a flashy, expensive harlequin tuskfish—seemed about to go belly-up in the tank. It was the third death in as many days. Maggie had agreed to stop by the restaurant to evaluate the situation, but from the owner's description of the harlequin's behavior, she thought she already knew what they were dealing with. And it didn't bode well for Sapphire Seas.

"It's not normal," Maggie agreed. She watched the beautifully striped fish do a one-sided spiral toward the top of the tank, its gills flared wide. She wished there was something she could do, but the poor thing was a goner. She gave Hank Price a regretful look. "He's been poisoned. He'll be dead in a few minutes."

"Poisoned!" Price gaped at her. Maggie was glad that the place had yet to open. Things might be about to get a little unpleasant since customers didn't like buying fish that died within weeks of being purchased.

"Impossible," the owner went on. "My people know they'll be pounding the pavement if they so much as touch these aquariums."

"Your employees haven't done anything, Mr. Price. This fish is probably suffering from sodium cyanide poisoning. Some of the other stock may be affected, as well."

"How could sodium cyanide get into the tank?"

"It didn't," Maggie said, shaking her head. "The local supplier who provided your fish—if he didn't catch them himself—probably bought them in the Philippines." She glanced back at the dying harlequin. Not long now. "There's an easy way for a fisherman to catch tropical ornamentals. You squirt sodium cyanide into the reefs where these fellows hide out. The poison stuns them. They usually hang on for a few weeks, then die of kidney failure. Kills the reef, too, but the suppliers don't care because it means big bucks for them."

"Why would you buy fish from people like that?" Price asked.

"I don't normally. We've been using a new supplier. I won't be using them again, and since this is illegal, I'll also be reporting them to the Fish and Wildlife Service."

Price's jaw had gone rock-solid. "I'm not paying for dead fish."

"Of course not," Maggie reassured him. She had a horrible headache this morning from spending a sleepless night thinking about Amy and Will and any future she might have with them. But she had to concentrate on the problem at hand, a problem that could have serious ramifications for her business. She gave Price her most apologetic, sincere look. "The company will replace any stock that doesn't make it. In the meantime, I'll adjust the chem numbers to give the rest of them the best chance for survival. I'm so sorry, but I want to assure you, we'll correct this, and there will be no further expense to you."

That promise seemed to lessen some of Hank Price's displeasure. Maggie stayed long enough to increase the oxygen content in the tanks, then dealt with the dead tuskfish, depositing the poor thing into a plastic bag in case the authorities needed proof. In the car, she went through her briefcase until she found what she was looking for, the address for Tropic Beauties, the company they'd recently contracted with.

Then she called Zack, who was already hard at work at the LaCrosse project. She explained the situation at the Blue Reef.

Her partner responded as she had, with frustration and concern. "Damn it! That makes three dead."

"I know. We made a mistake, Zack."

As a favor to Harry, one of their regular crew members, they had been willing to give a new supplier—his cousin—a chance to furnish stock.

"I knew in my gut that Harry was pitching us a load of bull about his cousin," Zack said. "I'm sorry, Mags. I know I talked you into it."

"What's done is done. I could have vetoed the idea, but I didn't. The prices were just too good to pass up."

"What do you want to do now?"

"Get in touch with Summerfield," she told him, referring to their usual supplier. "Let him know we may need a complete Level Two package in case we have to restock the Blue Reef from the ground up. In addition, tell him I want a couple of showy ornamentals to add to the tank—clowns, butterflies—whatever he has on hand."

Freebie fish, particularly the more flamboyant tropicals, might go a long way toward assuaging Hank Price's feeling that he'd been ripped off. Zack sighed heavily, stating the obvious. "This could end up being expensive."

"We don't really have a choice. I don't want a customer with a sour taste in his mouth. Damage control, Zack."

"I know, I know. Are you heading back?"

"Not for a while. I want to pay a visit to Tropic Beauties and talk to Ken Branigan. See what he has to say for himself."

"What!" Zack's voice boomed through the cell phone. "No. Don't go anywhere near him. Come back here."

"Why? The company's only a few miles away in Pompano Beach."

"I don't care if they're on the next corner. Stay away from Branigan. If he deals in illegals, you don't want to mess with him."

"I'll be fine," Maggie said quickly. She squinted through the windshield at black clouds darkening the horizon. Bad weather up north, right where she was headed. "Do me a favor, will you? Get Fish and Wildlife on the phone. Find out what we have to do to report this guy or start an investigation. I'm not taking this sitting down, Zack. If he's using cyanide instead of nets, someone needs to put him on notice."

Zack was practically yelling at her now. "It doesn't have to be you. Mags, don't go. Don't do this."

"Too late. I'm already on the interstate."

"Then get off."

"I'll let you know what I find out."

"Mags—"

Closing the phone on his objection, Maggie moved into traffic. What Tropic Beauties had done was inexcusable, cruel and harmful to the reef environment, and could have devastating consequences to Sapphire Seas' business. Trust was everything in this industry, and she couldn't afford to lose even one customer because of an unscrupulous supplier.

She felt compelled to check out Tropic Beauties, see for herself if they were as corrupt as she suspected. Truthfully, she was almost looking forward to paying them a visit. The last couple of days, fretting over her possible relationship to Amy, trying hard not to let herself sink any deeper in lust with Will, those things had conspired to leave her restless, longing for action.

If nothing else, with all she had bottled up inside

her these days, Maggie knew she was ready to give someone one heck of a tongue-lashing.

TEN MINUTES LATER, she pulled into the dirt parking lot of Tropic Beauties just as the long, low bank of dark clouds over the Atlantic began to pelt the ground with fat, cold raindrops.

Thunder rumbled as she sprinted toward the office, a one-story Florida bungalow with an attached warehouse, surrounded by other small businesses and fast-food restaurants. She entered the building quickly, shaking rain off her hair as the door banged behind her. The reception area was a tiny, utilitarian space with yellowing tiles and threadbare furniture. The room was empty.

Determined not to be deterred, Maggie went through a swinging door she hoped would lead to the owner. She came into the warehouse area and saw right away that it held numerous waist-high tanks with open tops—temporary holding tanks for fish.

The place was dimly lit. At the moment, the only light came from the open roll-top door at one end where a truck could be parked for loading stock.

She saw a man hosing down a walkway between the tanks. A guy with a greasy comb-over who was built like a linebacker. He looked up when he realized he had company. Probably Branigan.

All Maggie's dealings with Tropic Beauties had been handled over the phone and through e-mails. That had been a mistake. In an effort to trim costs, she and Zack had relied too heavily on their employee's recommendation of his cousin. They hadn't taken the time to fully check out the supplier, and she blamed herself for that.

"Are you Ken Branigan?" Maggie asked.

The man nodded. "You're not supposed to be back here."

It went downhill from there.

Maggie spent the next ten minutes explaining who she was, why she'd come and the suspicions she had about his stock. Branigan listened, grim and silently hostile in the way he stood—arms crossed over his broad chest, a frown carved between his bushy brows. He offered no excuses, no explanations. And no apologies.

"For the last time," he said, coiling the hose in his beefy hands. "I did not sell you sick fish."

"I know what I saw. I've been in this business a long time."

Annoyance streaked across Branigan's features as he threw down the hose. "Then you ought to know what a chance you take importing any kind of live cargo. Fish get stressed out. They're left out on tarmacs in below-freezing temperatures or boiled in their crates from the hot sun. Customers mess with them even when you tell them not to, then lie about it." He shrugged. "So you got a few dead ones. Crap like that happens. Get over it."

"That isn't the case here. I witnessed the last one die. Typical sodium cyanide poisoning."

"My fish are clean. They cleared Customs. I get them from honest, hardworking fishermen in the Philippines who net in spite of the fact that they could make a lot more money just squirting that shit into the reefs."

Irritation spiked through Maggie. She was getting nowhere with this guy. "Maybe they're honest," she said in low anger. "But you're not."

Branigan took a step in her direction. "Listen, honey…"

The rain was coming down harder. The thunder had gone from occasional rumbling to something with a real kick to it, causing the aluminum sides of the warehouse to shake ominously. Because of all the noise, Maggie didn't notice that it was no longer just the two of them in the building until Branigan turned his head toward the front office.

"Now who the hell are you?" he demanded, and Maggie swung around to find Will coming toward them.

Surprise left her momentarily speechless. He was the last person she expected to see here. Dressed in a gray suit spotted with raindrops, he looked completely out of place in the warehouse. As he approached, his gaze swept over them as he quickly assessed the situation. His eyes were flinty, his lips nothing more than a tight line of displeasure. He might be here, but Maggie knew instinctively that he sure didn't want to be.

He gave Branigan the barest nod of acknowledgment. Maggie, determined not to be sidetracked, turned back to the fish supplier.

"Do you think I can't recognize the signs?" she told the man. She pointed at his wrist, where the flesh was red and ugly-looking. "You ought to get that checked by a doctor."

"What are you talking about?"

"That rash is from handling sodium cyanide. Dangerous stuff if you don't know what you're doing."

"Maggie..." she heard Will say in a low, hard tone.

She ignored whatever warning he intended. "As far as I'm concerned, our contract is null and void. I won't be giving you any more of our business."

Branigan looked as if he were holding on to the thinnest filament of control. "You can't do that."

"I can. I'm not stocking my tanks with your fish."

"You have no proof. You cancel and I'll sue you."

"Fine," Maggie snapped. "You'll be suing me from behind bars. I'll get proof. What you're doing is inhumane and illegal, and I intend to make sure you pay for it."

Color flew in Branigan's face like a flag. "Listen, you little bitch—"

He took another step toward her, but Will was suddenly between them. He lifted a hand to stop the man in his tracks. "Hold on, hold on," he said reasonably. "There's no need for this to get out of hand."

Branigan wasn't the only one who was angry. Maggie's own blood had heated up to a dangerous level, and she didn't feel the need for Will's interference. "Stay out of this," she told him. "It isn't your concern."

His eyes caught hers, full of dark alarm. "I'm making it my concern."

Branigan snorted. "You need to keep your girlfriend here in line, buddy. She has a mean mouth on her."

"Yeah, I know. But she has other gifts that work in her favor."

"I can see that."

After that remark, all Maggie saw was red. She took a step forward, too, but immediately felt Will grab her upper arm. His hold was light, but there was steel in it. "Come on, Maggie," he said. "Let's go back to the office and talk this out."

"I don't—"

He turned toward Branigan. "We'll be in touch."

She didn't like Will's attitude, the way he'd just commandeered the situation. It brought her mind to a furious boil, and she tried to pull away as he swept her hurriedly out of the warehouse. "You can't—"

He pulled her closer to his side so he could bring his mouth against her ear. "If you don't keep walking, I'm going to go all caveman on you and take you out of here over my shoulder. Don't think I won't do it."

Infuriated, Maggie hardly had time to react before Will had pushed her out the front door. The rain hit her, cold enough to elicit a gasp, but when she moved in the direction of her convertible, Will tugged her toward his car.

"Get in," he yelled over the storm. "I'm taking you home."

Dripping water, she fell into the front seat, breathing as hard as if she'd run a marathon. Will joined her a moment later on a gust of chilly wind that made her shiver. He started the car without a word and swung out of the potholed parking lot so quickly that Maggie was practically thrown from her seat.

"Stop," she said before they'd even reached the corner. "Take me back to my car."

"No. You think I'm going to let you drive that piece of junk in weather like this?"

"There's nothing wrong with my car."

"All right. The car's fine. You're not. In this frame of mind, you'll end up wiping out on the freeway. I'm not having that on my conscience."

Maggie's gaze jerked to him, furious. "I don't care about your conscience. Who wants you to take any responsibility? I don't. Nobody asked you to come up here and rescue me."

"Actually, Zack did," he said in a tight voice. "He was worried about you. With good reason, it seems. Why in hell would you go toe-to-toe with that guy?"

"I had it under control."

Lightning needled the sky, strobing the interior of the car with an eerie, pale glow. The rain ran down the windshield in solid sheets, and though it was swept away instantly by the wipers, visibility was so poor that Maggie was amazed Will could see to drive.

Suddenly, muttering a curse, he pulled off the road.

The windows had steamed up. Maggie couldn't make out where they were, but from the lush greenery and a glimpse of the churning Atlantic beyond the dunes, she thought it must be a seaside park.

Shutting down the engine, Will turned in his seat to look at her. He was still breathing hard, and she could feel the weight of his anger. "No, you *didn't* have it under control," he told her. "All you had was a full head of steam about to explode all over that Neanderthal. What did you think would happen then? Tears and a full confession? Then what?"

"I don't know. I didn't have the chance to find out because you decided to march me out of there like a whipped puppy."

With a heavy sigh, Will brought his hands to his head to scrape water out of his hair. His eyes closed for a moment, as though he could will away her existence. "Lord," he muttered. "If this woman ever gets the common sense to go with the *cojones,* there'll be no stopping her." He shook his head. "Just tell me one thing. Are you ever going to think before you act?"

That did it. Over the rush of blood in her ears, Maggie launched out of her inertia and reached for the door handle. "Go to hell. I'm walking back to my car."

"No, you're not."

She pulled several times, but the door refused to open. Will, damn him, must have set the child-protection locks. Maggie swung back to face him, now even more furious. "Let me out this instant."

"No."

"Now who's the Neanderthal?"

"Maggie, for all I know, you'll go back in for round two with that guy."

Feeling cornered, Maggie glared at him. Outside, the weather enclosed the car in a heavy, gray cloak, but inside, the electric antagonism between them felt like a living thing. "If I did, it would be none of your business," she said over the pounding agony of her headache. "Don't you get it? I don't need your help. I don't *want* your help. In fact, when it comes right down to it, I think I hate you."

"No, you don't. I don't know what your feelings for me are exactly, but it's not hate."

"Don't flatter yourself."

Will chuffed out a weary sigh. "It's a damn shame we can't get past wanting each other. My life would be so much simpler if I could just get over the constant desire to kiss you."

"Kiss me! If you did that right now, I'd—"

Unexpectedly, Will covered the distance between them. He kissed her, so hard that Maggie was pinned against the passenger-side window. His mouth was hungry, violent on hers, and left her feeling as though a piece had been stripped from her soul.

"You'd what?" he whispered when they surfaced at last. "You'd want more?"

"No," she said, but without a lot of steam behind

it. She couldn't seem to move, as though she might shatter something important.

"You're such a liar." He touched his mouth against hers again briefly, a smile making the corners tilt. "I've always loved the look in your eyes when you're angry. As though gunpowder has been tossed into them and ignited."

Like a massive wave, instinct broke over her. She felt inside something as unavoidable as destiny. She grabbed his tie, pulling him against her. "Oh, shut up," she breathed. "Just kiss me."

Because of the rain and the gloom of the storm, they were webbed in shadows, but as Will's eyes met hers, Maggie knew his feelings. No chance for either of them now. They were unwound, unsettled, and no scrap of logic, no common sense would allow them to stop.

Whatever walls had been between them, they must have been embarrassingly transparent and flimsy. Whatever moment of sanity told her that they mustn't do this—not here, not now—her brain refused to get the memo. How long had she been waiting for him? There was no way she could turn away and refuse to savor this sinful fantasy.

Her arms tightened around him, clutched at his shirt. When she brought her lips against the pulse pounding at Will's throat, he made a rough, growling sound, then burned a hot, damp trail of kisses along her collarbone. He dug both hands into her loose curls, bringing her head back so he had complete access.

In no time his mouth seemed *everywhere,* making

her yelp in startled delight, making her gasp in pure pleasure, making her nearly jump out of her skin.

Her fingers tangled in his thick, wet hair, but in another moment she was pulling apart his buttons, tugging, desperate to feel the warmth of his bare flesh against hers. The sound of his voice encouraged, all low and sexy and silky, making her heart flutter like a tangled bird's. Her body was all one ache now, almost beyond bearing.

Dimly she heard the fumbling rasp of a zipper. She fought to get her own jeans down. Having sex in a car—no matter how luxurious—wasn't easy, but she had to smile at how inventive they both were, how quickly they dealt with obstructions.

When Will slid inside her, Maggie gave a soft cry of sharp, throbbing pleasure. She lifted her knees as much as she could, encouraging him to reach places that had not been touched in so long, places where only the holes of her life had been. He claimed her, each thrust deep and delicious until she felt her senses dissolving. There was nothing but heat and friction then, and Will's breath coming in tortured gasps close to her ear.

She hauled in a ragged breath herself, feeling the warmth, the spark of pure, undiluted sensation take hold within her. The spasms began to flash through her, one after another after another, sweet and glorious and so strong that Maggie thought she would never surface from them. She shuddered, her body losing itself, losing its identity.

Just when she thought that surely she'd hit bottom soon and stop falling, the shock waves within her settled down. She began edging toward normal, though words were impossible. The only thing that would form in her mouth was a sigh.

Will gave her a gentle kiss, then dragged his mouth and body away from her. They began rearranging their clothes. The quiet interior of the car felt awkward, alien and too warm. Outside, the downpour still pounded the windows, and the sky was so pale that it looked like it had been erased.

After an excruciatingly long time, Will let out a short, dry chuckle. "God. You're the only woman I've ever known who can make me behave like a horny teenager." He lifted one hip, withdrawing his personal organizer. "I think you broke my BlackBerry."

She supposed that, after what had just happened, he meant to keep things light between them, but it didn't work. Maggie felt her eyes cloud with tears. She had spent years missing this man. Wanting him.

The reality of it crouched like a tiger in the corner of her mind. *I'm still in love with him. I've never stopped being in love with him.*

She supposed there were no formulas to account for the idiosyncratic yearnings of the human heart. There it was. Plain as day. Now what was she going to do about it?

The blood rushed through her as though Will's hands had returned to her body. Her gut coiled, even as a warm sense of calm and purpose settled over her.

Whatever hope she might have for the future, none of it would be possible if she and Will weren't honest with one another.

She turned so that she could see him clearly.

He looked over at her. "Hell," he said with a muffled laugh. "I feel so energized right now… Let's go back to your fisherman friend. We'll *both* beat the crap out of him." When she said nothing to that, he asked, "What's wrong?"

"Tell me the truth, Will," she said in a clear, strong tone. She knew she could not afford to let emotion color her words. "Is Amy my daughter?"

# *CHAPTER SIXTEEN*

"YES," HE replied simply.

For one agonizing, improbable moment, Maggie's spirits zoomed. But then, just as quickly, something like gnarled driftwood twisted her insides. She mustn't kid herself. There weren't going to be any easy resolutions here.

Will stared out the windshield. "How long have you known?"

"I realized it the day we went to the aquarium."

She saw him grimace. "I knew that was too much time for the two of you to be together."

His words turned her stomach to ice. As she had feared, he had tried to keep Amy a secret from her. She swallowed a shaky breath. "How did it happen?"

He stiffened. There seemed to be an ocean of space between them suddenly. How could it have been that only moments ago they'd dissolved into one another? "What do you mean, how did it happen?" he asked her. "You gave her up for adoption."

"But how did she end up with you?"

He expelled a huge sigh. Then he nodded, as

though coming to an enormous decision. "After you left, I had a private investigator track you down. I saw you in Key West coming out of the free clinic. You were obviously pregnant, and I felt sure the baby was mine."

The knowledge that Will had followed her brought a little hope, but she knew she couldn't count on that. "Why didn't you ask me?"

"I saw you with Zack. I thought he was the new man in your life. I thought you were trying to move on, and you were going to take my child with you without ever telling me."

"So you went home."

"Yes. Do you remember Ernie Becker?"

"Your father's attorney?"

"Yes, and a good friend to Lisa and me."

"I think I recall him."

"I went to him for help. I was angry with you—enough that I fully intended to fight for custody. But then he found out that you'd made arrangements to give the baby up for adoption. I thought—what the hell—if anyone's going to adopt my kid, why shouldn't it be me? You might not have wanted the baby, but I did."

He stopped then, as though aware that it was a lot for Maggie to absorb. He jerked down one sleeve of his shirt, taking a ridiculous amount of time buttoning the cuff.

Maggie, still trying to find her bearings, shook her head. "It wasn't that way for me. I wanted to keep her. But when I went to stay with Zack, I left everything behind. I had very little money, no job, a beat-up car. I was sleeping on his couch." She tossed a quick glance at Will, wanting desperately for him to understand. "How was I supposed to raise a child on my own? I thought I was doing the best thing for the baby."

"You could have put your pride aside. You could have asked your parents for help."

"Why do you think I left Miami in the first place? My father's idea of a solution was to let my sister raise the baby."

He stopped adjusting his cuff and frowned at her. She could tell that he hadn't been expecting that little tidbit of information. Whatever bulging file folder of her life he might have accumulated, the knowledge of how her parents had tried to push her hadn't been part of it.

She bit her lip, remembering those awful, early days of her pregnancy as though they were yesterday. "Maybe leaving town was a selfish decision, but I knew, no matter what, I couldn't bear pretending that the baby was my niece instead of my daughter. Even after I signed the adoption agreement, I didn't let my parents know where I was. It was a couple of years before we spoke again, and even now, we don't discuss it."

"You should have come to me."

"I didn't think I could. Not after the way we'd left things."

"We'd have worked something out."

"How do you work something out with a guy who's said he never wants to see you again?"

"For the sake of our child, you might have tried."

She flinched slightly from the harshness in his voice. She could have predicted this response. But she wouldn't give up trying to make him see her side of it. She'd empty her heart if it would just make him realize what it had been like for her.

She dragged in a tattered breath. "I'm not saying it wasn't a bad decision. But at the time, adoption seemed like the only sensible option." She brought her fingers to her throat, trying to untie the knot of misery that seemed to be lodged in her windpipe. "There hasn't been a day since the baby was taken out of my arms that I haven't thought about her. Wondered where she was. *Who* she was."

Will made a restless movement. "I'm trying to understand how you could have done such a thing. But when I look at Amy… When I think that my child could have been living with complete strangers all this time. Even good parents—"

"Hindsight is always twenty-twenty, isn't it?" she flashed out. Her flaws belonged to her like wrinkles on her own face, and she'd accept them. But he wasn't entirely guilt-free. "Maybe you never will understand," she said wearily. "Maybe you'll never be able to forgive me for what I did. But at least I was doing what I *thought* was the right thing. I haven't been telling Amy a pack of lies about her mother all these years. I didn't do anything underhanded to get her."

A moment passed during which neither of them spoke. Then he looked at her. His features were hard and cold, and seeing them, the ripples of Maggie's unhappiness widened.

"I did nothing illegal," he said tightly. "I simply stepped in to adopt my own child. It's called exercising a putative father's rights, and it's surprisingly easy. I suppose I could have told you, but since you were willing to give Amy up, I didn't think it would matter to you. I didn't see any need to complicate things."

"Well, they're certainly complicated now. What's Amy supposed to think about her mother? What about your fictitious friend Tina in Paris? Are you going to kill her off one day so you and Amy can properly mourn?"

"I fully intend to tell Amy the truth when she's old enough to handle it."

Will's cell phone rang suddenly, slicing through the stillness and making Maggie jump. He snatched it off the dashboard where he had tossed it earlier, glanced down at the caller ID and frowned.

"I'll call you back," he said into the phone after he punched the Talk button.

Whoever it was, they ignored Will's response. Instantly a man began to talk, loud, excited words that Maggie could clearly make out.

"I've got good news, son," the voice said. "Mama Maggie has no recourse. I spoke to my friend, and he says if she tries to make trouble for you she'll end up wishing she'd never left Key West. Breathe easy, my boy. Amy's yours and always will be."

"I'll have to call you back," Will said again, clicking off.

He tossed the phone back on the dash.

The silence in the car—awkward and difficult before—became deafening now. Maggie sat there, air pushing out from between her lips with slow care as a deep sense of despair washed over her. Amazing how powerful a punch the death of hope could deal.

Finally she turned her head to catch Will's eyes. She could see nothing in them. Nothing. Across the wide gulf between them she said quietly, "I was going to ask you what we could do now to fix things. I was going to ask where we could go from here. But I guess I have my answer, don't I?"

THAT EVENING, after getting off the plane from Hilton Head Island, Alaina headed for Zack's hotel. A front-desk clerk, with her salaried smile, connected her by telephone to Zack's room. There was no answer. Disappointed, she hung up, feeling the slow pulse of her heart in her ears. She had wanted so badly to talk to him.

On the way out, she passed the coffee shop, a bright alcove filled with a few people having an early dinner. A man sitting in a booth closest to the door, alone, caught her attention—Zack. Trembling, Alaina drew herself up in tight control. She knew what she wanted to do. Now she just had to do it.

Sliding into the seat across from Zack, she smiled at him. "Feel like buying a girl a cup of coffee?"

He didn't show even the slightest sign of welcome. "Coffee's bad for you. Ask Maggie."

"Well, maybe I've decided to spend the rest of my life living dangerously."

One brow went up. "What are you doing here, Al?"

"A few days ago, Maggie mentioned you were staying here while you finish that South Beach job. I needed to see you." When he said nothing, she almost lost her nerve. Luckily, the waitress wandered up just then to take her order and keep her from bolting from the room. "Coffee," Alaina said. "Black, please."

Zack already had a plate of bacon and eggs. She remembered that about him, that he loved to eat breakfast for dinner, a habit Alaina had never found appealing and had often teased him about.

When they were alone again, he said quietly, "So you've tracked me down. Any particular reason why?"

"I came to tell you something. Something I should have said a long time ago."

He couldn't possibly know what she was about to say, so it surprised her when he lifted a hand to stop her. "Whoa. If someone's told you about confession being good for the soul, it's not true. It only makes things more complicated."

"That's funny, because right now I'm trying to *un*-complicate my life. And it feels like I have to start with you." She drew a deep breath, determined, even though her stomach felt knotted with fear. "I wanted to tell you that I'm sorry. For what I did to you that summer after high school. I'm not saying 'I'm sorry' the way I did back then, trying to get through it fast and easy and make it as painless as possible for me."

She bit her lip. Her well-rehearsed speech sounded lame, even to her own ears. But she knew she had to go on. "Looking back on it now, I can't believe I was such a bitch, hurting you like that when you'd done nothing but be the kindest—"

"Alaina, stop," Zack ground out harshly. "For God's sake, I don't know what's brought this on, but consider your apology accepted and go home."

In the face of his impatience, she nearly *did* leave. But she wouldn't be that kind of coward. Never again. "I don't have a home," she said softly. "Well, not one I want to go to."

"What the hell are you talking about?"

"I'm leaving Gil."

His gaze was disconcertingly steady for several seconds. She dropped her eyes, watching the long, blunt grace of his fingers as he set down his fork. A working man's hands. Nicked and boney, but somehow beautiful, too. She swallowed, willing her gut to stop quaking. She couldn't quit now. She couldn't allow this chance to fall into the same deep crevasse all the rest of her life had plunged into.

She looked at him. "Turns out Mr. Perfect hasn't been so perfect after all. I just got back from Hilton Head. I walked right into Gil's hotel room and discovered him with not one, but two of the prettiest, youngest, blondest bimbos you could ever imagine." She chewed the inside of her cheek. "You should have seen his face."

The waitress came back with her coffee. She sipped it, burned her tongue and set the cup away from her with a grimace. Without saying a word, Zack used his spoon to fish a couple of ice cubes out of his water glass and dumped them into her cup. He stirred the dark liquid until they dissolved.

"Try it now," he said.

She took another taste, pronouncing it better with a quick smile. Hadn't that always been Zack's way? Looking after her, making things right even before she could voice a complaint? Why would anyone give up a guy like that? Why had *she?*

He wiped his mouth with a napkin, then tossed it on the table, though the meal in front of him had barely been touched. "So you're moving out of the mansion. Giving up the good life?"

"Hopefully for a better one. The house is big enough for the four of us, I guess, but even a coward like me can't pretend that a home shared with your husband and his two lovers is normal. So the three of them can have it. I've always hated that monstrosity anyway."

"Where will you go?"

"I'm not sure yet. Mom and Dad's for the short term, I guess. Or maybe a hotel. Are you surprised?"

A beat or two passed, and then he said, "I stopped being surprised by anything a long time ago." She watched his jaw harden, his mouth thin. "So what exactly do you want from me, Al? You want me to applaud the fact that you've left your husband? I do. I get all my information from Maggie secondhand, but from what I hear, he's a bastard who's never appreciated what he had in you. But more than that…"

He frowned, as though he'd grown tired of the conversation and wished it would end.

"Mostly I just wanted to say I'm sorry. And I guess I'd like to know that it's not too late."

"Too late for what?"

She leaned forward, as far as the edge of the table would let her. "Too late to start fresh. I've been such an idiot all these years, trying to breath life into a marriage that was DOA almost before it began. It was stupid of me to throw away what we had for something so completely foolish."

She sensed him stiffening. "So you took a long walk and reached the wrong destination. You want me to step in and take Gil's place now?"

She shook her head. Her heart felt as though it was punishing her ribs, but hope continued to whimper inside her. "No, nothing like that. I couldn't ask such a thing. And truthfully, I think I need some time by myself to try and sort things out. I've made such a mess, but I'd like to believe it can be fixed."

"Then what do you want from me?"

"I guess I just want to know that if I really do set the wheels in motion to change my life…I guess I'd like to hope that you might…"

She had to stop and regroup a moment. After so many years of avoiding the difficult things in life, after running away from any unpleasantness, this was so tough. In spite of the restaurant's too-cool air-conditioning, a trickle of perspiration was actually making a run for it down the middle of her back. She shook her head again, trying to jar loose the mild, buzzing sensation in her ears.

She locked gazes with Zack. "I know I can either stay in my safe, empty excuse for a life. Or I can have a real one. I feel ready to take that plunge. But it would be so much less frightening if I thought you were there, willing to help me find my way."

Silence hummed between them for several seconds. Finally, Zack leaned back in his seat and said with lethal softness, "No."

Alaina blinked. She didn't know what to say. She stared down at the cup of coffee in front of her, wondering how she would ever be able to speak with tears clogging her throat and a heart that had cracked in two.

"Al, look at me," Zack said.

She did. And when he placed his hand on top of hers, she tried to act as if everything was just fine, when all she really felt was drained, drained of energy and courage.

"Al..." His fingers traced the veins along the back of her hand. "I want you to be happy. I will always want what's best for you. But I'm not a trained circus poodle. I can't be in the wings waiting for you to want me. Ready to fix things just because you've decided it's time. That was who I was in high school. But it's not who I am now. I'm not going back to being that kid who couldn't get through a single day without a look or a smile or a word from the popular, beautiful Alaina Tillman. I'm still a fool about you in a lot of ways, but that big a fool I'm not."

"I'm not asking you—"

Zack released her and slid out of the booth. The waitress had left his check on the table and he tossed a twenty-dollar bill down on top of it. "I'm sorry, Al. I hope everything works out for you. Get healed. Get the new life you crave. I want that for you. But I can't be the one to help you get it."

AFTER ZACK LEFT, Alaina sat a long time in the diner's booth. Long enough that the smell of the cold eggs began to turn her stomach and she had to ask the waitress to take the plate away. She felt numb, uncertain what to do now, but there was no strength left in her legs, no thought of where she should go from here. So she merely continued to sit.

After about thirty minutes, Alaina blinked up in surprise to see her sister settling into the seat Zack had vacated.

"Maggie… What are you doing here?"

Maggie reached across the table, grasping Alaina's fingers in hers. "Zack called me and asked if I'd check on you. See if you were all right."

Even in her current mood, Alaina couldn't help a small smile. He might have felt compelled to keep her at arm's length, but Zack was still Zack, and obviously he couldn't bear to think of her alone and miserable. "Did he tell you why I came to see him?"

"Most of it. I take it things didn't go well in Hilton Head?"

"You could say that."

She told Maggie what she'd walked into up there, how surprisingly civil it had all been. Neither she nor Gil had raised their voice. No heated words at all. Just the understanding that their mirage of a marriage was over, that radical change could come in a heartbeat.

When she'd finished explaining to Maggie about the two lovers in the bed, Maggie sat back in her seat. "Wow," she said quietly. "I wasn't expecting something that…"

"Sleazy? Me, neither. But I suppose it could have been worse."

"I wish the son of a bitch was sitting here right now. I'd love to take out some frustrations by rearranging that snotty, uppercrust nose of his."

"He'd just buy a new one. A better one, even."

They both laughed then. They ordered drinks from a passing waitress, then a second one. Funny how you could still function even when you felt like you were swimming in tar.

At last Maggie set down her empty margarita glass. "So what can I do to help?"

"I'm not sure."

"Well, what do you want to do?"

"Divorce Gil, I suppose. Find a place to live. Get a job. Get my damned life back."

"That's a pretty tall order. Especially that last part. Getting a life back can be really tough."

Something in her sister's voice made Alaina look up sharply. For the first time since Maggie had joined her, she noticed dark circles under Maggie's eyes, as though she hadn't been sleeping well, and there was a sadness in her features Alaina had never seen before.

"Is everything all right with you?"

Maggie shrugged. "The project is going well. We should be finished ahead of schedule."

"What's wrong? Zack came to see me recently. Something about your baby's adoption, but he wouldn't elaborate."

"It's nothing you need worry about," Maggie said. "Let's see what we can do to fix *your* problems."

"I'm tired of talking about me. I want to help *you.*" She leaned across the table. "I know I let you down, telling Dad your business. But I'll never do such a thing again without your permission. You look miserable. Please trust me."

Her sister hesitated for a long moment. Alaina squeezed her hand, encouraging. To her complete surprise, she saw tears fill Maggie's eyes, and soon, the whole story spilled out.

"It's unbelievable," Alaina said when Maggie finally sat back in the booth, seemingly spent. "Amy is your daughter, and she's been right here all this time."

"The question is, what can I do about it now? Will may fight me tooth and nail to keep me out of Amy's life."

"Surely he wouldn't be that cruel."

"I don't know *what* he'll be." Maggie shook her head, offering Alaina a small smile. "Oh, sis, we do make one heck of a pair, don't we? We have really messed up."

Alaina nodded. "Yes, but it's nothing we can't sort out. Starting right this minute, we can do better."

"We can?"

"I'm going to stop being afraid to disappoint, stop being afraid to make waves," Alaina said, straightening. "I'm going to get my act together, and not be terrified if I make a few mistakes along the way and don't live up to everyone's expectations. What I want is the only thing that matters."

Maggie laughed a little. "Poor Gil had better watch out."

"As for you," Alaina continued, "you have to stop letting pigheadedness get in your way. You've always acted like you don't need anyone else's help. Like you have to do everything on your own. That's part of why you left town years ago. But this is different. You need to include the family in this, Maggie. Dad still has connections. Let him put them to good use if it becomes necessary."

"He'll try to take over."

"He might. But if Will really does fight you on this, isn't Amy worth using every weapon at your disposal? Don't let pride keep you from asking for help from anyone. Including Dad."

BRIGHT AND EARLY the next morning, Maggie went to see her parents. She found them together in the open garage, struggling to clear a space for something.

She heard them bickering even as she walked up the driveway.

"I don't understand how you can need to build a workshop in here when all your tools look brand-new," Maggie's mother complained. "You haven't even taken the skill saw out of the box it came in, and I gave that to you two Christmases ago."

Her father wiped sweat from his brow. Even on a spring morning, the Florida sun could be brutal. "That's because I don't have a proper workshop to use it in," he told his wife.

Maggie knocked on the side of the garage door. "Hey, you two," she said in her most pleasant voice. "Feel like taking a break?"

"Did you come here to help out?" James Tillman asked.

"I will. But first I'd like a chat."

They adjourned to the kitchen. Her father plopped into a kitchen chair. Her mother, evidently sensing something serious, started to pull breakfast stuff out of the refrigerator. She had always believed that anything could be resolved over a good meal.

Maggie returned the carton of eggs to the fridge, then laid a hand on her mother's shoulder. "Mom, please. Just sit down so we can talk."

Connie Tillman took a seat next to her husband. Maggie sat down across from them. She sighed heavily, not knowing precisely where to start. She'd been nursing a headache for days now, and the confrontation with Will in his car, finding out just how nasty things between them might get when it came to their daughter, hadn't helped to lessen it any.

"Honey," her mother said. "What is it?"

She looked up to see two sets of concerned eyes staring at her.

*Get it out, Maggie. Just start at the beginning.*

So she did. They already knew she'd put her baby up for adoption, but they'd never really discussed such a sore topic. She told them everything she'd originally refused to divulge—the hows and whys of her decision, the emotional toll it had taken on her over the years, the hope that one day God would forgive her for something she'd never been able to forgive herself.

They listened silently, carefully. And when she could not talk about it anymore, her father surprised her by reaching across the table to place his hand over hers. "Maggie," he said softly. "We've never spoken about this before. But your mother and I—we should never have done what we did. We drove you away…"

"Why did you think Alaina should raise my baby?" Maggie couldn't keep herself from asking. "Did you really have such little faith in me?"

"It wasn't that," her father replied. "It's what I thought was best. Your sister was married, settled. She was ready for children. You…you were just finding your way, a world of opportunity just within your grasp. I wanted you to have every chance. Children are wonderful little creatures, but for a young woman, still struggling to make a start—well, I saw the baby as a burden holding you back. I know that was wrong, but there it is."

Regret tightened within her. Yes, her parents had come up with a solution to her pregnancy that she couldn't accept. But she'd insisted on doing everything on her own terms, just as Alaina had said. She'd resented their interference and acted without thinking. She'd run away, when she should have stayed and battled it out.

She shook her head. "I made the mistake, Dad. I shouldn't have run away to Key West. I should have…"

Her father squeezed her hand, then sat back. "I suppose there is only one truth in this, Maggie. We all come to crossroads in our lives, and half of us are destined to take a wrong turn. We can't erase the fact, or wish it away. We just have to live with it the best we can."

She thought suddenly of the story her mother had told her about her father, that he had always blamed himself for his little sister's death. She could see how that could be, because it was the same for her. You could make a decision—a poor one—and it could change your entire universe.

Her father stared at her. "There's something else I want to tell you. When you first told us you were pregnant, my first thought wasn't concern for you. It was for me. I've operated by a very upright, strict code of conduct all my life. I couldn't bear the thought of having an unwed mother in the family, and I was desperate to think of a way around it." He shook his head. "I know that's ridiculous in this day. Old-fashioned. Considering the way things have turned out—

the knowledge that my chance to have a beautiful granddaughter in my life is gone—I should never have given it a moment's thought."

"The whole situation may not be as irreparable as you fear. As least, I hope not."

Her parents exchanged a curious glance. Then her father said, "What do you mean?"

She told them about her discovery that Will had adopted their daughter. The fact that she was still in love with him in spite of everything. Finally, she explained that there could be horrible days ahead if what she feared turned out to be true—that Will might refuse to allow her any access to Amy.

When she finished, Maggie steeled herself for their reaction. They were two people who were used to getting their way, used to taking charge, but perhaps they weren't *impossible* to deal with. You just had to know how. The problem was, Maggie wasn't sure she'd ever sat in on that particular lesson.

Her father crossed his arms over his chest. She winced inside. He was the one who worried her the most, and nothing in his face boosted her confidence.

"It may come down to a custody battle in court," she said cautiously. "I dread the thought of it, but now that I know where Amy is, I can't go back to the way it was. I can't simply forget. I need to be part of her life."

"What do you need us to do, Maggie?" her father asked. "Just tell us."

She had never heard him speak this way before.

It gave her hope. However difficult the future might be, maybe, just maybe, she wouldn't have to go through it alone.

"No matter what, she's our granddaughter," her mother added. "I thought we'd lost her, but if there's a chance we could have her in our lives, too, both your father and I will do whatever it takes to support you."

Maggie smiled a little. "I know I've done nothing but push the two of you away all my life. I know that we've hurt each other in so many ways, but it can't continue. It's time I stopped blaming you for everything that goes wrong. Whatever Will decides to do…" Her courage started to unravel. She had to swallow hard to reel it back in. "If…if there's a fight ahead, I'll deal with it. But I don't think I can do it alone. This isn't the time for me to be too proud to ask… I need you both—to give me hope and advice. I need your help."

She watched her father's eyes. He smiled, just slightly. "Maggie, Maggie. No matter what happens, you will always be our daughter. And we will always be there to help you in any way we can."

He held out his hand. She took it, and in the joining of their fingers Maggie felt the love that had always been there but which she had spent so many years denying.

# CHAPTER SEVENTEEN

IT TOOK WILL an hour longer than it should have to modify some of the computer schematics he'd worked up for Hallandale's new city hall. Instead of coming home, he would have been better off staying at the office a little longer.

Where there was peace and quiet.

Lisa was in her bedroom, picking out love songs on her guitar, presumably to enchant her boyfriend, Charlie. From the sound of it, she needed a lot more practice.

He cut a glance away from the computer monitor toward his daughter. Amy sat cross-legged in front of the coffee table, noisily engrossed in some fantasy play with her Princess Valentina doll. Her voice, excited and filled with drama, was gaining altitude. Evidently, the princess was in one heck of a battle with some wicked magician.

"Amy," Will said to grab his daughter's attention. "Keep it down, will you?"

"Okay, Daddy."

The battle of good and evil subsided a little as Amy whispered commands to her doll, marching the princess over the table's surface.

Will pushed out a sigh and turned back to his laptop. His concentration was shot. He couldn't seem to dig in tonight, couldn't seem to focus. He knew that wasn't anyone's fault but his own. From the moment he'd left Maggie yesterday, he hadn't been able to get anything to make sense.

Sure, he supposed he could get past the idea that live-by-the-rules, play-it-safe Will Stewart had actually had sex in his car. In broad daylight. With a woman he lusted after, but supposedly couldn't wait to see the back of.

He could even accept that the truth about Amy's adoption was now out in the open. That there might be tough days ahead when he'd have to come to some kind of arrangement with Maggie over their daughter's future. But they'd work something out. Ernie's telephone call probably hadn't helped much, but he could explain. To tell the truth, he was sort of relieved that she finally knew. He felt ten years younger, as if the weight of secrecy that had been crushing the life out of him had finally been removed.

What he *couldn't* seem to figure out was what to do about Maggie. Was there any hope for the two of them? Did he *want* there to be any?

He'd spent the night tossing and turning, just trying to come up with answers. But orchids would grow in Antarctica before he understood how he could still want a woman who had done something as unforgivable as putting their daughter up for adoption. No matter how valid she thought her reasons had been, how was *he* supposed to ever be all right with that?

He had to stop having all these wayward, albeit intriguing, thoughts about her. It had just been sex, for God's sake. *Great* sex. But that's all.

Annoyed that he was unable to stuff images of Maggie into some dank, dark corner of his brain, Will clicked out of the software program he was in and pulled a blank page up on his screen. He was a man whose mind, with pleasure and from long habit, made thoughtful decisions. To add up pros and cons, to devise a plan and then follow it. It was natural to him. Maybe what he needed to do was list all the ways—both good and bad—that Maggie affected his life.

He began typing, quickly, determined not to overthink it. Then, almost immediately he deleted what he'd written. What the hell was wrong with him? Matters of the heart shouldn't be sorted through this way. Surely he must *know* in his gut whether he wanted Maggie in his life or not. Why was everything he did so planned and precise?

Disgusted, he shut down the computer. Damn, he was tired.

Amy's voice, going into a spiral again, knifed into his head. It was already past her bedtime, and he hoped there wasn't going to be a fuss tonight. He listened to her chattering nonsense to her doll, then frowned when he realized that it had something to do with Princess Valentina trying to save Antarctic penguins.

He definitely didn't want to listen to *that.*

"Amy," he said sharply. "Get ready for bed."

"But, Daddy—"

"*Now.* Don't give me an argument."

The moment the words were out, he knew he'd been too harsh, that he shouldn't have taken his frustrations out on Amy. For the briefest of moments, she looked stunned. Then her eyes lost their liveliness as they filled with tears. She jumped up, tearing off for her bedroom.

Will swore under his breath. He seemed destined tonight to say, do and think all the wrong things.

Hearing the water running in the bathroom—Amy brushing her teeth—he got up and went into the kitchen to fix a cup of coffee. He'd apologize, of course, but he didn't want to do it in the heat of the moment, when Amy might still be too furious to even speak to him.

When he was fairly certain that she'd hopped into bed, he went down the hall and into her room. The lights were on. As usual, she lay under the covers, waiting for a good-night kiss.

He sat on the edge of the mattress. "All set?"

She nodded.

"Let me see."

She showed him her teeth, a gap-toothed, minty smile destined for braces one day. Nothing in her features suggested anger, though she did give him a long, speculative appraisal through her dark lashes.

Will pushed her bangs away from her forehead, then planted a kiss on her brow. "I'm sorry I yelled at you."

He looked down into her sweet, trusting face. His daughter, this beautiful, breathless miracle who was all warm sunshine and bursts of laughter and careless grace, who even during her worst tantrums had a melting effect on his insides. No matter what the future held, he would never regret that he and Maggie had created this child.

Amy lifted up on one elbow. “It’s okay, Daddy. I forgive you ’cause you worked really hard today. I wish I could make it all better, but I don’t know how. So I’ll just be good and go right to sleep, and then tomorrow it will be all new.”

She dove forward into his arms, burying her face into his chest like a kitten making itself comfortable. Will’s heart swelled. He was lucky. So lucky. How stale his world would be without Amy to teach him where the flavors lay.

“I love you,” he whispered, though he could hardly speak. He gave her another kiss, tucked the blanket close, then turned out the bedside lamp.

Lisa lounged at the bedroom door, her guitar clutched in one hand. She’d evidently heard the commotion and had come to investigate. His sister had poetry in her soul and a kind heart, but as Will closed his daughter’s bedroom door, Lisa’s lips were pursed in sour disapproval.

“Are you still trying to figure out how to be a good father?” she asked softly, shaking her head at him.

“It looks that way. Fortunately, Amy doesn’t hold a grudge and is willing to work with me.”

“Good thing she has such a forgiving nature.” Lisa gave him a curious look. “Wonder where she gets that from.”

THE NEXT DAY, Maggie ran the last panel of chem numbers that would balance the tanks for the South Beach project. She'd been at the construction site until long after midnight last night and had come back first thing this morning to put the finishing touches on the living reefs she'd designed and to transfer the fish to their new home.

She loved this part of the job. All the inhabitants were in now. The brilliant hues of exotic tropicals glided in elegant tranquility behind the lobby's viewing panels.

Teddy had left the choice to her, and Maggie knew she'd outdone herself. Intensely colored yellow-tailed damsels, neon Fiji blue devils, vibrant flame hawkfish, the shimmering silver bodies of hi-hats. So many different species of saltwater ornamentals—and all of them needing her right now.

In a few days they would acclimate, but until then she would have to create nooks where they could hide, visual barriers of live rock they'd feel safe in, temporary aquascapes to colonize and make their own.

She pressed a finger against the glass, then smiled as an inquisitive trio of little candy basslets, with their striking orange and purple stripes, came to investigate. Basslets were timid, but very quick, and watching them school was fascinating and fun. The kids who came to stay here with their parents would be enthralled.

Thinking of the future, Maggie couldn't help wondering if one day she'd bring her daughter here. Would she ever share with Amy the love she found in this work, the pride and delight she took in creating these living pieces of art? In spite of all the wrong turns she'd made, there had to be *some* compromise she and Will could reach.

She wanted to believe it was possible, but there was no sure way of knowing what would happen if she tried to push him. Overhearing Ernie Becker's voice on Will's cell phone, she'd been deeply shocked to discover the steps he'd taken to prevent her from being part of Amy's life.

Shocked, but oddly enough, not angry. He'd only been trying to protect Amy. And no matter what, he had done the right thing by their daughter—adopting her when Maggie had lacked the courage to raise her child as a single parent.

No, she didn't want to hurt him. To tell the truth, she was in love with him. It was that simple. And that hopeless.

But as she had told her parents, now that she knew the truth, there was no going back to the way things were.

Being within Amy's orbit put her in a world of pure feeling, unlike any she had ever known. Just thinking of spending more time with her made Maggie feel like a convalescent leaving some terrible sickness behind. All those long, lonely years, gone forever in the blink of an eye.

If Will was willing.

Her stomach clutched. How would she endure it if he was not?

But she wouldn't think about that right now. She would concentrate on finishing this job for Teddy, a project that might result in more changes in her life. All of them good. Sapphire Seas would finally gain the place it deserved in the industry.

The small school of basslets darted in a tight circle toward the bottom of the tank. As Maggie ran her finger along the glass, they followed it. They were hungry.

"Hang in there, little gluttons," she told them. "Any minute now Zack should be here with feeder shrimp. How do you like your new home?"

"They ought to love it," a male voice said behind her. "It's spectacular."

She turned to find that Will had entered the lobby. She put a hand against the aquarium, just to be certain that she'd keep her balance. Dressed in jeans and a shirt in a blue the shade of heaven, he looked so handsome as he came toward her. No matter what, just the sight of him could still make her throat go dry.

Trying for nonchalance, Maggie swung a glance back to the viewing panel behind her. "It isn't quite finished," she said, hoping she didn't sound as nervous as she felt. "It will take about another week for everything to settle and for us to make any minor adjustments. Then we'll be ready to turn it over to whoever Teddy's chosen to do regular maintenance."

"I'm sure he'll want your advice on that." He tilted a smile her way. "You can keep him from dealing with someone like your friend from the other day. Incidentally, what's going to happen to him, by the way?"

"Fish and Wildlife say they'll start an investigation."

"Good. Good." He seemed suddenly interested in the tank's inhabitants, following the flitting progress of a couple of black and white clown fish. A bright blue, orange and yellow fish swam up close to the glass, catching his attention. "He's a pretty little guy."

*"Pseudochromis aldabraensis,"* Maggie explained, and, seeing his raised brow, she added, "Neon dottyback. They're very curious. If you were to put your hand in there, he'd investigate it."

He shook his head ruefully. "I'd never take a chance and do that."

"Why not?"

"After the way we left things between us? I'm not sure you wouldn't have me shake hands with a piranha."

They were both silent a good, long, terrible minute. At last, Maggie said softly, "I suppose we ought to talk about it."

"Yes. I know you must be upset."

"I am," she agreed, but managed to give Will a look of quiet understanding. "But not for the reason you imagine. I'm not angry with you for adopting Amy. If anything, I'm glad. You did something I couldn't find the strength to do. You kept our daughter from disappearing out into the world. You kept her in your life. You gave her a home."

"She needs more than a home, Maggie."

"I know. And as much as I don't want to hurt either of you, I can't just go back to Key West and forget about her. I made a huge mistake. I turned my back on her once, but I can't do it again. I just can't."

"Is that what you think I'm asking you to do?"

"But your phone call the other day? That was about keeping me away from Amy."

"Yes. I'll admit it. When you first came back here, I wanted you as far from her as possible. I wanted to be certain I could ward off any claim you might make. But that isn't the way I've come to see things. I realize you need to be part of our daughter's life."

She looked up at him sharply, her breath squeezing tight in her lungs. "Does that mean we can work out some sort of joint custody? That maybe she could spend time with me? Christmas, perhaps? Or a few weeks in the summer?"

"No. That's not what I want."

That statement hit her like a slap. "Then what are you willing to do?" Maggie asked, her voice hushed and filled with a primitive, unspeakable fear.

"Amy needs a mother, Maggie. A real mother." He reached out to catch her hand and bring it to his lips. "I want you to marry me."

"So that Amy can have a mother."

"Yes. And so that I can have *you.*"

She tried to tug loose her hand, but he only tightened his grip. This was insane. He couldn't be serious. Marriage. But for all the wrong reasons.

"What are you talking about?" she asked, feeling a flare of panic ignite within her. "You can't marry me."

"Why not?"

"Well…for one thing, you hate that I gave Amy up for adoption."

"Yes, I can't bear that you felt compelled to do that," he said. "But I don't hate you for it."

"But you'll never forgive me, either."

He sighed heavily. "Well, a week ago, I would have said you were right. But last night, a strange thing happened. I yelled at Amy, some stupid fuss I made over too much noise. Later I tried to apologize, and our daughter…" He laughed lightly. "She's the most amazing little creature. She told me she forgave me. Just like that. No grudge. No resentment. Just, 'I forgive you, Daddy.' That's the way she is. Loving and kind." He smiled at her, letting his lips brush gently across her knuckles. "Just like her mother."

"She's a wonderful child, but—"

"You're missing my point. I'm trying to tell you that if our little girl can forgive me for making a mistake, then who am I not to forgive you for doing the same, especially when you felt you had no other choice?"

She frowned at him, too afraid to expect much, but wanting to believe what he said so badly that the depth of it terrified her. "Do you mean that?" she asked at last.

"With all my heart." He stood back, studying her thoughtfully. "Say you'll marry me, damn it. You know we'd be good together."

"Having great sex doesn't mean we're right for one another. We're so different. We always have been."

Will made a sound, something like a groan. "I've never proposed to a woman before, but I'm almost sure it's supposed to be easier than this. At least, when the answer is so obvious."

"It isn't obvious to me."

"Then let me clarify." He pulled her up against him, wrapping his arms around her waist and letting his lips touch her brow, her temple. "Yes, we are different," he agreed, and she could hear the smile in his voice. "But that's part of what makes me so sure. The things I loved about you eight years ago haven't changed. You are, and always have been, one of a kind. You drag me out of my comfortable rut. I tried so hard not to fall for you, but the truth is, the day I met you I stumbled into love, and I've been stuck there ever since. Maggie..." His hands tangled in her hair, bringing her head up so that their eyes met. "Listen to me. I can't fight it. I don't even want to try."

"You know I'll drive you crazy."

"Yes, you will. But you'll also make life exciting. The joy I lost when you left will come back. You'll keep me from turning into my stuffy, tedious, boring father. Just tell me that you love me. That you can imagine spending the rest of your life with me and Amy."

"Imagine it? Will, you don't know..." She felt euphoric in the wake of his words. Coaxed out of fear and into hope, her lonely heart opened and took him in even as her arms tightened around him. She pressed her cheek against his chest. "I thought this job would keep me from thinking about anything else. But when I'm with you, when I'm *not* with you—all I do is imagine that we're together. I love you and always have."

He pulled back again, giving her a lazy smile. "Then imagine kissing me."

That was easy. She leaned into him once more as he caught her mouth in a long, lingering connection. She felt it then, all the possibilities. The chance to forge a new life together. The soul-deep satisfaction of Will's lips on hers banished the last pockets of darkness. Of fear. Of loneliness.

When they had to come up for air at last, his husky chuckle sent delighted shivers up Maggie's spine. "Can I assume I've finally convinced you that I love you?"

"You have."

"Then marry me. I want you in Amy's life, Maggie. But I *need* you in mine."

He kissed her again, sinking into her mouth with a skill that melted her. She savored it, cherished it.

It was some time before they became aware that they were no longer alone. They looked up to see that Teddy LaCrosse had entered the lobby. His broad grin told them that he hadn't missed that last embrace.

"Well!" he exclaimed as he reached them. "So I assume this means you two have settled your differences?"

Will, who had not turned her loose, chuckled. "I guess you could say that."

Teddy seemed pleased. He nodded slowly, then went past them to inspect the aquariums. "So let's see what we have here."

The developer had not given her any feedback during the construction of the aquariums. To Maggie's knowledge, this was the first time he was seeing the nearly finished product. In spite of her best intentions, she felt a wave of nervousness creep over her. As though sensing it, Will pressed her closer to his side.

After what seemed like an eternity, Teddy swung back to face her. "I love it," he told her, in such an enthusiastic tone that Maggie felt her mouth form into an ear-to-ear grin. "It's everything I wanted and more. I'm delighted. The grand opening is next week, and I predict that shortly after that Maggie Tillman is going to be very much in demand." Teddy's gaze traveled back and forth between Maggie and Will. "But then, it looks like maybe you already are."

"She is," Will responded with a laugh.

Teddy winked at them. "Will, I'll see you this afternoon." He reached out, took one of Maggie's hands in his. "Miss Tillman. Congratulations, and thank you."

"My pleasure. Thank you for having confidence in Sapphire Seas. And me."

When Teddy had gone, Will turned her into his arms once more. He looked as pleased and proud as she felt. "Sounds like you're going to be a very busy lady," he said. "But I hope you'll let me hire you first."

"You?"

"The Hallandale city hall project. I was thinking it could use something different, something eye-catching in the front lobby. What do you think?"

"Something whimsical?" she suggested, linking her hands behind Will's neck.

"Precisely."

"I could do bubble walls or curtains of sea fans," Maggie said, starting to get excited. "Or maybe a terraced deep-reef environment. People don't see that very often."

Will began to shower little kisses across her upper lip. "Uh-huh," he whispered. "Whatever you want."

Keen anticipation shot through her at his touch. She closed her eyes, seeing bright-hued waves of color, jeweled fish streaming past her eyelids. Her world with Will was going to be magic, a miracle, and she was going to love every moment of it.

"I think we should go to my house," Will said against her ear. "Right now."

She nodded. "I can leave Zack a note."

He pulled away, taking her hand to tug her toward the entrance. "We have plans to work out."

"For the Hallandale city hall?" she asked, puzzled that he would want to get started so soon.

He shook his head. "For how to tell Amy you're her mother."

Maggie pulled up short, her heart beating a mile a minute. A feeling of dread was curdling in her stomach, a feeling that never lied. "You mean today?"

He looked back at her, his eyes full of understanding. "You don't have to be afraid. I'll be there with you. We can get through this."

"Suppose...suppose we tell her, and she hates me? I'm not anyone special. I'm just me."

He pulled her so swiftly into his arms that she nearly lost her breath along with her balance. Against her lips he said, "She's not going to hate you. She's been waiting for you her whole life. And as for just being you, I think she's going to think that's pretty wonderful. I know I do." When she remained silent too long, he ducked his head to make her meet his eyes. "All right?"

Slowly, the steady squeeze of fear eased up on her insides. She nodded, knowing suddenly that she could do this.

"Good," Will said in that practical, no-nonsense way he had of making anything seem possible. "We made one heck of a mess eight years ago, Maggie. Now let's go make a family."

# *EPILOGUE*

BY JULY, it felt as though Maggie's entire existence had changed.

The unveiling of Teddy LaCrosse's South Beach project was an enormous success, and just as Maggie had hoped, her contribution to the restoration sparked a lot of interest. Sapphire Seas had contracts lined up until long past the end of the year.

But it was her personal life that had morphed the most—into something she'd never have dreamed possible.

She was married to Will. Blissfully married in a charming, low-key ceremony held in her parents' backyard with her sister as her maid of honor and Amy her only bridesmaid. The child had looked like a tiny angel come down to Earth in her fluttery pink chiffon dress with miniature rosebuds woven into her dark hair.

But it was the look in Amy's eyes. Excited. Happy. Full of so much love that it had put Maggie's breathing on hold. There were some mistakes that you never got to erase, but having given up Amy wasn't one of them. All those years without her—gone forever. Could she have asked for anything more?

Right now Maggie sat on a long stretch of beach protected by dunes and high grasses, one of the last places near Miami where sunbathers could find a little privacy. She wasn't alone, of course. Will lay beside her, having played hooky from Jacobson and Duquette for the day. A few feet away, at the water's edge, Amy sat sifting through the sand, intent on building a lopsided castle.

With a sigh of happiness, Maggie shaded her eyes against the warming sun and watched her daughter play. The child seemed to love the ocean as much as Maggie did.

Beside her, Will stirred, rubbing the back of his hand along her arm. "What are you thinking?" he asked softly.

She turned her head to smile at him. For an architect who spent a lot of time in a suit, he really did have the most marvelous body—powerful and tanned, with muscles in all the right places. It wasn't the effect of the warm day. Just looking at him, everything slowed inside her: her heartbeat, her breathing, her blood.

Slipping to one hip, she leaned over to run a fingertip across Will's bare chest. "I'm thinking about all those years ago, when I wanted you to sneak off to the beach with me. To this very spot, in fact. And now here we are at last."

She bent to place her lips against his sun-warmed flesh, felt his quivering response against her mouth, delicious. Will's hand slipped into her loosened curls, tilting her head back so that she could meet his sparkling eyes.

"We can't misbehave, you know," he told her with a rueful look. His glance swung toward the ocean, where Amy was busy examining shells she'd excavated. "Not with an audience."

Maggie settled back. "That's all right. I know where to find you tonight."

Will grinned, bringing her hand to his lips so that he could kiss the pad of each finger. "And tomorrow night. And the next night, and the next night…"

"You're such a creature of habit."

"You're a habit I could never break."

"Good. Being your wife. Being Amy's mom. That's the kind of routine a girl could fall in love with."

He reached for her, letting his palm cup her face. "I love you, Mrs. Stewart."

"I love you, Mr. Stewart."

"Daddy! Mommy! Look what I found!"

Amy dropped to her knees on the blanket between them, flinging sand and cold drops of seawater like a clumsy puppy. She uncurled her fingers, revealing a pockmarked pebble about the size of a dime. Within it glimmered bits of mica.

"I'll bet it's gold," the girl said on an awed breath. "It looks like gold, doesn't it?"

Always practical, Will started to shake his head. "Honey, if there's a spec of gold on this beach—"

"I'll bet you could find it," Maggie finished for him. She jumped up from the blanket. "You know what?" she said to Amy. "I think you may have found pirate treasure. Lots of Spanish ships sank off this coast, and all kinds of exciting stuff must wash up all the time." She held out her hand. "Come on, matey. Let's see what else we can discover."

Grinning, Amy rose immediately and reached for Maggie's hand. They ran toward the water.

"Wait!" Will called after them.

Maggie turned back. She supposed Will might have a hard time entering into the fantasy of searching for pirate loot, but she wasn't going to miss this opportunity to play with her child.

But instead, her husband smiled at her as he came up off the blanket. "If we're going to search for gold, we need something to dig with." He lifted his hand, and Maggie saw that he'd rescued one of Amy's best beach shovels from her bucket.

With a laugh, Maggie grabbed hold of it, used it to bring Will close enough for a quick kiss, then pulled him down to the water, where they could join their daughter on her latest adventure.

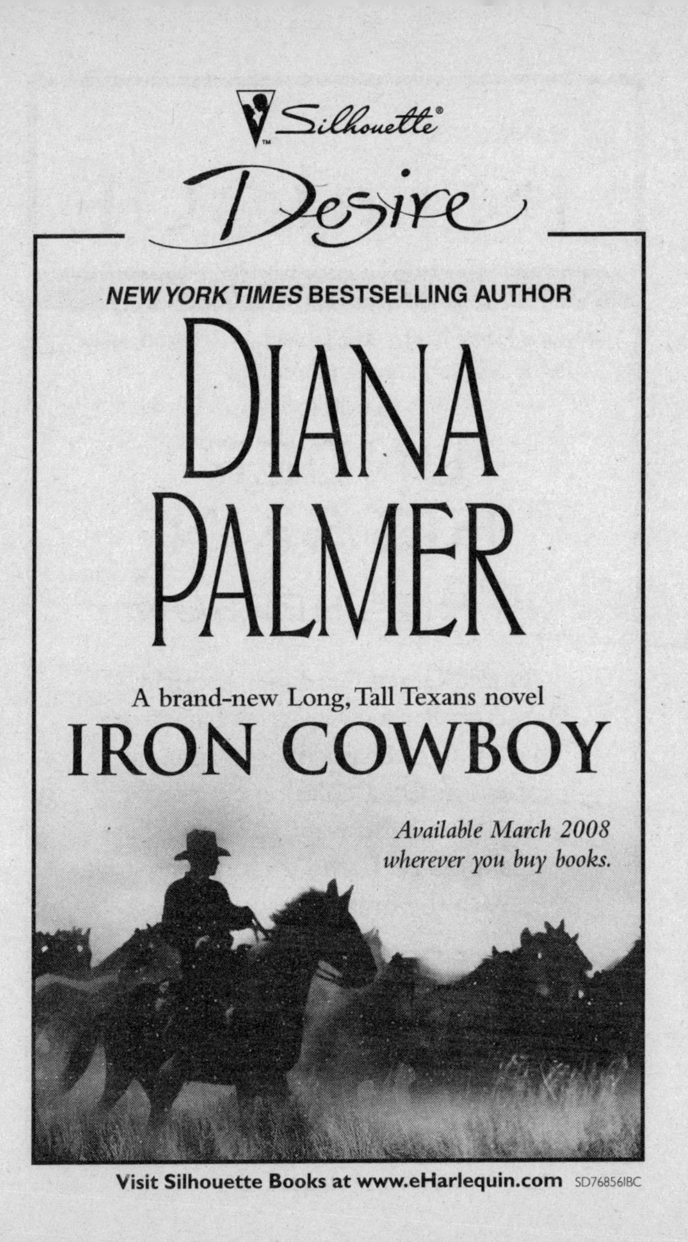

The bestselling Lakeshore Chronicles continue with *Snowfall at Willow Lake,* a story of what comes after a woman survives an unspeakable horror and finds her way home, to healing and redemption and a new chance at happiness.

***On sale February 2008!***

---

**SAVE $1.00** **off the purchase price of SNOWFALL AT WILLOW LAKE by Susan Wiggs.**

Offer valid from February 1, 2008, to April 30, 2008.
Redeemable at participating retail outlets. Limit one coupon per purchase.

**Canadian Retailers:** Harlequin Enterprises Limited will pay the face value of this coupon plus 10.25¢ if submitted by customer for this product only. Any other use constitutes fraud. Coupon is nonassignable. Void if taxed, prohibited or restricted by law. Consumer must pay any government taxes. Void if copied. Nielsen Clearing House ("NCH") customers submit coupons and proof of sales to Harlequin Enterprises Limited, P.O. Box 3000, Saint John, N.B. E2L 4L3, Canada. Non-NCH retailer—for reimbursement submit coupons and proof of sales directly to Harlequin Enterprises Limited, Retail Marketing Department, 225 Duncan Mill Rd., Don Mills, Ontario M3B 3K9, Canada.

**U.S. Retailers:** Harlequin Enterprises Limited will pay the face value of this coupon plus 8¢ if submitted by customer for this product only. Any other use constitutes fraud. Coupon is nonassignable. Void if taxed, prohibited or restricted by law. Consumer must pay any government taxes. Void if copied. For reimbursement submit coupons and proof of sales directly to Harlequin Enterprises Limited, P.O. Box 880478, El Paso, TX 88588-0478, U.S.A. Cash value 1/100 cents.



MSW2493CPN

# Texas Hold 'Em

When it comes to love, the stakes are high

Sixteen years ago, Luke Chisum dated Becky Parker on a dare...before going on to break her heart. Now the former River Bluff daredevil is back, rekindling desire and tempting Becky to pick up where they left off. But this time she has to resist or Luke could discover the secret she's kept locked away all these years....

*Look for*

## TEXAS BLUFF

*by Linda Warren*

#1470

*Available February 2008*
*wherever you buy books.*

HARLEQUIN® Super Romance®

# COMING NEXT MONTH

**#1470 TEXAS BLUFF • Linda Warren**
***Texas Hold 'Em***
Sixteen years ago, Luke Chisum dated Becky Parker on a dare...before going on to break her heart. Now the former River Bluff daredevil is back, rekindling desire and tempting Becky to pick up where they left off. But this time she has to resist, or Luke could discover the secret she's kept locked away all these years....

**#1471 THE DAD NEXT DOOR • C.J. Carmichael**
***Three Good Men***
Allison Bennett isn't looking for a family and commitment. Then Gavin Gray and his young daughter move in next door. Allison is drawn into their lives and begins to think she's found a home...until Gavin's ex-wife returns seeking a second chance.

**#1472 CAITLIN'S COWBOY • Barbara McMahon**
***Home on the Ranch***
Caitlin is down on her luck, and she's in Wyoming for one reason only—to sell the ranch her distant relation unexpectedly left her and get out of town. But the beauty of the ranch that has been in her family for generations starts to get under her skin—just like the sole remaining cowboy, Zack Carson.

**#1473 SINGLE-DAD SHERIFF • Amy Frazier**
***Count on a Cop***
Following in the footsteps of her hotel-magnate father landed Samantha Weston in rehab. Now clean and sober, she's settled in North Carolina's Blue Ridge Mountains seeking a new life under a new name. Her quest may end before it begins, however, when single dad Sheriff Garrett McQuire starts delving into her past.

**#1474 THE BROTHER RETURNS • Jeannie Watt**
***Home on the Ranch***
After betraying his brother years ago, cowboy Brett Bishop has tried to make peace with himself. Which has meant keeping his family at arm's length. But the arrival of the town's new teacher, Claire Flynn, with her close ties to his family, could change everything.

**#1475 MR. UNFORGETTABLE • Karina Bliss**
Luke Carter can never forget that he was once an abandoned child—and that's why he's driven to build his camp for underprivileged kids. But he can't do it without the support of the beautiful widow mayor, Liz Light. Their shared efforts make Luke wish she'd stop grieving long enough to prove that more than her loyalties lie with him.

HSRCNM0108